Night of Seduction

～∽～

Heaven's Gate

This is a work of fiction. Names, characters, places and incidents are either the product of the author's imagination or are used fictitiously, and any resemblance to actual persons, living or dead, business establishments, events, locales is entirely coincidental. The lyrics to the beginning of the song was created by Iris Bolling

Night of Seduction/Heaven's Gate
Copyright©2011 by Iris Bolling

All rights reserved. No portion of this book may be reproduced in any form without the prior written consent of the publisher or author, excepting brief quotes used in reviews.

ISBN-13: 978-0-9801066-5-7
ISBN-10: 0-9801066-5-6

Library of Congress Control Number: 2011904736

Edited by: Gaye Riddick-Burden
Cover and page design by: Judith Wansley

Acknowledgements

Thank you my Heavenly Father and my family. Raymond Washington, thank you for your love, support and patience.

Judith Wansley, thank you for sharing your talents, your kindness and your unyielding dedication and belief in the dream.

Roz Terry, LaFonde Harris, and Gemma Mejias: the roots to my tree, thanks for always answering the telephone. Monica (Helesi) Simon, and Cathy Atchison, thank you for your time, knowledge and encouragement.

To Shannon Purnell, and Monica Jackson, may God's blessings always be with you.

Victoria Wells, your friendship is worth my weight in gold.

To Beverly Jenkins and Gwyneth Bolton, thank you for sharing your knowledge and experience.

To Sistah Girl Reading Club of Miami and all my readers: Thank you for your encouragement and support, book after book. You make us what we are.

This book is dedicated to Heather Jones-Marable
A remarkable woman and friend.

*Books by
By Iris Bolling*

The Heart Series

*Once You've Touched The Heart
The Heart of Him
Look Into My Heart
A Heart Divided
A Lost Heart*

*www.irisbolling.net
www.sirient.com*

Book One

Night of Seduction

Chapter 1
Siri and TeKaya

Life as Siri knew it changed in a matter of moments. A two minute conversation began a string of lies that turned her world upside down. Today she was going to reclaim her life. The past was no longer going to control her. Glancing into the mirror, the questions and doubts still swirled through her mind.

"Don't you dare!"

Siri turned to the one person that knew the turmoil of the last year. Gracefully placing her hands on her hips, she asked, "What?"

"Don't what me. You know exactly what I'm talking about." Her baby sister TeKaya Kendrick scowled at her. "I can see your pathetic little mind over there working. You are not backing out of tonight. I have VIP tickets, a limo filled with champagne and a date with, Silk Davies, crooner extraordinaire. The man that can make your panties wet with one song. There is no way I'm going to miss this concert. Let's go."

Before she could mumble a word, Siri was snatched by the arm, dragged down the stairs, out the front door, and thrown into the waiting limo.

An hour later, as a crew cleared the opening act's equipment from the stage TeKaya suggested they go to the bar. A drink was the last thing Siri needed or wanted. On the other hand, hanging out with her baby sister, TeKaya, whom everyone called TK, a drink might be exactly what she needed. Why she ever agreed to this outing, she would never know. Friday's At Sunset was one of the best outdoor concert series Richmond, Virginia had to offer. The artists that appeared ranged from old school funk to jazz and all points in between. It was August and this was the last concert for the season. The evening was a delightful seventy degrees with a nice cool breeze trickling through the crowd of close to thirty five hundred concert-goers.

As the official photographer, TK had VIP tickets to the event and immediately deemed it as her opportunity to entice "*Mr. Romance*" himself, Silk Davies. Siri smiled at the thought—she would probably get a handshake and picture, then be sent on her way.

"What are you smiling about?" TK asked turning to her sister.

For a brief second, Siri thought she should be honest and tell her that fairytales and dreams only end up as nightmares over time—but, that would be cruel. Although life had thrown her a few curves, she certainly did not want to rain on TK's fairytale. So instead, Siri replied, "Just enjoying some of the sights out here tonight."

"I know what you mean. Did you see the sister with the blue-blonde hair? What could she have been thinking when she stepped out of the house?"

Leave it to TK to be blunt. "You should stop. Someone could be saying the same thing about you." Siri knew before the thought was finished it was not true. TK was a fashion photographer that looked like she should be on the other side of the camera. Everything that touched her body was the latest fashion from a variety of up and coming designers. Tonight she was wearing an original design by her friend,

Chanin Rachel, out of Atlanta. The outfit was simple, but on TK, with that perfect size six body, any man would stop and stare.

TK turned and posed. "That may be, but I looked in the mirror before leaving the house. She struck another pose, "And I look fabulous." She retrieved her drink from the bartender and began walking back to their seats. "Speaking of outfits, you are definitely wearing that two-piece skirt set, showing off your navel. I don't understand why you always wear old maid clothes. If I had your flat stomach and big booty, you wouldn't be able to handle my strut."

Siri smiled brightly at her little sister, "I'm not sure I can handle your strut now. But thank you for the compliment and the outfit."

Happy to see her sister smile, TK took her seat. "Are you having fun?" She did not know the reason for her sister's failed marriage, but she did know it left a dispassionate view of life. When they were growing up Siri had a zest for life unmatched by anyone else she knew. Living each day to its fullest had been her motto and she had followed it vigorously. Then she married Carl Austin. Not only did he snuff the life out of her, it seemed he also took a part of her soul. Tonight it took TK three hours to coerce Siri into coming with her. After a year of seeing a shell of her sister, she wanted to see a genuine smile on her face.

That's it. Something had to give. Siri did not like the look from her sister. It was one thing to hear strangers question her sadness, but quite another to hear your little sister pitying you. She was going to enjoy herself tonight, even if it killed her. Taking the glass of wine out of TK's hand, she took a sip and sat back in the lounge chair. She returned the glass, removed the pins that held her hair up, allowing the breeze to blow through it as it fell down her back. She leaned over and returned the glass to TK, "I'm having a wonderful time. Thank you for inviting me."

The look of relief on TK's face was priceless. The sun was about to set and the main act was about to take the stage.

"I hope your camera is ready. I want a lot of pictures of this man."

Picking up her camera TK adjusted the lens. "You realize sometime during the performance I will have to leave you. But it shouldn't be for too long."

"Do you girl, I can take care of myself."

With that said, TK stood and began doing just what she loved, capturing moments of a lifetime.

"Ladies and gentlemen," the announcer began as the lights on the stage dimmed. "The moment has arrived. If you came with a special someone, now is the time to pull them close. If you came alone, grab your neighbor. If you are still alone, I have the number to an escort service. No one is going to want to leave alone, tonight. The man referred to as, *'the baby maker, the guaranteed panty dropper* and *Mr. Get Her Wet,'* The man with the voice so smooth, they had to change his name. Ladies and gentlemen, put your hands together for the incomparable, Silk... Davies."

The crowd stood on their feet and enthusiastically greeted the Grammy award-winning artist to the stage. As if on cue, the band merged with the rhythm of the applause from the audience. Just as the sun set, magically, Silk Davies appeared center stage dressed in white pants and a long sleeve linen shirt that stopped at his thighs. The band stopped. The applause settled and the man's voice was all that could be heard. There were no instruments playing, not a sound from the crowd, just a man with his eyes closed and a microphone at the moment soothing all the ills of the world. If anyone ever wondered if Silk Davies could sing, the answer was loud and clear. The sound of his voice was mesmerizing.

At the conclusion of the first song, he opened his eyes and smiled at the crowd. Then in the smoothest voice, Siri had ever heard he said. "Good evening. I am Silk Davies. Welcome to a night of seduction." Now she understood exactly what the announcer meant about panties getting wet. Instinctively she crossed her legs and gripped the arms of the lounge chair as her eyes followed the man across the stage to the white baby grand piano. Meticulously he began exactly what he indicated, seducing every female in attendance.

Siri sat and listened. It was uncanny how the selection of songs seemed to follow a journey through a relationship. From the uncertainty and excitement in the first stages, to the hurt and sorrow at the end. Tears slowly slide down her cheeks as he sung through the hurt of a dream being shattered. After the first set of songs, the band continued to play as Silk left the stage. Upon his return, he sat center stage on a stool, dressed in a pair of jeans and a white tee shirt that hugged his body displaying his muscle bound arms. He wasn't a big man, Siri thought, but lord, what he had was well defined. He picked up his guitar and smiled. "I'm an incurable romantic who could never leave you hopeless. After every cold, harsh, winter, there comes a fresh, new, spring. Let's continue the journey."

An indescribable urge, to hear what this man was about to say, consumed her. Siri sat forward anticipating the next note. It seemed, for a moment, he searched for something or someone in the crowd. His eyes scanned over her, but then quickly returned. The intensity of his stare caused her to turn around in her seat to see who he was looking for. Turning back, she found his eyes directly on her. Certain it was her imagination, she settled back and listened. This time when he began to sing, it felt as if no one else was there but him and her. Every note, to each song, touched her heart. The tears dissipated and the doubts she felt about her life began to dissolve. By the time he reached the last note, Siri's outlook on life had changed. The man on the stage had given her hope again. It was foolish of her to think he was singing only to her, but what the hell, that's the way she felt. One day she had to find a way to thank him.

"Did he put on a show or what?" TK exclaimed as she rejoined Siri.

Standing and folding the lounge chair, Siri stopped, looked towards the stage nodding and agreed with her sister. "If I had the nerve I would take off my wet panties and give them to him."

Shocked at her words, TK stopped and stared with her mouth open at Siri. Then she laughed, "Well I'll be damned. Look out world, the real Siri is re-emerging. Come on," she said while gathering her things. "I have to get a few shots of the after party at the hotel."

Making their way through the crowd, the privileged few, including TK and Siri, climbed the steps from the park area into the breezeway leading to the lobby of the hotel. Showing press passes, TK and Siri entered the elevator leading to the penthouse suite of the hotel. Upon entering the reception area, they joined a small entourage of people that traveled with Silk. "Wow. I've lived in Richmond all my life, but I never knew this was here." TK marveled at the room. Before Siri could respond, a man with a determined swagger approached TK. "Ms. Kendrick?" he extended his hand. "Good evening. I am Jason Davies. I understand you are one of the photographers for this event."

"Yes I am," TK replied smiling. The air between the two was electric as she took his hand. They faced each other staring. As if suddenly remembering, she turned to Siri and introduced her. "Um, this is my sister Siri."

Extending his hand Jason smiled, "It's nice to meet you. Would you mind terribly if I steal her away for a moment? I promise it won't be long."

"No, not at all," Siri replied as she released his hand. Jason turned to call someone over, while TK raised her eyebrows at Siri and mouthed, "He is so fine." Siri nodded her head in agreement.

"Stan, would you keep Siri company for a moment?" Jason patted the young man on his shoulders and turned back to Siri. "Here," he gave her the glass of wine he was holding. "Thank you," Jason said as he placed his hand on the small of TK's back and guided her away. Siri took the glass and watched as the two strolled away. They made a stunning couple. She smiled as a pleasant thought crossed her mind. This was not going to be the last time she saw the two together.

"Is that smile for me?" Stan asked with a wide grin and what appeared to be drool coming out of his mouth.

This is going to be a long night, Siri inwardly sighed and then took a sip of wine. Certain wines always had an adverse effect on her and she usually stayed away from alcoholic beverages for that very reason. However, trying to keep Stan in check would cause anyone to drink. His hands seemed to continuously touch her in places they shouldn't. To make matters worse his conversation was limited to, "You sure are fine," or "You know I'm with the band" or "I got a room a few floors down." Doing the best she could to be civil, she scanned the room. She noticed Jason and TK on the balcony engaged in what appeared to be a very enjoyable conversation, for they were both displaying smiles bright enough for a Crest toothpaste commercial. The last thing she wanted to do was interrupt that, but she needed a reason to escape Stan. The third glass of wine was affecting her system and she would never forgive herself if, in the morning, she awakened with Stan next to her in bed.

Reaching deep into the recesses of her mind, she found the one thing that always got rid of a man. She downed the remaining portion of her third glass of wine and cleared her throat, "Stan would you excuse me? I need to find the ladies room. It's—you know—that time of the month." The deflated expression on his face was exactly what she wanted. Walking away, she smiled triumphantly. *That's right buddy you will not be getting any tonight.*

In search of a quiet place to wait, Siri ventured down the hallway until she reached a set of double doors. She tentatively knocked. Receiving no response, she tried the door handle. It was unlocked. Stepping inside she called out, "Hello. Is anyone here?" Receiving no response, she closed the door behind her. It was amazing how the noise from the party evaporated once the door closed. "Finally, a quiet place," she exhaled. She reached into her purse, pulled out her cell phone, and pushed a button. Looking around she noticed the room was a bedroom suite and a very elegant one at that. She sat on the sofa near the door while waiting for TK to pick up. "Hey. I could see you are in the midst of a deep getting-to-know-you conversation and did not want to interrupt. I'm taking a cab home. Enjoy the rest of your night." She teased.

"Did you drink that glass of wine?" TK asked with a giggle.

"Yes, that one and more, Mother. You apparently have never been in the company of Stan, the man with the hands. It took everything in me not to slap him and cause a scene," Siri replied with a bit of a slur.

"I'm coming to get you. Where are you?"

"Girl, please. I'm a twenty-nine year old woman. I can take care of myself. You stay put and take care of that fine man you are with."

"Are you sure?" TK asked concerned.

"Yes, I'm sure. I'll talk to you when you get home." Siri disconnected the call and laid her head back. The wine had affected her more than she thought. She decided to lie down on the sofa for a minute, to get herself together. Then she would have the clerk in the lobby call her a cab to take her home. She stretched out on the sofa and before she knew it, she was sound asleep.

Refreshed from a long relaxing shower, Eric wrapped a towel around his waist and grabbed another for his head of dread locs that hung to his shoulder, then walked into the bedroom of the luxurious hotel suite. He sat on the side of the bed and laid back. As with every performance, the day was long. The stage check was at ten, but Eric was up by six that morning. With every performance, there was an uncertainty and nervous energy that always hit him early in the morning. With the addition of interviews with the local television and radio stations, there was no time for relaxation. Thankfully the regular meeting with the crew after the performance was cut short. Apparently, his brother, Jason had other plans for the evening.

Running through the performance in his mind, he thought things went rather well. Tonight he felt the crowd was with him every step of the way, especially that one woman on the front row. As always, he attempted to find one person to connect with in the audience. At first sight, he was drawn to her. After a song or two he would normally move on, but tonight, this woman held his attention. Several times, he walked around the stage, but found himself drawn back to her. There was something so longing in her eyes that he could not pull away. Suddenly words to a song came to mind. He sprang up from the bed to search for his laptop—he had to get the words that popped into his mind down.

Remembering his bag was in the sitting area, he purposely walked into the room. Reaching for the bag on the desk, he stopped midway and looked towards the sofa. He could not believe what he was seeing. He closed his eyes, thinking he must be seeing things. Slowly reopening his eyes he could not believe the woman from the audience was actually there, on the sofa. He looked around the room to see if Jason was lurking somewhere waiting to jump out and yell, "Punked!" It didn't happen. Taking a step forward he took a closer look. Standing less than ten feet away from her, he could see she was asleep. Had she been waiting for him to come out of the shower? Disappointment spread through him, as he realized, Jason, his brother and manager must have sent her. Since the beginning of this tour four months ago, Jason had been on him to get a woman to help him release his pent up stress. Jason's way of getting him to relax was sending him a woman. That was probably why she had front row seats. *Damn*, he thought, *I must be losing my grip. I was about to write a song for a call girl.*

Disappointed or not, the woman did have an effect on him. The provocative position she held on the sofa exposed her entire body, and what a body it was. Her arm was over her forehead, with her other hand resting on her stomach. Viewing her profile from head to toe, her curves were a feast for his eyes. From the v-shape of her spaghetti strap top, he could tell her breasts were more than a hand full and firm. The skin beneath the hand resting on her flat stomach seemed so smooth he was tempted to touch it. The skirt covered her thighs, but the portion of her legs that were not covered revealed the same even toned cocoa brown skin as her face. She had the daintiest feet, he had ever seen in a pair of open toed sandals. He loved a woman with pretty feet. If a woman took care of her feet, she took care of her body just as well. His lips curved into a cryptic smile. He wanted to taste her toes—run his tongue over her navel—taste her lips. *Damn, am I that horny?* He thought for a minute, *when was the last time I had a woman.* Well over a year, he remembered. Nodding his head, okay that makes sense. That's why his reaction was so strong towards this woman.

Returning to the bedroom, he retrieved a blanket out of the closet, unfolded it, then walked back into the sitting room to place it over her. He gently removed her shoes and placed them beside the sofa. Looking into her face as he covered her, he wondered. How someone that looked so much like an angel could be a call girl? Kneeling next to her he stared intently at her. She just did not fit the profile. But who knows, circumstances could have forced her in that direction. With his finger, he removed a single curl from her face. He smiled at the way her lashes rested against her cheeks and the way her lips were shaped. Surprisingly, there was no makeup on her face, not even lipstick. Frowning he wondered what kind of call girl did not wear makeup? Rethinking his first assumption, he examined her hand. *No ring.* For some strange reason, that revelation pleased him. The sudden movement of her head startled him, but her whispering his name in her sleep amazed him. Well, it wasn't exactly his name—it was his stage name, but it was still him. *Is she dreaming about me,* he wondered. Unable to resist he leaned over and whispered in her ear. "I'm here."

Her lips curved into a sensuous smile. He grinned in response.

"Thank you," she whispered so sincerely it sobered him a little.

Why was she thanking him? Whatever it was, there was certainly no reason to be rude. "You are welcome," he replied. The expression on her face softened and that touched him deeply. His entire body began to spring to life. A man could spend a lifetime looking into that face. Other than moving the single curl from her face, he had not touched her. The urge to do so became overwhelming. He stood and braced his arm against the wall above the sofa to keep from touching any other part of her body, then he slowly touched his lips to hers. The first kiss was a soft, barely touching the center of her lips, and then he feather kissed the left side of her mouth. When he reached the right side, he saw her lashes flutter open. That was his undoing. The longing he saw there during the concert was reflecting back at him now, through the most beautiful black eyes he had ever seen.

Am I dreaming? Siri thought as she gazed into warm hazel eyes. His breath against her skin felt so real and his lips so tender. Unable to stop the action, she swallowed as the intensity of their stare continued. *If I'm dreaming, don't wake me. I want to enjoy every minute.* Afraid the dream would end, she closed her eyes and continued the kiss. The pressure increased and she instinctively parted her lips.

Not one to miss an opportunity, Eric eased his tongue inside her parted lips. Their tongues began to move in a slow enticing rhythm, producing a sweet moan from her. Encouraged, he eased his hand around her waist pulling her body closer to his. The kiss deepened as she wrapped her arms around his neck. Not sure if the second moan came from her or him, he returned to his knees while removing the blanket from between them. As their bodies made contact, he could feel her nipples harden against his bare chest. Leaving her lips, he placed a trail of kisses along her neck and down her shoulders. His previous thoughts were right. Her skin was smooth as silk. Easing the strap to her top down, he immediately captured the tempting peak of her nipple between his lips. His tongue roamed the erect bud as he felt her cradle his head with her hands to hold him securely in place. She began to place kisses on top of his head and the side of his ear. Her breath was so tantalizing against his ear, it caused him to return to her lips. She greeted him with the desire of a woman demanding more to quench her thirst. Giving what was demanded he slid his hand down her flat stomach and inched his way beneath her skirt. His hand encountered silk lace material that was wet with her desire. He eased his fingers to the soft mound and gently stroked. She tightened the hold around his neck merging their bodies closer. As he eased a finger inside her, he heard her slight intake of breath and felt a shudder. The reaction brought him inexplicable joy. He slid another finger in and began to stroke her. Her body moved feverishly against his hand as her head fell backwards, breaking the kiss. There was a strong need for him to see the expression on her face, he opened his eyes. He watched as her expression changed from anticipation, to need for fulfillment, to astonishment as her body exploded.

Her eyes flew open as she stared, stunned at her reaction. "I'm not dreaming am I?" she asked wistfully.

"If we are don't wake me now."

Placing her head on his shoulder she tenderly kissed his neck. "Thank you." She said again.

He had no idea why she was thanking him, but he would gladly take her gratitude. He captured her lips again as she rubbed her hands over his chest. When her hand caressed his nipple, he moaned. The fire was building so fast within him he couldn't control what was happening. He quickly lifted her from the sofa onto the floor as she clung to him. Holding her against his chest, he pulled her top over her head. She held her arms up to allow the top to fall, and then returned to the assault of kisses against his chest. Unzipping her skirt from behind, he lifted her and pulled the skirt away. Not wanting to place her almost naked body on the floor, he carried her to the bed. Standing above her looking down he could not believe how beautiful she was with the rich cocoa brown skin, the long lashes covering her cheeks, the pint size nose, and her sensuous lips. Nothing about her read call girl to him, as she shyly laid there. "What's your name?" he asked.

She opened her eyes and he could see the realization that he was half naked appear there. Then the look changed to appreciation—she liked what she saw. He raised an eyebrow. "Are you sure you want to look at me that way?" he hungrily asked.

She sat up and came to the edge of the bed on her knees. The man was perfection with muscles in all the right places. He wasn't as tall as her ex-husband, but he had to be at least six feet tall. Curiously, removing the towel from his waist, she inhaled as the evidence of his need was revealed. She reached out and encircled her hand around him.

Reactively he closed his eyes and moaned, "Hmm. What's your name?" he was barely audible.

"Siri," she replied in a whisper.

She slowly began stroking his already engorged member. "Are you sure you want to be here?" he asked reaching out threading his fingers through her hair.

Moving closer, she kissed his chest, then ran a single finger down his abdomen counting the muscle ridges. She stopped at four before answering, "Yes."

Not wasting a minute, he reached into his wallet that was on the nightstand and pulled out several foils packages. He dropped them on the bed and pulled one apart. She grabbed his hand, "May I?" Taking the condom from his hand, she tenderly covered him, then laid back across the bed. "Thank you for protecting us."

If she thanked him one more time, he was going to lose it. He reached down and slid her lace panties down her legs. Smiling he joined her on the bed and wondered, *What kind of call girl wore panties and not thongs?* Mesmerized by the shear essence of her body, he leisurely ran a finger down the inside of her breast down to her thigh. He journeyed up the inside of her thigh until he reached her center. He placed his full palm against her and began to massage. He placed his head in the crook of her neck. The feel and smell of her was intoxicating. She moved and straddled him. Her hands braced against his chest as she closed her eyes and eased down on him.

There were no words to describe the way he felt embedded inside of her. They both laid there immobile adjusting to the overwhelming feeling that flowed with their joining. Eric closed his eyes, basking in the moment. His hands traveled up her thighs and gently massaged the muscles. Feeling the pressure of her hands against his abs, his eyes opened just as she eased up, then back down on him. His eyes rolled back and closed again as she continued the movement slowly over and over and over. When the momentum reached the point of no return, he flipped her onto her back. She wrapped her legs around his waist tight, drawing him in deeper. Suddenly, time disappeared. There were no sounds in the room, only the overwhelming melody that began playing in his head. As his tempo increased, so did the rhythm in his mind. Holding her waist, he continued the sweet torment until he and the melody reached the crescendo. Every vessel in his body exploded as he desperately tried to control all of the melody flowing through his mind. He lay on top of her as she embraced him. She gently rubbed the back of his head as he relaxed in the crook of her neck. He kissed her neck and whispered, "Thank you, Siri." He rolled to her side and pulled her into his arms. Exhausted, Eric surrendered to the melodies playing in his mind while thinking; *when I wake up I definitely want to take that journey again.*

Chapter 2
Eric and Jason

Eager to feel the incredible pleasure of before, Eric reached out for the woman. This one was definitely worth whatever price Jason had shelled out. Instead of cursing him to the core, as he had planned to do, he had to thank his brother. Apparently, he needed a woman more than he thought. As his body reacted physically to his thinking, he reached further across the bed. Void space. He adjusted the direction of his hand. Opening his eyes dubiously, he raised his head slightly off the bed and looked around. She was gone. The thought bothered him. Why would she leave without being paid? Sitting there contemplating the situation, he decided to check the bathroom. Wrapping the sheet from the bed around his waist, he walked into the bathroom and looked around. There was nothing out of order. He frowned as he scanned the room. There was no sign of her clothes anywhere. When his vision reached the nightstand, he noticed his wallet was there. Exhaling and shaking his head, "the oldest trick in the book." He disappointedly stated. Picking it up, and checking the contents, his brows formed into a frown again. Nothing was missing from his wallet, which contained a thousand dollars in cash, plus two credit cards he carried when he traveled.

Dumbfounded, Eric never noticed Jason standing in the doorway watching his frantic movements from the other room. He turned to look at the bed. Had it been a dream? Was she a figment of his imagination? Lifting his hand up to run it down his face, a portion of the sheet fell to the floor.

"As amusing as this scene is, I've had enough," Jason joked raising an eyebrow out of curiosity at his brother. "It's good you slept late. It gave me a chance to take a good look at the schedule for the week."

Turning to his brother, Eric wrapped the sheet back around his waist and sat on the edge of the bed, a bit perplexed. "Who was she? He asked with a quizzical look.

"I ordered a couple of cups of cappuccino from Starbucks." Jason stated nonchalantly as he stepped into the room and sat the paperwork in his hand on the table by the window. He took a seat and continued reviewing the schedule for the week.

A little irritated with his brother, Eric's replied, "The woman you sent here last night. Who was she?"

"What woman? Which one? Where? Who?" Jason teased as he continued reading, unconcerned with his younger brother's question.

"The call girl you sent here last night. I assume she was from an exclusive agency."

Jason looked up, "You had a woman here last night?"

His brow creased with a frown. Jason did play games, but not to this extent. "Did you send a woman to my suite last night?"

"No, I was busy with a woman of my own," he replied with a smooth smile.

Eric looked around the room as Jason looked on inquisitively. "You don't know who you were with last night? Huh, I'm proud of you little brother. You needed some release. You've been kind of uptight lately."

"I'm not uptight." Eric stated as he abruptly stood, walked over to bathroom and closed the door just as he heard Jason's last comment.

"You're right—you look very relaxed this morning. That's what a good lay will do for you."

When he returned from his shower, Jason was in the sitting area on his cell phone. Eric pulled on a pair of jeans and a t-shirt then sat on the bed to put on his socks and shoes. On the floor near the nightstand was a pair of black lace panties. He picked them up and yelled, "I haven't lost my mind!"

"I'm glad to hear it!" Jason yelled back. "Now can we hit the road? We are already running behind schedule."

Smiling at the discovery, Eric placed the panties in his suitcase with his dirty clothes and closed the top. Questions surrounding the woman still lingered in his head. *Who was she and why did she leave without payment?*

The midday warmth from the sun was the catalyst that snatched Siri from her dream—correction—the memories of the night before. If the Lord came down to take her home, she would have no complaints. Only a heavenly being could have made her feel so precious, so sensuous, so complete. Thinking back to the night, she covered her eyes and turned her face down into her pillow smiling. She held her breath for a moment, and then released a scream into the pillow. She sat up in the bed and pinched herself. "Ouch," she exclaimed and rubbed the spot. "Okay, it wasn't a dream." She pulled her knees up and hugged them, trying to remember everything that happened.

She awakened earlier that morning in the arms of Silk Davies. Not wanting to face the man she had been so provocative with, she slid from his embrace and quickly dressed. Never in her life had she been so aroused by a man just from his look.

Four years with her husband and never once did he make her feel the way Silk did. She closed her eyes and exhaled. *Was he satisfied?* The thought frightened her. That was the real reason she left. The unsatisfied look on her ex-husband's face was one thing, but to have Silk Davies tell her that would have been too much for her ego.

She placed her forehead on her knees and closed her eyes, ashamed. She had never been with another man before her husband. She had no idea having sex could be so exuberating, so wonderful. Her head snapped up. "No. I refuse to let something that was so beautiful become corrupted in my mind." The moments she spent with Silk Davies were wonderful and she refused to reduce it to something sleazy. Suddenly the words that escaped her for months to end her first novel came to her. Not only that, she had the title.

Excited, she got up, sat at her desk, and opened her laptop. After she pulled up her document, she inserted a title page to the novel she had begun writing during her divorce and typed; **Night of Seduction,** by Siri Austin.

Chapter 3
Siri and TeKaya

Two weeks later Siri stood in her classroom at the elementary school wondering where to start. The room she was assigned was more like a penitentiary than a classroom. The walls appeared to be blue-grey, she thought, but the windows were definitely grey. How are children supposed to expand their minds in such a dreary environment? She asked herself. Something had to be done.

Well, first things first, she thought as she started to place her purse on the desk, but then thought again. The desk was just as dirty as the windows. She turned and left the room. When Siri reached her car, she opened the trunk and put her purse inside. She pulled out her cell phone and put it in the back pocket of her jeans. Siri reached back inside the trunk and pulled out the plastic container with cleaning supplies. She closed the trunk, put the alarm on, and walked back to the classroom. As she walked past the principal's office, she noticed a few people gathered, but did not bother to stop. She had a lot of work to do and no time for conversation.

Thankfully, when she returned to the room, the janitor had left the bucket of water she had requested earlier. The cleaning process began at her desk, and then carried on to

Night of Seduction 21

the blackboard and students' desks. As she cleaned the desks, she moved them out and stacked them in the hallway to make room so she could scrub the floor. On her hands and knees, she began scrubbing each square of the floor. After what seemed like an eternity, finally she reached the door and was backing out of the room when a voice interrupted her.

"I don't believe you ever got into that position for me Mrs. Austin."

She looked over her shoulder and was surprised to see Carl, her ex-husband, staring down at her. *Lord, why now? Of all the times, why would you have him see me on my knees in dirty jeans with my hair sweated out?* Trying hard to ignore the urge to clean herself up, she continued with the task and responded, "Mrs. Austin is your mother. If you ask I'm sure she'll try."

"Mrs. Austin that was cruel and uncalled for. Mr. Austin is here out of concern for the conditions in our facility. I will not have you being disrespectful," declared Roscoe Ford, the principal.

Siri closed her eyes and hung her head; she should have known butt-hole number two was not far behind. He always had been a foot deep up Carl's butt. "If you two haven't noticed, I'm busy. I don't have time for idol chit chat."

"I suggest you make the time. Would you stand please?" Roscoe the butt-hole demanded. Siri threw the sponge into the dirty water and did as she was asked.

"You always treated me like I was beneath you. What you don't realize is Mr. Austin is the only reason you are working here. If I had my way you would never work in another school."

"If I had my way you would have taken a tic-tac before talking to me, but we all have our crosses to bear," Siri replied.

Roscoe took a step towards her and Carl stopped him. "Roscoe let me handle this. Oh, and by the way, don't ever speak to my wife in that tone again."

The look of disdain was clear on Roscoe Ford's face. "Of course Mr. Austin," he replied as he sneered in her direction and walked away.

Carl turned to her and stared. She could be wrong, but it seemed he was pleased to see her. She cleared her throat, "I'm no longer your wife. Your mother made sure of that. If there's nothing else, I'm busy."

"I can see that. Why are you scrubbing the floor?"

"Because the floor is dirty, the desks are filthy, the windows are dingy, and the room is basically unsanitary. But you don't care because none of your family will have to go here."

"Let me take a look." He looked at her standing in the doorway. If only his mother could see the beautiful woman, he saw whenever he looked at her. If only he could have stood up for her, she would still be his. Seeing her standing in the doorway as if defending her territory he remembered how passionate she was about children and regretted he never gave her a child. "Please."

Siri looked down the hallway at the number of teachers that were standing outside their door listening. Most were afraid of saying anything to her because they feared the wrath of Queen Austin, mother to butt-hole number one. She was one of the most powerful women in Richmond City Government and a member of the School Board. One word from her and you could easily be transferred to one of the worst schools in the district.

Cashmere Wagstaff, the only friend Siri had at the school, stood in the doorway of her class across the hallway. She always had a soft spot for Carl. She nodded her head indicating to let him see the room. Siri stepped aside and allowed Carl into the room.

Stepping inside, he immediately felt the despair Siri was referring too. He could only imagine what it was like before she began cleaning. "What do you need to make it presentable?"

There were times when Carl showed he had a heart, but as soon as he mentioned anything to his mother, the kindness would disappear. She had witnessed his efforts to do things and his mother talking him out of whatever she could, stripping him of his self-pride. "Thanks, but I'll pass on the unrequited hope."

"Siri, I'm serious. Tell me what you need and I will have it done before the week is out." He knew she'd heard the words before, but what she did not know was that he had learned how to get around his mother. His only wish was that he had learned that lesson a year ago.

Knowing he meant well, mixed with the fact that as a member of city council he had the influence to get the job done, Siri looked around the room. "Paint and clean windows would be a good start," she stated. A fan or two and a working heater for each of the rooms couldn't hurt. A good supply of books, computers for every student and more staff would be nice."

"Okay Siri, you and I know that's not going to happen. Painting and windows will be done by Friday." He reached into his pocket and pulled out his cell. Placing his call, he looked into her suspicious eyes. "I promise it will be done if I have to come and do the job myself." During the call, Siri moved the clean desks back into the classroom. The call ended about fifteen minutes later. "The Grounds Department indicated it would be cost effective to do the entire building, which would have to be scheduled. The supervisor can't put together a team by this weekend. Do you think you could get some volunteers together? I'll pitch in."

Not sure if she should believe him or not, Siri hesitated. "What about Ford? Will you get it cleared through him?"

"Roscoe will do whatever I ask."

"I can get a few people to join in," she replied. Silence pursued for a few seconds. "Why are you here Carl?"

Carl leaned against one of the desks, folded his arms across his chest, and smiled. "I knew it was your first day and how much you love Roscoe, so I wanted to make sure you were okay."

"Yeah, is that why you assigned me here?"

"No Siri. You were assigned here because these children need someone to give a damn about them. That someone is you. The whole time we were married you begged me to let you come here to teach. I wanted to give you something to show you how much I care." Catching his error, he stood and walked towards the door then stopped before exiting. "I didn't do a good job of making you happy during our marriage. I thought I would try again." He hesitated then walked out the door.

That evening Siri appeared in the kitchen with dirt from head to toe. TK was sitting at the breakfast bar fumbling with her camera equipment. She looked up at Siri and smirked, "What dumpster did you crawl out of?"

Looking at her sister whose appearance was dangerously sensuous tonight, she asked, "Going somewhere?"

Placing her equipment on the counter top, she stood and posed. "I have a date and I'm going for elegant, sensual, and irresistible. Does this outfit qualify?"

The form fitting, backless, red dress stopped above her knees and clung to every curve of her body. Her red sandaled heels and a diamond ankle bracelet completed the ensemble. "If you are planning on his tongue hanging out, I'll say the dress will do." Their mother, Kerri stared as she walked into the room. "Who are you going out with tonight?"

"She took a seat at the table. A friend from Atlanta is in town and we're having dinner."

Her mother looked over and frowned at Siri, "What dumpster did you crawl out of?"

"My classroom," Siri replied as she sat at the table in a huff. "Do I have enough time to shower before dinner?"

"Sure, I'll wait for you, since TeKaya is eating out." Kerri turned to TK. "What is this man's name?"

"I didn't say it was a man."

"You didn't have to, the dress said it, and from the looks of it, he must be special."

Siri chuckled, "Don't come home pregnant."

TK scowled and poked her tongue out at he sister, "He is not getting any tonight, maybe next time."

"Name TeKaya, his name," her mother asked again.

She sighed deeply, "His name is Jason Davies, and he is a music executive based in Atlanta. He is single, one daughter and a partridge in a pair tree."

Siri sat up, "You're going out with Silk Davies brother?"

"Yes, I am." She smiled sheepishly.

"I take it you are referring to the singer. How well do you know this man?" her mother asked.

"I met him two weeks ago, but I feel as if I have known him all my life. Is that possible Mommy? Is it possible to meet someone whose aura is so in tune with your own that you believe life would be pointless without him?"

Siri and her mother looked at each other. "That sounds pretty serious, but yes it is possible."

"TK, is um, Jason here alone?"

TK looked up at her, "I suppose, why do you ask?"

"I was just wondering," Siri exhaled with relief.

"It sounds as if you are developing feelings for this man," her mother probed.

"Mommy, the minute I saw him standing on the side of the stage, my heart stood still. At first I thought it was just the atmosphere of the night....it was so sensually charged wasn't it Siri?"

Siri thought back to that night. "Mmm-hmm, more than I would ever say."

"But then later that night we talked for hours, until the sun came up and the connection was unmistakable. I have not had a decent nights' sleep since. He called about a week ago and said he was having a hard time getting me off his mind. I want to believe him, but you know me. I have to play it cool, take my time, and make sure this is what I want. Jason said he's not in this for a game, he wants a serious relationship. I want to be sure before I make a commitment to him, you know what I mean Mommy?"

Siri smiled at her sister's revelation. She knew she would see the two together again, it was written on both of their faces. Then her experience from that night came to mind. She closed her eyes and allowed the memory of Silk's hands roaming her body to play blissfully, his voice caressing her soul like a soft violin and his lips, oh those lips kissing her in places she never would have imagined. Her toes were still tingling. When she opened her eyes her mother and TK were staring at her with questioning glares. She cleared her throat.

"Well," Kerri smiled, "It seems my daughters had quite a night. Siri came home that morning with a renewed zest for life and it seemed you came home with something as well." She looked at Siri who was the spitting imagine of her father with the dark cocoa brown skin, cool black eyes and wavy black hair that stopped below her shoulder blades. Then there is TK who was a mirror of herself. With her light mocha skin with huge brown eyes and long straight black hair that reached her waist. Physically, her girls were beautiful. She did all she could to keep them grounded and teach them the importance of real love in their lives. All she wanted was for each of them to experience the love she had

Night of Seduction

had with their father. "You know, in 1976, no it was '78, I was at Montclair State College at the time."

Siri and TK looked at each other and rolled their eyes as they recognized the signs of a lengthy sermon on the horizon. "Mommy if this is going to be a Heathcliff Huxtable moment, I have to go take a shower."

"You will do no such thing. You will sit here and listen until I finish talking." Kerri turned away and continued her story.

Siri looked at TK who mouthed, "I am so sorry."

Siri replied mouthing back, "I will get you for this." They both sat and listened.

The private jet was at the airport fueled and ready for the short trip to Richmond. Eric was downstairs in the limo waiting. It seemed he was more anxious about this trip than Jason, which seemed impossible.

At thirty-two, Jason was ready to settle down and the woman he wanted to make a permanent part of his life was in Virginia. A satisfied smile creased his lips as he remembered the twenty six year old photographer with the eyes of an angel and the looks of a goddess. Nothing had entered his mind for the last two weeks without her face preceding or following. The night they spent together remained prominent in his mind. They talked about his daughter, who meant the world to him, and her mother who he simply wanted to choke half the time and stomp the other half. He told her about their living arrangement and explained his reasons for living in the same house with his child's mother. He thought she would have walked away, but she did not. She stayed and listened without judgment or question.

Walking down the stairs that led into the east wing of his house Jason could hear the giggles before he reached the room. Peeping inside the room decorated with teddy bears and space ships, three-year-old Sierra ran to him, "Daddy, Daddy look."

Jason reached down, picked her up in his arms, and kissed her chocolate covered cheek. "Hello pumpkin. Is the candy good?"

Bobbing her head up and down she replied smiling, "Yummy Daddy, want some?" She pushed the remaining chocolate bar toward his mouth.

He bit a small piece. "Mum yummy. Where's Mommy?"

"She went out Mr. Davies," Gabby the live-in babysitter replied as she began picking up toys.

"Did she say when she would return?"

"Not really, but I don't expect her until later or in the morning."

"Alright," Jason replied a little upset. "I have to go out of town, but I'll return tonight. It may be a little late." He looked into the face of his precious little girl. "Daddy loves Sierra."

She put her chocolate covered hands on his cheeks and kissed the tip of his nose. "Sierra love Daddy," she giggled.

Gabby reached out while laughing. "I'll take her Mr. Davies. I'm afraid you're going to have to change your shirt."

"It's alright Gabby. We'll walk out to the car so she can give her Uncle Eric a chocolate kiss."

After cleaning his cheek of the chocolate kiss from his adorable niece, Eric sat on the eight seat private plane ready to take off for Virginia. While he waited for Jason to change his shirt, he began strumming notes that continued to invade his mind on his guitar. Closing his eyes the vision that awakened him each morning came to mind. She laid asleep in his arms, her eyelashes fluttered open, the most incredible black eyes he had ever seen looked into his, and a smile as warm as the sun graced her face. Transfixed, he allowed the image to transfer and the music to sooth his soul. The melody began smooth, soft, intriguing; then the heart of the music began its crescendo as the images of the woman from Virginia filled his mind and reached the crest just as he ventured into the sweetness of her love. The mellow peaks slowly began to return to the smooth rhythm of the beginning.

"Whoa that was sweet. Something new you're working on?" Jason asked from the seat in front of him.

Eric never heard Jason return to his seat, he was so engrossed in the music. "No just something that's been playing around in my head for a couple of weeks."

"Since we left Virginia," Jason asked with a questioning look.

Lowering his eyes and putting his guitar to the side, Eric sat forward and rested his elbows on his legs. He cuffed his hands and looked intently at his brother. "Something happened that night in the hotel."

"Um yeah, you had an encounter with a call girl."

"Hmm, I'm not sure she was call girl. I mean I've been around and this woman was not that experienced."

Jason sat forward and joined his thirty-year old brother. "You know last month I would have teased you and told you to go get laid." They both snickered. "You took my advice and you've been distracted since then. If the woman touched you in some way, maybe you need to find her. I just don't want you to be punked. If this woman is in the life, you need to accept that and move on. If she's not then I say go for it—I am."

That was an unusual take from his brother who was generally on the, "Don't let one woman tie you down," trip. Eric knew why he wanted—no had to go back to Virginia. But it was not clear why Jason was in a hurry to get back there. "Ahhh, so this trip is about a woman that you need me to seduce for you," Eric asked as he sat back grinning.

"You know this game of me getting them and you sleeping with them is getting a little old."

"No, it's about the woman," Jason replied as he sat back. "I don't want you to seduce her, I have her interest, at least I think I do. I need you for insurance, just in case she needs to be serenaded." Jason grinned then looked out the window of the plane. "You remember when Mom used to say, 'you will know when the right woman comes along. 'And we would ask, how? Then she would say, 'you just will'."

"Yeah, I never understood that answer," Eric laughed.

"I didn't then either, but I do now." A knowing smile appeared on his face, "Her name is TeKaya Kendrick, they call her TK. I met her at the concert you gave in Richmond. Eric, this woman is so beautiful I knew she had to be a model, actress, or somebody trying to make it in the business. I tried to keep my distance, but something about her kept drawing me to her. When we went back to the hotel, I was given the name of the photographer and it was her. You met her. Remember the woman we took pictures with on the balcony before you went to your room?"

"I do remember her, she was stunning."

"Yes, she is, and intelligent. More importantly, she is real and has no interest in being in front of the camera." He stated shaking his head in disbelief. "I don't know how, but I'm going to make her mine. Whatever it takes, she will be mine."

"What are you going to do with the woman that lives with you; the mother of your child?"

Dropping his head, he shook it, "I don't know. When I moved Latoya in, I truly believed it was in Sierra's best interest. You know how badly I wanted my baby girl with me. But, these antics that Latoya keeps pulling are getting ridiculous. Most of the time I welcome the disappearing acts she pulls, but the arguments and fighting with other women over me is getting crazy. I don't want Sierra around that type of atmosphere."

"Have you given any thought to what Mom suggested?"

"Moving out? Nah, I can't leave Sierra."

"Then, out of curiosity, big brother, why are you going to bring this other woman into this situation when you already know how Latoya is going to react?"

Jason sighed, "It's something about this woman that I can't ignore. She's calling out to me and I can't say no."

"That's deep from a man who doesn't believe in commitment to one woman."

"Yeah. The other night I was with Brandy, one of the background vocalists for Kenny, I could not get into her. TeKaya kept slipping into my mind. After an hour or so, I just gave up, came home, and called her. We talked through the night and I slept like a baby." He sat back in his seat and sighed. "For the past two weeks my mind has been consumed with a woman and I can't do a damn thing about it."

Eric sat back in his seat and sighed with his own thoughts of a woman. "I know exactly what you mean."

Chapter 4
Jason and TeKaya

The car service arrived precisely at 6:15 p.m. to transport TK to Seducciόns, a private restaurant located near the Canal Walk in downtown Richmond. The 12th floor where the restaurant was located was circular, with a glass elevator that traveled though the center of the building. Once the doors opened, the maitre d' greeted the guest and asked their names. As the couple in front of her responded, TK looked around and immediately wished she had brought her camera to capture the exquisite view from the windows.

As the couple was taken to their table, behind the area where the maitre d' station stood, another maitre d' greeted her. "Mademoiselle, may I help you?"

"Yes, thank you. I am meeting Jason Davies."

"Ah, Mademoiselle Kendrick," he smiled.

"Yes," she returned his smile.

"Right this way." The Maitre d' took her behind the elevator area to a smaller, and as hard as it was to believe, more beautiful room than the exterior. The combination of the soft gold lighting, the mellow music, and the skyline of downtown Richmond as a backdrop, created a sensuous mood in the room. In the middle of the room was a water fountain with a statue in the center of a couple lovingly

Night of Seduction 33

embracing. Tables were stationed in each corner of the room, giving the appearance of privacy in an open environment. Standing at a table in the far corner of the room was Jason. TK wasn't sure what was more breathtaking, the city skyline in lights or the man standing before it. In either case, they both astounded her. She stepped forward and the decision was clear. It was the man who stood more than six feet tall, dressed in a navy blue suit by Miguel of Atlanta. The suit apparently was made just for his body. She was sure no other man could wear that suit and look that good.

There was nothing on this earth that could describe the woman walking towards him; she had to be a heavenly being dressed in red with her hair parted in the middle and flowing straight down her back. That thought alone should have warned Jason he in was about to take the journey of a lifetime. There was no skin showing with the exception of her arms and legs. It wasn't difficult for him to determine why his manhood sprung to attention. He mentally ordered that part of his anatomy to relax, this is not going to happen tonight, too much is at stake. The smile that greeted him made it difficult to concentrate on anything but the woman he was about to touch. His dreams of her over the past weeks paled in comparison to her presence. It wasn't just her outer appearance, but the aura around her that created the total package. Jason reached out his hand to her, "Hello TeKaya." That was supposed to be his greeting, and then they would sit, eat a meal and talk. That was all he wanted. But his lips wanted something more. One hand held her hand, the other caressed her cheek and his lips gently touched hers. The reality of the kiss was sweeter than any dream or imagination. The touch of her hand at his waist was titillating to say the least as heat surged through all regions of his body. His hands circled her waist merging their bodies together. The pieces to the puzzle of his life now all fit. This was the missing piece and he was never going to let her go.

Magnificent was the only word that came to mind as the simple hello kiss turned into a mutual uniting of two souls. TK was in awe of the man holding her so securely in his arms. Nothing her mother ever told her could have prepared her for the onslaught of feelings poring through her veins. She had only met this man once, yet his kiss was swaying the "take your time approach" she had planned. Her instinct, to hold on to this man for the rest of her life, was so strong that she was afraid to let go of him. It was clear that regardless of how many times the man in the background cleared his throat, Jason was not going to end the kiss, and she was just as sure she did not have the strength to pull away.

Jason's retreat was slow and sensuous as he lightly brushed a kiss on her cheek. Holding her close he could see the cloudiness of her eyes. "Please accept my apology for taking certain liberties with your lips, but they were quite irresistible."

"Your apology is not accepted and I would be offended if you never took such liberties again," TK replied with a sensuality she did not know she possessed.

A beaming Jason caressed her lower back. "I certainly don't wish to offend you, however, if I kiss you again we will not have dinner, dessert or breakfast."

With a raised eyebrow and a twinkle in her eye TK smiled. "You know, I'm okay with that."

The slight tilt of his head indicated he was contemplating accepting that invitation. He slowly took a step back, took her hand, and seated her on the opposite side of the table. He leaned over and whispered, "We will have the rest of our lives to make love. Tonight I want to get to know the woman who captured my heart with a single kiss." Once he took his seat, the waiter, who stood patiently waiting for the hello to end, approached the table.

While Jason spoke with the waiter, TK leisurely observed the virtual stranger that caused her to act so brazenly in public. The more she watched him the clearer the reason became. It was the olive toned, smooth skinned man, with hazel eyes, dressed as if he'd stepped out of GQ. He had a confident demeanor, and a mustache that promised to both tickle and drive any woman to lose her mind. Clearly, she had lost hers. This man is a music executive. He travels around the world with his brother, who is a chick magnet if one was ever created. *How could one family hold claim to two magnificent men?* She asked herself. "It's unfair, it's just unfair."

"What's unfair?" Jason asked.

Crossing her legs and surrendering to the inevitable, she sat forward, folded her hands under her chin, and relaxed. "I did not mean to say that out loud. I was just wondering why a man with as many women around as you would fly here just to see me."

"What's unfair about that?"

"You have me at a disadvantage. You are a man that has traveled the world, in private jets, no less. I'm a simple girl from the south. The furthest away I've been is Washington, DC on a field trip when I was in the fifth grade. I've had one boyfriend in my life. You have women at your disposal. It's very clear you know how to seduce any one of them. So, you tell me what about this evening is fair?"

"You don't mince words do you?"

"I never learned how."

Taking her hand in his he gently stroked her fingers. "It's you that have the advantage over me TeKaya. Your simple life is what I want. I would give up the money, the plane, and the women without a glance, if you were in my life. Match, point, set. Who was the boyfriend?" TK laugh quietly. "I'm serious TeKaya. Does he live here? Did he hurt you? Is he still in the picture?" He stopped questioning and laughed with her. "I'm serious woman and you're laughing."

Dinner was served and the two spent the next hour talking about each of their lives. TK talked about her mother, sister, and Nana, as they referred to their grandmother. Jason talked about Sierra, his mother, who was a jazz singer touring Europe at the time and of course his brother. He also talked more about the situation with Latoya and their living arrangements.

Just as the uncomfortable silence filled the air, Eric appeared on the makeshift stage with his guitar and began playing softly. The other three couples, whom Jason and TeKaya had not noticed, clapped as he ended the first song. He began the second song with the words, *believe in the experience, believe in the feelings, believe in me.* Jason stood and held his hand out to TeKaya who hesitantly joined him in the dance. The other couples joined in, as each reveled in the aesthetic sounds. When Eric's songs ended, Jason continued to hold TeKaya. "Believe in me enough to know I will work through this situation. I don't want to lose my little girl or my new girl."

Resting her head in the crook of his shoulder TeKaya sighed. "I believe you will Jason," she kissed his neck. "Just don't hurt me in the process."

With his finger on her chin, he brought her eyes up to his. "You have my word. I will never hurt you." Easing his hand across her shoulder and down her back, he kissed her softly, "That's my promise to you."

Sensing the moment was right, Eric stepped closer to the couple. Jason took her hand in his and faced his brother. I know you two met briefly, but I would like to introduce you again. Eric, this is TeKaya."

Eric kissed her cheek, "It's apparent from the silly grin on his face, you make my brother happy. I owe you."

TK blushed. "It's nice to meet you again Eric. But it's I that owe you."

"Is the car out front?" Jason asked before Eric could question her response.

"Yes, it is."

Turning to TeKaya, "Would you ride with us to the airport?" Jason asked.

"Sure," she replied a little disappointed he had to return to Atlanta.

As they took the 15-minute ride to the airport, Jason explained, "I'm sorry I have to return tonight, but Sierra is home alone."

Startled, TK jerked away, "You left her home alone? Are you crazy leaving a baby alone?"

Tickled by her immediate motherly instincts showing Jason laughed, "She's with her nanny."

"Where's her mother? You indicated the reason she lived with you was so Sierra would have both parents around her."

"That's true, but..."

"There are no but. Tonight she doesn't have either you or her mother. A nanny should not be raising your child. I'm not saying anything against the nanny, but whose values and beliefs do you want Sierra to have yours or your nanny's?"

"Isn't that the same question Mom asked you?" Eric grinned.

Jason changed from the surprised look at TeKaya to the irritated look at Eric. "Do you mind?"

"Sorry," Eric replied and looked away.

"I have to have someone dependable at the house for Sierra because I travel so much. When I'm home she is with me constantly. I can't depend on Latoya staying home with her."

Not understanding the logic, TK stammered. "But she's her mother. Where else would she want to be?"

Seeing the lost look on his brother's face, Eric knew he needed help. "TeKaya,"

She turned from Jason to Eric, "TK is fine."

"Thank you. Earlier you stated you owe me something, why?"

As if the answer was understood, she simply replied, "My sister." She turned back to Jason with a questioning eye.

"Your sister?" Eric questioned.

Realizing she had not really answered his question, she apologized. "Oh, I'm sorry. My sister was with me the night of your concert. She was going through a difficult year with her divorce and everything. She had fallen into a kind of funk, if you know what I mean. But something happened to her the night of your concert and she became alive again. I have my sister back and she swears you are the one to thank." She smiled. "If she was here I'm sure she would thank you in some elegant way. But since she is not you have to accept mine. Thank you for helping her through a very difficult time."

Eric looked to Jason, "I like her." He then looked back to TK. "What can I do to keep you around?"

Smiling brightly she started to answer but stopped. "You know, there is something you can do, both of you." She looked to Jason then back to Eric, "If you don't mind."

"Name it," Jason and Eric said in unison.

Surprised by their eagerness to please, "I like that. But you may not want to after I tell you what it is."

"Try us," Eric said with a smile.

"Okay, my sister teaches at an elementary school that is in dire need of a paint job. The school board will supply the paint but she has to gather painters. Before the divorce, it would not have been an issue, but you discover who your true friends are when you go through adversity. To date she only has four volunteers. If you two could help that would give us six people. What do you think? Will you help?"

"Let me get this straight. You don't want us to give you the money to hire a team to paint the building—you want us to help you paint?" Eric asked.

"Yes."

Eric and Jason smiled at each other. They were both used to people asking for funds or for Eric to sing to raise funds. This woman simply wanted their help. "When is this going to take place?"

"That's just it, her ex husband will only be available this Saturday, so she did not have a lot of time to pull things together."

Jason smiled and asked, "Would you mind if I bring a few friends?"

"No, not at all," she eagerly replied. "Just let me know how many, my mother is going to prepare lunch for everyone."

"Why don't you allow us to bring lunch?"

"Oh, I can't ask you to do that. Just your muscle will be appreciated."

The car came to a halt, to Jason's despair. Eric reached behind him and grabbed his guitar case. "TK it was a sincere pleasure to meet you. If I'm free, I will see you Saturday."

"It was nice to see you again Eric."

Jason turned to TeKaya. "The service is going to take you home." He pulled her close, "I'm so glad you agreed to see me tonight. I wish I could stay."

She kissed his lips softly. "I wish we had more time, but Sierra is waiting for you."

Her concern for his daughter touched him. "Thank you for understanding." He bent his head to kiss her and she stopped him with her hand on his chest.

"I understand your love and concern for your daughter. But I do not play second to any one. Before you and I go too much further, you should really look at your relationship with your ex-girlfriend. Be sure you are honest with yourself as to why she is living with you."

"That's fair," Jason nodded. He kissed her goodbye, "I'll call you when I get home."

He watched her standing at the car as the plane took off, and knew, TeKaya was his future.

TK walked into the house and joined her mother and sister in the family room watching television. Siri looked at the clock as TK sat on the sofa next to her. "You're home early. Was he that bad?"

Slipping out of her heels, TK sighed, "No, he was that good," she replied as she pulled her legs up and crossed them on the coffee table.

Siri and Kerri glanced at each other. Kerri smiled and turned off the television with the remote. "Details."

"Mommy I'm going to marry Jason. I don't know when, I don't know where, but I am going to be his wife—just as soon as I get rid of the girlfriend."

"That's taking it slow," Siri teased.

"What girlfriend?" Kerri asked.

TK exhaled, "Latoya Wright. She is his daughter Sierra's mother. From what he said they live separate lives, but under the same roof."

"I don't like the sound of that TeKaya. I didn't raise you to be a fool. He has to finish cooking in that kitchen before he starts storing food in another, you know what I mean?"

TK looked at Siri then back to her mother. "No Mommy, we never know what you mean when you say things like that."

Kerri sat up in her seat. "He needs to finish his business with that woman before he starts a relationship with you."

"I have to agree TK. I don't want you putting your time into Jason, as fine as he is and end up hurt. It took you three years to get over Cain. That was one boyfriend you could have done without."

"Well the Kendrick's fall quick and love long. I fell for your Dad in...."

"Two hours twenty-three minutes and ten seconds," TK and Siri responded together and laughed. Then continued, "Without ever saying a word to him, just watching and wondering when he was going to make his move."

"Laugh if you want to, but it is the truth," Kerri grinned at her daughters.

"I'm not laughing at you anymore Mommy. I've fallen for Jason hard. I can still feel his kiss lingering on my lips."

"Wow," Siri exhaled.

"My question is did he fall for you?"

"Yeah, Mommy he did," Siri answered for her. "I saw that the night they first met. He couldn't take his eyes off her."

"Then it will work out. You just might have to fight a little harder. When will I get to meet this man?"

TK picked up her shoes and stood. "Saturday, he's helping with the school job."

Siri sprung up. "Is he coming alone?"

"He mentioned bringing some friends."

"That's wonderful Siri. A few more people and you may get more than just the classrooms painted," Kerri replied excitedly.

"Um, yeah." Siri replied then asked, "Is Silk coming?"

"I don't know. I asked him, but he never said for certain."

"Silk was here, tonight, in Richmond?" Siri's question raced out before she could stop herself.

Both women turned to her with questioning eyes. "Yes, why?"

Siri noticed the look from them and decided to change the subject. "I was just wondering if he was going to be performing near here again anytime soon."

"Oh, he didn't say. But he did indicate he might be busy on Saturday. So I don't expect him." TK said as she walked toward the stairs. "I'm a little out of it. I'll talk to you guys in the morning."

"Good night TeKaya," Kerri said with a concerned mother's smile. When her baby girl was up the stairs and out of hearing range, she turned the television back on. "Is there something you need to tell me about Silk Davies?" She asked Siri who appeared to be unaffected by the question.

Looking away from her mother's eyes she shook her head and replied, "He has a wonderful voice." Then added, "You know I have another busy day cleaning tomorrow so I think I will turn in for the night." She walked over, kissed her mother's cheek. "Good night Mommy."

"Good night Siri." Kerri sat back, put her feet up and shook her head, "Who does she think she's fooling?" She smiled and settled back to watch her favorite program, reruns of the Cosby Show.

Chapter 5
Siri

Jason, Eric and a van of eight other men arrived at the school a little past nine Saturday morning. TK met them at the door and escorted them through the hallway. She introduced them to a few people along the way. She was so flustered by seeing Jason again she forgot a few names, but he corrected her blunder. If it was possible, he was more handsome in his jeans and t-shirt then the last time she had seen him. Since that night, he had awakened her every morning with a call and they fell asleep on the telephone together every night. She learned more about him in a week than most people would learn in a lifetime, and yet she still wanted to know more.

"This is quite an undertaking. How many volunteers did your sister get?" Jason asked.

"Not enough, but your friends will definitely help the outcome. My sister gave up having her room painted so the cafeteria could be done. That's where you guys are going to help. Are you ready?"

"Point me to the paint and brush," Eric smiled. Looking around it was clear that the building had been neglected. It felt good to be doing something to bring a school back to life.

Upon entering the cafeteria, a few people were standing on tables and ladders painting. There were buckets of paint and brushes near the door. A few long handles were leaning against the wall and a few rollers on the floor next to them. The huge room looked more like a penitentiary common area than a cafeteria for children. The few windows had bars on them and looked as if they had not been cleaned in years. This was definitely a place that needed a lot of TLC.

TK looked around but did not see Siri. She asked one of the workers and they pointed to the kitchen area, where it sounded as if a confrontation was in progress.

"We did not agree or discuss painting this area. Now it may have been your ex-husband that put you here, but you answer to me."

"Roscoe what difference does it make where the paint goes. I gave up painting my room so we could do the kitchen. It does not make sense to paint the outside and not in here. The children eat out there but the cooks work in here. They need to be comfortable with their surroundings as well as the children." Her back was to the door as all five feet three inches of her stood with a brush pointing at a man that stood at least six feet and a clear three hundred pounds.

"My name is Mr. Ford to you. I have had enough of your disrespect. Just know, Mrs. Austin, is well aware that you were the one that talked Carl into this and she is not pleased. I think it would behoove you to remember how persuasive she can be. You may be able to sway him; God only knows why, but me, huh, I know what you are."

"Is there a problem here?" Jason asked with the authoritative voice that was natural to him.

The two turned and Siri dropped the brush she was about to swing at Roscoe. Her eyes widened and her lips separated apart, but not a sound came out. She turned away quickly, but not soon enough.

"Siri?" Eric called out as he stepped towards her.

"You know my sister Siri?" TK asked smiling.

Night of Seduction

Eric looked at TK, then at Jason then back to Siri. He wasn't sure what he was reading in her eyes. Surprise was definitely one of the emotions, and he certainly understood why. But there was something else.

"Who in the hell are you?" Roscoe demanded.

Jason stepped forward, "I'm Jason Davies, manager of Silk Davies standing right there. We came to assist Siri with her painting project. And you are?"

"Oh," Roscoe quickly changed his tune. "You're Silk Davies, the singer. I didn't recognize you." He extended his hand grinning broadly. "Welcome, welcome to our little project here." When Eric was slow in extending his hand, Roscoe turned and grabbed Jason's. "We were having a little disagreement on the extent of the project. As you can see this is a huge undertaking."

"What's the problem Roscoe?" TK asked defiantly and ready to back her sister up.

Eric stepped closer to Siri who was still avoiding his eyes. He extended his hand, "Eric Davies, I've heard so much about you from your sister."

Siri was still motionless. *What in the hell was he doing here? What would Roscoe do if he found out about that night? Would she lose her job? Be humiliated all over again? Did he always look so good, so kissable?* Her eyes traveled down the t-shirt that covered the defined muscles she knew were underneath. Then on to his slightly bow legs she remembered straddling her, that were now covered in jeans. Then back to the eyes that had completely captured her that night. "Hello," she replied so low, she wasn't sure he heard her.

Cashmere walked in, "Mr. Ford you better come see this, you too Siri."

"What is it Ms. Wagstaff, can't you see we are busy here?" Roscoe responded.

"I'm pretty sure you want to see this," she replied.

They stepped back into the main cafeteria and were shocked to see the number of people standing there. "They heard Silk Davies was here to paint and they decided to help too." Cashmere whispered then winked at Siri.

Siri looked around and smiled brightly, "I think we now have enough people to do the entire school. What do you think Roscoe?" She slapped him on the back then walked out to the crowd to begin taking names and passing out equipment. She was sure that someone upstairs was looking out for her. If she had stood in the room with Silk Davies for another minute, she would have lost her dignity—that, she was sure of. Even now, she could not concentrate on the names people were giving her, for the sense of him staring at her. She chanced it and looked up. Yep, he was staring at her.

Seeing Siri was busy, Cashmere began organizing which classrooms workers would go to. Soon they had at least two people in every classroom, several in the cafeteria and kitchen, and several in the auditorium. A few hours later, some men came in with spray guns to help speed the job along.

Because the number of helpers had increased so dramatically, Kerri's lunch spread was not going to feed all of them. Jason gave one of the band members his card and instructed him to bring back whatever was needed to feed the volunteers. TK, Jason, Eric, and Kerri were all seated at the back of the cafeteria eating when Siri emerged from the kitchen. "Siri, come here, sit down, and have some lunch with us." Kerri ordered. "That child is going to work herself to death trying to clean up this school."

"You know how she is about the kids Mommy, don't fuss," TK pleaded.

Siri slowly made her way over. The last thing she wanted to do was be near the man whose presence affected her so deeply she could barely breathe. Eric who was sitting at the oblong table next to Kerri never took his eyes from Siri as she approached. She was more beautiful than he remembered. Something inside him stirred as she came closer. He had hoped that when he saw her again she would not have the same effect as she had that night. That hope faded when he saw the bluish gray paint on the tip of her nose and in her hair that was held up by a clamp. The gray midriff shirt and sweat pants that hung seductively low on her hips were stained as well. He swore there was nothing more exquisite than the woman standing before him.

Kerri reached into the cooler and pulled out a container. "Here I fixed your favorite salad, with grilled chicken, tangerine, green peppers, sweet peppers, raisins mixed with spinach and lettuce." She sat the container on the table then reached down and pulled out a bottle of water.

"Thank you, Mommy," she replied softly. She looked around and knew she could not sit at that table with Silk. "I'm not very hungry. I think I'll go get started on my room."

Kerri frowned. "Nonsense, girl. You've been here since seven. You didn't eat breakfast and have been working since you got here. Of course you're hungry and if you're not sit down and eat anyway." Kerri reached down into the cooler again, speaking her mind as she did. "If that ex-husband of yours was any kind of a real man, he would have paid someone to do this. Not sucker you into going out with him again. Where is he anyway? Some kind of councilman he turned out to be." She finished just as she pulled out her famous strawberry shortcake."

Normally Siri would have been fighting with TK over the dessert, but her nerves were too in tune with Silk. Noticing she was still standing and not fighting over the cake, which TK and Jason were now sharing, Kerri became concerned. She stopped fidgeting and looked up at her daughter who was busy trying not to look at the man sitting next to her. Kerri looked from Siri to Eric, who was not even attempting not to look at her daughter. "Siri, honey, are you okay?"

Smiling fictitiously she replied, "Yeah, Mommy, I'm fine. I just want to get things finished before people start leaving." Avoiding the eyes she knew were watching her, she nervously picked up the bottle of water and the container. "I'll eat this in my classroom." She started to walk away then stopped and turned to the people at the table. "Thank you for coming to help with the school. I truly appreciate your help. I'll make sure the children know who you are and what you did today." She smiled bashfully and walked away quickly.

"Has that man been here bothering her today?"

"I haven't seen him or his mother. You know they only come around if the news cameras are here," TK replied.

"I certainly hope she is not going back into her shell again. I hate what that family did to her." Kerri stated as she angrily began putting things away.

"What happened to her?" Jason asked, concerned with the conversation.

"Carl and Mable Austin happened," Kerri replied angrily.

"Carl is Siri's ex-husband." TK explained, "He divorced her because his mother Mable decided Siri was not the type of wife Carl needed to further his career in politics. The divorce was played out like a soap opera on the local news. Siri refused to comment on any of the accusations that were levied against her and Carl was too spineless to contradict anything that his mother said. The media reported her as having a questionable relationship with a minor and accused her of marrying Carl for his family's money. She lost her teaching job at the high school and the respect of the community."

"What happened with the minor?" Jason asked.

"The boy was seventeen years old and very taken with Siri." Kerri replied. "Siri was tutoring the boy one evening when the boy made advances towards her. Well, Siri's a fighter; at least she was before this. She whipped that boy's behind good and sent him home to his parents. The boy went around school telling people he and Siri were getting it on. Mable refused to have her son's name attached to such a scandal and ordered Carl to divorce her. The boy's father discovered it was all a lie and convinced his son to tell the truth. But it was too late; the damage had been done. Siri lost her job, her husband, and her self-respect. The irony of it all is I believe Carl truly loved her, he just can't stand up to his mother."

"What's really sad is Carl is the only man Siri has ever been with and he knows that to be the truth. I'm afraid if she goes back into that funk she was in before, she will never let another man into her life," TK sighed. She looked up at Eric. "You know you really touched her the night of your concert."

"Yes, you did." Kerri added with a smile. "The next morning she was full of life and ready to take on whatever was to come. A few days later, she reapplied for a teaching position and she finished a novel she had begun last year. I was so happy to see her back to her old self again, until today."

Jason looked at Eric, who was listening intently to the conversation. Eric looked up at his brother. There was no way he could know he touched her in more ways than the music. "I think I'll go down to her room. What number is it?"

"Number 12, right next to the office so the principal can keep an eye on her," TK replied very disgustedly.

Eric cleared the table, picked up a bucket of paint, a brush, and a roller and walked down the hallway.

Appalled with her behavior Siri sat at her desk and ate in silence. *I acted ungrateful to people that came to help the school. TK must be so angry with me for not spending time with her and Jason. How am I going to explain the way I behaved to my sister or her mother?* "How do I fix this?"

"It's really not that bad. A little TLC cures most of the ills of the world." Eric's six feet frame stood in the doorway with a bucket of paint in one hand and the roller in the other looking sexier than any person had a right to.

"Not all things," she shyly replied. Embarrassed by his presence she looked down at her barely eaten salad. "Silk, I know I don't have the right to ask, but please don't mention that night to anyone, please."

Concern with the tremor in her voice, he stepped into the room and closed the door. "My name is Eric. Silk is my stage name." He sat the items in his hand down and sat at a desk directly in front of her. "I was never one to kiss and tell."

The vicinity of his seat was a little too close for comfort. Siri stood and opened the door. "I'm not allowed to close my door when another person is in the room." She stood by the door and looked around nervously.

The sexual tension was in the air as they stared silently at each other. The shock of seeing her again had not completely diminished for Eric as he fought the urge to kiss her as thoroughly as he had before.

"I think it's important for you to know, I don't sleep around with men."

A devilish grin appeared on Eric's face, "Do you sleep around with women?"

"No!" She swallowed, "I--what I meant to say was I don't sleep around. You know like what happened between us." She whispered while looking out the door to ensure privacy.

"Oh, so that was your first time?" he whispered back.

"No. Umm--yes." She replied flustered as she stepped away from the door so the conversation would not be overheard. Standing directly in front of him now with her arms folded across her chest she whispered, "No, it wasn't my first time with a man; it was my first time with a stranger."

"You should try it again, you are pretty good at it," he teased.

Sure, she had misunderstood what he said she frowned. "I can't go around sleeping with strangers. My reputation is stained as it is."

"Well you could just sleep around with me. I won't tell anyone."

Siri's hands went to her hips and her eyebrows furrowed. "As enticing as that may be, I can't do that. I don't know you."

He took her hand and motioned for her to sit at the desk next to him. "I beg to differ," he said as she sat in the chair. "I think you and I know each other better than some married couples."

Blushing, Siri lowered her head. "About that night--"

"Yes about that night of seduction," he interrupted her. "You left something behind."

"I did, what?"

"Your panties."

Siri sprung from the seat and gasped.

"Will you relax?" Eric laughed. "It's not that serious. No one will ever know Siri. You have my word on that."

With tears appearing in her eyes Siri whispered, "You don't understand. I just went through a really, really bad period in my life. If something like this gets out about me it would be catastrophic. I'm just beginning to get my life back in order. I could lose my job, and the little respect I've managed to earn back. Please, I beg you, please don't tell anyone."

Eric stood and embraced her. The fear in her eyes annoyed him. "Siri, I will never tell a soul about that night." He kissed the side of her head and held her protectively in his arms as her tears captured his heart. "Look at me Siri."

Slowly she raised her head until their eyes met. He wiped the tears from her cheeks with his thumbs. "That night was very memorable for me. I hope it was the same for you. I certainly don't want you to stress over it."

Mesmerized by his eyes and his voice, Siri wasn't sure which was causing the serenity within her, but whichever it was, she was grateful for it. "The memory of that night soothes me to sleep at night and awakens me refreshed each morning. I never thought I would have to explain it to my family."

Touched by her words he smiled. "I hope you will explain it to me one day. But not now. We have a room to paint and you have people to thank. Where shall we start?"

Realizing she was still standing in his arms, Siri slowly pulled away. "My room isn't going to be painted. I compromised and did the kitchen instead."

"I have never volunteered to do manual labor with these hands. Are you turning down my offer?"

Touched by his confession Siri smiled. "Thank you for the offer, but my boss will have a cow or two if this room is painted."

"He looks as if he could have two cows." Siri smiled so brightly at his comment, Eric was certain somewhere on earth the sun was rising. Thinking to himself, *I would love to see her smile like that every day.* "I'm sure he would look and feel a lot better if he had at least one cow, so what do you say we help him along."

"Hmm, you are asking me to do something that will tick my boss off. Let me think about that for a moment." She acted as if she was contemplating. "Works for me," she declared. "Let's start with the back wall."

Smiling contently, "The back wall it is," Eric replied.

The local radio station was on as the two worked silently. The deejay announced, "*We have a request from a volunteer over at the elementary school on the north side of Richmond. It seems they have a paint party going on over there and I wasn't invited. My feelings aren't hurt, just bruised a little. Especially since Silk Davies is there. That's right folks the one and only Mr. get them sticky and wet is in town working to help our community. Way to go Silk, and just to show you how much love we have for you here in the capitol city, the next hour we will give a little of the old and new from you. To my loyal listeners, let Silk Davies be an example to all of us. It's the little things that make the biggest difference. Enjoy the smooth sounds of Silk Davies, The Little Things."*

"That's an interesting nickname you have," Siri commented as she painted the low area and he did the high.

"Yeah, they tell me it is well earned," he replied reaching over her head with the roller.

"I can testify to that," she said while looking up at him.

He looked down and all the attraction he was trying to hold in began seeping out. Her black eyes reflected the mutual understanding of the moment. They may agree not to speak on the night they met, but both were deeply affected. She stood slowly as if something unspoken commanded her. A drop of blue paint from the roller landed on the tip of her nose. Reaching out he touched the spot. The sensation that surged through him was stronger than he had ever experienced. "If you keep looking at me like that, I am going to kiss you and we will relive that night right here in this room."

"Hey did you guys here the announcement on the radio?" TK asked from the doorway.

The two did not answer for a moment, which seemed to be missed by TK who was now standing by the radio turning the volume up. Jason on the other hand noticed a little more. His brother was zoned in on Siri as if she was the only woman on earth. To keep her distracted and quench the urge to hold her close, Jason turned to TK with his hand stretched out, "Dance with me TeKaya."

"I would love to," she smiled sensuously.

Placing the roller against the wall, Eric extended his hand to Siri. Afraid to take it, but terrified not to, she joined him in a dance as his voice echoed in the room. Kerri stood in the doorway and admired what she witnessed. The room was filled with a sense of oneness, which only surfaces when there is love in the air. Leaning against the door Kerri wondered, *now I know about Jason, but when and how did Eric happen?* The thought pleased her, but concerned her as well. The last relationship her oldest daughter was in was public and it almost killed her, this one could be worse. Eric's popularity was worldwide, not local. If this were to go badly it could destroy her.

"Doesn't appear to be much work going on in here!" Mable Austin yelled to be heard over the music. "Siri I believe your behavior at the moment is in conflict of your contract. Would you mind turning that blasphemous music off?"

Siri walked towards the radio. "I'm rather enjoying that music and since this is a Saturday and not a school day, the contract you mentioned is not in affect Maybelline," Kerri spoke as a mother protecting her cub.

"Regardless of what day it may be, her behavior reflects on the Board. If she wants to keep her job, it's best that she remembers that."

"I understand the contract Mrs. Austin. I don't need to be reminded," Siri replied.

"It appears you do. Oh just so you know, from this point on, any ideas or suggestions you have for this school will come directly to me, not Carl."

"Hey I just checked out the cafeteria and some of the rooms. It really looks great. Siri this was a wonderful idea." Carl commented enthusiastically as he walked in from the hallway. When nothing was said, he looked around the room at the sullen faces, and then looked to his mother.

"Excuse me," Mable said as she left the room.

"Hello Mrs. Kendrick, TK, Siri." He extended his hand to Jason who stood close to the door, "Carl Austin."

Jason shook his hand, "Jason Davies."

Carl walked over to where Eric stood and extended his hand. "Silk Davies, I'm a huge fan. Thank you for giving us a hand."

Eric shook his hand and looked at Siri. "I'm here to help Siri and the children. Do you normally make it a habit to insult people who volunteer to help in the community?"

The smile on Carl's face dropped and he looked at Siri and exhaled. "I don't know what my mother said to offend you, but please accept my apology. We do appreciate anyone that steps forward to help with our schools. It's clear that your participation brought others in the community forward to help as well. As hard as we may try, it's difficult to get people to understand if they give, the community will prosper. Sometimes bringing in a celebrity encourages others to do what they can to help themselves. Thank you for coming forward."

As much as he wanted to, Eric did not dislike the man that was once married to the woman he could not get off his mind. "You're welcome. If we are planning on finishing this room, we better get back to painting."

"Sure I'll get out of your way." He turned to Siri, "Umm, may I speak with you outside for a minute?"

Siri walked past her mother and kissed her cheek. "Go home Mommy, I'll be fine," then stepped outside the room.

"Will you guys be okay while I walk my mother out to her car?" TK asked.

"Sure, we're straight," Jason, replied with a smile as the women walked out. He walked over to the wall Eric was angrily painting. "I don't like what I just saw. It's as if she is surrounded by people who are openly disrespectful to her. The mother-in-law is at the forefront. We have to fix this Eric."

It had been a year and a half since he had been inspired. Everything he wrote in that time was garbage to him, even if his team disagreed. Eric knew deep down it was not up to his standard. Fate was a bitter pill to take. Someone has had come along that touched him so deeply he was creating music in his sleep. The past few weeks, the vision of this woman and the music in his mind were one. He thought he would never see her again. Now she's here with more baggage than the lost and found at LAX and just as exquisite as he remembered. There were women all over the world who wanted to be with him, give their lives to him, be at his beck in call. He could simply settle for one or two of them and be happy. But no, he had to have a woman with a reputation of a child molester, an ex-husband that clearly still has feelings for her and an ex-mother-in-law from hell. What he was about to say was clearly a sign that he had lost every ounce of good sense his mother had given him. "Find me a condo and studio in Richmond." Disregarding the surprised look on his brother's face, Eric continued painting. "Let's finish this room."

Chapter 6
Eric and Siri

How could such a wonderful day turn into a huge mess? Every room in the school had a fresh coat of paint and the floors were clean. The number of volunteers increased as the news of Silk's presence leaked out. Of course, Mable was contributing the successful undertaking to Carl through every news media source that would listen. But Siri didn't care. The important thing was that when the children arrived at school next week, they would have a better learning environment.

Carl crossed her mind as she walked through the hallway ensuring all trash was gone and there was nothing out of place as Roscoe had ordered. He did step up to get the paint they'd needed to do the job. For the first time she actually heard him apologize for his mother's behavior, that in and of itself, was an accomplishment. She was still leading him around like a puppy, at some point Carl would have to cut the apron strings. As much as she loved him at one point, there was no way she could go back to him. The cut was too deep and the wound had just begun to heal.

Putting the keys Roscoe had left with her in the office and locking the door, she looked around one final time. Eric "Silk" Davies did this. At least his celebrity status did. If it had not been for that, they probably would have gotten only half the number of rooms painted. People loved him and his music so much that they came out and accomplished a great thing. "Of all the people you could have sent into my life, why him Lord? The man is walking temptation to every woman on earth. I couldn't resist him that night and as much as I try I can't resist him now." She shook the outer doors to make sure they were locked then walked around the building towards her car thinking—Jason and TK seemed good for each other. She didn't know a lot about him, but she had never seen TK so happy. Young love is a wonderful thing, she thought, but it also had the potential to hurt. Carl was her first and the only man she had ever been with until Eric.

Tired to her bones and starving, the thought of him eased her weariness. He was quite a man. She certainly understood why women all over the world went crazy over him. That extraordinary night was proof. Never in her life would she have slept with a total stranger, much less want more. She stopped walking as the thought settled in. She wanted to make love with him again. The first time was unplanned, spontaneous, uncontrolled. The next time she wanted to be fully aware of all that occurred. Easing into her car she placed her head on the steering wheel and wondered what was she going to do? She had the hots for the brother of her sister's new man. He was a music superstar who woman would kill for and she wasn't sure if he felt the same for her. "You really got yourself in a fix this time Siri Octavia."

When she reached the two story split-level house she called home, there were two SUV's parked in front. Shrugging she pulled around them and parked in the driveway. The sounds of laugher and conversation could be heard from the front porch as she inserted her key into the doorknob. The sight that greeted her was unusual, but very familiar. It reminded her of the way the house was when Daddy was alive. It was always filled with people laughing, eating, and just enjoying life. Closing the door, she walked through the foyer and searched the small crowd of about ten people to identify at least the residents of the house. As she stepped down into the family room TK and Kerri were sitting near the fireplace, on the floor, flagged by Jason on one side and Eric on the other. The guys from the band were around them with plates piled high with food and laughing at photos. As if sensing her presence Eric looked up and smiled then looked back down at the pictures. Siri's eyes followed the direction of his and she gasped. "Mommy are you showing my baby pictures?"

"Hey Siri," TK beamed looking up at her. "It's about time Roscoe let you go. Is he locking up?"

"No, Roscoe left the building around six. I just finished cleaning and locking up."

"He left you in that building alone, this time of evening?" Kerri asked in a motherly tone.

"I was fine Mommy." Feeling a need to get all eyes off of her, she looked to the guys. "Did you guys leave any for me?"

"Nope, J-bird ate it all," one of the men joked. The man she assumed to be J-bird sucker punched the other guy and the battle was on.

"There's plenty in the kitchen." Kerri stood with Eric's assistance. "You worked so hard today, baby. Why don't you go up and shower while I prepare a plate for you."

"You worked just as hard. I'll run up and make a quick change. Then I'll come down and eat. You guys continue, but not with the baby pictures please."

"Why not? She embarrassed me. Now it's your turn," TK laughed. "Besides, Eric asked to see them."

Her eyes found his. The warmth of his stare streamed over her like the effect of a waterfall. Looking around she wondered if anyone else noticed the tremors flowing through her. "I'm afraid there isn't much to see." Turning she walked up the steps and hoped everyone would be gone by the time she returned—well maybe not everyone.

An hour later as she emerged from the well deserved shower, dressed in a short jean skirt, a sleeveless midriff top, and flips flops, Siri's wish seemed to have been granted. The family room was empty of everyone, including her mother and sister. Walking through the kitchen, disappointment touched her with the realization that Eric was not there. What could she have been thinking; he would have no reason to be there. To him she was just a one night stand, regardless of how she felt. In the kitchen, the plate her mother prepared for her was on the stove. Having worked all day and having her appetite taken away by Eric's presence, she was now starving. Taking a seat at the table, she savored each taste of the meal as she closed her eyes and chewed.

A sound startled her and she turned. Standing behind her at the open patio door was Eric. Looking stunned she asked, "Where is everyone?"

"The guys went back to the hotel. They are flying back to Atlanta tonight. Jason and TeKaya went out for the evening. Your mother indicated she had a very long day and asked if I would stay to keep your company while you ate dinner. I decided to wait on the patio." Before he could stop them, the words came out even though he deplored them, but he had to know. "Are you still in love with your ex-husband?"

That was the second time today she had been asked that question. When she stepped out into the hallway with Carl earlier today, he apologized for being several hours late. It seemed his mother had set up appointments for him to meet with contributors who requested a dinner meeting in order to continue the conversation. Therefore he had to cancel their date. Anger had set in from his mother's earlier attack and she released her frustration on him.

"It's the same old thing with you Carl. Your mother tells you to jump and you just keep jumping until you think she is satisfied. Contrary to what you say, you will never change, you will never be your own man. We could never think about starting over as long as your mother controls you."

"Things have changed I just can't discuss them with you right now. I want to make things right Siri. I want to make up for all the hurt my Mother caused. I love you Siri, I never stopped."

"Then why didn't you defend me against your Mother's attacks or her public humiliation of me. You stood back and allowed her to destroy my reputation and career. You don't do that to someone you love."

"Siri I've been taking steps to correct all of that. I got your job back. I made sure you got here, where you wanted to teach. I had to stand up against my mother to get those things accomplished. I admit I made some mistakes with us, now I am doing all I can to right a wrong. All I need to know is that you still love me—that's all I need."

At the time, she did not have an answer for him. She just replied, she didn't know. Now she was being asked the question again and not sure, why he asked the question, she had to think it through. The love she had for Carl was damaged along with her reputation, simply because he could not stand up to his mother. "I can never go back to Carl."

"That's not what I asked you."

"I don't know. I haven't thought about it much since the divorce." She wiped her mouth with the napkin and sat back in the chair as she tried to think it through. "There were so many harsh words between us, it's hard to forget. I care for him and would not want anything terrible to happen to him, but I don't think I'm in love with him any longer."

The answer pleased him more than he wanted to admit for the sight of this woman was rendering certain parts of his body out of control. "I'm glad to hear that. He seems like a nice enough guy, but nowhere near man enough for you."

Dressed in a pair of black slacks, a black silk blend t-shirt, his locs hung neatly around his shoulders. He had the most amazing face anyone could imagine. He was certainly man enough for her and probably a few other women. Uncertain of her reaction, she stood and put her plate in the sink. His presence was too much for her to control. "It was nice of you to stay, but I'm sure you have plans for the evening. You don't have to hang around."

"Actually I do. Jason drove, and I don't know my way around."

"Oh. Would you like for me to take you back to your hotel?"

"No, but I would enjoy you sitting with me out back."

With her insides tightening at the memory of the last time they were alone, she smiled. "Sure." Sitting out back couldn't hurt anything.

When she reached him he took her hand. His touch caused sensations to surge throughout her body. Maybe she was wrong.

Pausing he took in the entire package of Siri Austin, from the fresh clean face, to the black doe like eyes that looked up at him. In flats, the top of her head fell right at his chin. He was tempted to kiss her standing there in the doorway, but knew that if he did he would not be able to stop. All day he'd endured people belittling her, shouting at her, and making demands on her. There was nothing he could do because she did not want anyone to know about them. All he wanted to do was to kiss her senseless, make her feel cared for, loved, and, at the very least, appreciated. Instead, he continued on to the secluded area he found in the back yard.

Siri followed as he guided her to the swing set behind the tool shed. Before the shed was built the area was where she and TK would play in the sandbox, on the sliding board, and swing set. Her mother had never removed the items. She was patiently waiting for grandchildren to come along and put the area to use again.

"Eric, why are we coming back here?"

He stopped abruptly, which caused her to run into him. "If I don't taste you soon I'm going to explode."

Shocked by his blunt honesty she looked up at him with sultry eyes. "Oh."

He growled, "If you continued to look at me like that I will drop you to your knees and take you right here and I won't care if your Mother sees us." He turned and continued pulling her around the tool shed. As soon as they cleared the end of the building, he pulled her into his arms, cupped her face in his hands, and gently kissed her lips. "That's for looking out for the children." He then trailed his tongue along her bottom lip and pulled it between his lips, gently sucking it. "That's for putting up with your asshole of a boss." He slid his tongue inside her mouth and played tango with hers. "That's for your spineless ex-husband. And this is for the bitch of the day." He placed her arms around his neck and pulled her up into an embrace as he allowed his kisses to sooth all the ills of the world that had touched her that day.

The first kiss loosened her resolve not to make out in her back yard with her mother upstairs in the house. The second kiss eased the guilt, but the third kiss killed any chance she had to resist the urges building inside of her. This kiss gave her the nerve to do exactly what she wanted to do from the minute she turned and saw him. She wrapped her legs around his waist and melted into the kiss that was again threatening to take her good girl status away again.

The moment her legs surrounded him the blood pumping through his groin increased. Bracing her between his body and the tool shed, his hands touched the smooth skin of her thighs. Fire ignited in his system from the touch causing a groan to escape his throat. Positioning her lower until the core of her connected with his undeniable arousal. The jean skirt moved up as her body was lowered. The only thing separating his fire and her desire was the silk of her lace panties and the cloth of his pants. Not thinking twice he reached in to remove the barrier by unzipping his pants and freeing his arousal. "Tell me to stop Siri," he murmured against her lips, "tell me to stop."

Her pulse was racing, her mind void of thoughts and her body leaping with desire, "Please don't stop Eric. Don't stop." Their tongues met in mid air. No lips. Just tongues touching until she couldn't stand any more. "Eric, please----."

Before she could complete her plea he inserted a finger under her panties and into the desire she was sharing with him. Moving the frilly material aside he entered her with an inexplicable urgency.

He swallowed her cry with a kiss as he filled her to the hilt and they both sighed with satisfaction, "Hmm." Neither moved, as they panted hard against each other.

A sense of completeness consumed him as it had that first night and he wanted, needed, to savor the moment. This woman was his muse. She inspired him in more ways than he'd first thought. "I want you, Siri," he said as he kissed her cheeks, her eyelids. "I have wanted you again since that night." He moved slowly within her savoring her moistness, the snugness, the warmth of her. She tightened her legs around his waist pulling him closer as pure unadulterated lust engulfed her. That was the only way she could explain her wanton behavior and she was powerless to stop. She had committed to memory the feel of him that night and had dreamed of it, craving him night after night. "Eric," she moaned against his ear.

He eased their bodies down to the cool green grass beneath their feet and gently placed her under him without breaking contact. His body began delivering deliberate thrusts within her leaving no space untouched by the sweet torture. He wanted her to feel every note of the music playing along with the rhythm in his mind. Her body responded to every beat as if she was hearing the music with him. Her hands moved down his back and her legs widened, allowing him to plunge deeper and deeper into her folds. He raised himself above her and began to move like a man possessed. And at that moment the only thought that drove him was to bring both of them over the crescendo of their joining. The intensity of their movement magnified as he called out her name. "Siri, open your eyes. I want to see us through your eyes." Drawn to his words, she wanted to see herself though his eyes, she slowly opened them.

The look in his eyes caused her body to explode into tiny pieces and moisture cascading over her body. Her explosion ricocheted through him as the words heaven's gate came to mind. That's where he was, at heaven's gate and the doors had just opened as the two of them flowed through. They were both spent, neither could move, think, or breathe. As his senses began to return, he realized he had taken her in a raunchy way. He wrapped her in his arms and turned onto his back pulling her atop him and held her. "I wanted you so badly Siri, but not like this. You deserve better." He continued to hold her as she panted against his chest.

"Why?" was all she could manage.

He rubbed her back as he spoke. "I don't know why. I just know I want to make love to you in a bed where I can kiss and taste every inch of you. I don't want a quickie or a one night stand. I want to see you, touch you, feel you, take my time showing you how much I enjoy your body."

Confused by his words, she breathily joked, "You know sexing a woman senseless, then leaving her to think it was only a dream could be interpreted as cruel and unusual punishment."

"Disappearing from a man's bed before he could get his fill the next morning should be punishable by death."

She gently laughed against him and replied, "Then we are both guilty and deserve whatever we get."

He liked the idea of making her laugh. "How did you end up in my room that night?"

She told him the story of leaving the party and searching for somewhere to hide. When she finished he told her he thought she was a call girl Jason had sent to his room.

"Ahhh, the reason you keep condoms in your wallet." She felt his body tense and his breathing changed. She looked up at him, "What is it?"

He moved her to the side, came to his knees, and began righting her clothes, and then his. He stood and held out his hand to her. She took it and stood. "Eric, what is it?"

"I was careless. I did not use protection."

Siri stared at him. "This wasn't planned. In the heat of the moment neither of us thought."

"That's what causes death these days, not thinking."

Sensing his anger she began brushing her skirt off. "I was tested after my divorce which was nine months ago. I'm clean. I have not been sexually active, well other then you, since that time. You're safe," she stated then proceeded to march off.

He grabbed her arm as she walked by. "I'm sorry, that came out wrong. I'm not angry with you. I'm angry with myself." He pulled out his wallet and retrieved several gold packets of condoms. "This may not have been planned by you, but it was by me, the moment I saw you at the school." He replaced his wallet. "After finding you, I was not leaving Richmond without touching you again."

Siri stood there, not sure how to respond. This god of a man who had women swarming over him planned to seduce her, a woman who had limited knowledge of how to please a man. "Why didn't you use them?"

"I couldn't stop, I didn't want to stop." He pulled her into an embrace, "You haven't asked me."

"I don't need too. I know about all the charity events you sponsor about HIV it is well documented."

He kissed her forehead, "You still need to ask. I get tested every six months whether I'm sexually active or not. I'm concerned about something a little different."

"What's that?" she asked now holding his hands.

"Pregnancy."

Siri laughed. "You don't have to worry about that. The entire time I was married I wanted a child, but it never happened."

"You're not using any type of protection?"

"No, I'm sorry," she replied solemnly looking up at him.

He placed her head on his chest. "We'll worry about that when and if it becomes an issue."

Subconsciously he knew what he was doing; he wanted to feel her with no obstructions, nothing between him and her. The cost of that moment may take a lifetime for him to repay. It was at that moment he realized what he wanted from her. "Let's go inside and clean up."

The two sat at the kitchen table and she listened as he talked. Eric talked about his career, the affect of constantly touring, performing night after night. He loved the fans, but it was hard work and you had to be dedicated to be successful. How much he liked the small intimate venues as opposed to the larger ones. He told her about his mother, whom he and his brother were close to although they were on different sides of he world. Then he talked about Jason. It appeared he worshiped the very ground his big brother stood on. There was nothing he would not do for him, including continuing touring. What he really wanted to do was write music for others. But since any changes he made to his career directly impacted Jason's, he was reluctant to stop touring.

Listening to him made her realize he was just as vulnerable as she was. Yes, he was rich and famous, but he had to make sacrifices to get to this point in his life. It also occurred to her that he was ready for a change. He talked about meeting someone and having children, but in his world it was difficult to know if someone is with you for who you are as a performer or a man.

They acknowledged that they had a strong sexual attraction to each other; however they both knew it would be difficult to pursue it any further, and neither wanted to over shadow the budding relationship between Jason and TK.

Siri went to bed that night tired, but refreshed. She had a new take on life and looked forward to what it would bring. She also had a man that had touched her soul and a clear understanding of the concept of sexual healing.

Chapter 7
Jason

"Daddy, Daddy," Sierra squealed as she ran into his office barefoot and sticky hands. She jumped into his outstretched arms. "Hello Pumpkin. What are you getting into?"

"She's being bad as usual," Latoya said from the doorway with her arms folded across her chest. She put her hands in the back pocket of her jeans causing her breasts to protrude further out, and stepped into his office. "Are you busy?"

That was the first sign that something was amiss. Latoya never cared one way or another about what someone else's agenda was, only hers. Not interested in whatever she was up to Jason sat Sierra in his lap and replied, "Yep, but she can stay." He turned his attention back to the computer console.

"Haven't seen much of you in the last month or so, what you been up to?"

The question startled him as he turned back to her. She was a beautiful woman, which had always been his weakness, but not anymore. Her stance reminded him of why he became involved with her in the first place; the fair skin, bewitching eyes and a hell of a body, even after the baby.

That was the bait she used to pull you in, and once she did, the real witch would appear and try to take over your soul. "What?" He asked looking bewildered.

"You haven't been around," she replied taking care to tread lightly. "That's all. I missed seeing you."

"How would you know I haven't been around? This is the first time you have been home in a month." Sierra reached for the keyboard and he caught her hand and kissed it. "No Pumpkin."

"Ahhh so you were looking for me?" she asked teasingly and took a step closer.

"No, I wasn't. Since you have a daughter I thought you might want to, oh I don't know, spend some time with her."

"I spend the same amount of time with her that you do. So don't give me that. You missed seeing me and you know it." She grinned and teasingly pushed his shoulder.

That was the second sign. They had not had the 'joking with each other' relationship in almost a year. Not since she had flattened his tires to keep him from going out. "I am here every night and every morning when she wakes up." She had now walked behind his chair and placed her hand on his shoulder.

"Most times I'm here. But sometimes I just need to get away."

"You are a mother, you can't just get away."

"You're a father and you do it all the time."

"I don't have an issue taking her with me when I work. Isn't that right Pumpkin?"

Sierra looked up at her father, "Yes Daddy." He kissed her cheek.

"We use to do that together. But lately you haven't asked me to go along."

"It may have something to do with the chaos following you wherever you go. I don't' need it and Eric is fed up with it."

"That faggot brother of yours is sensitive about everything." He looked back at her with a warning. "Hey, I haven't seen him around any woman I call it like I see it."

"Not when it comes to Eric," he replied angrily as he stood with Sierra.

"Alright—alright. I'm not here to talk about your brother."

He sat Sierra in the playpen he kept in his office for her. "Why are you here?"

"Well, I was thinking it would be great to get away as a family; you, me and Sierra."

Sign number three. They had never been referred to as a family. They simply had a child together, nothing more. "We are not a family Latoya. You are the mother of my child, nothing more. You seem to have a difficult time remembering that when we are in public."

Standing in front of him, she put her arms around his waist and looked up at him. "Jason, I was more than that to you at one time. It could be that way again." He looked down at her hands, then at her. She took a step back and put her hands on her hips. "Jason, all I'm asking is that we do something together with Sierra as her parents. What's wrong about that?"

"Nothing's wrong with the theory, it's the application that seems to be difficult for you."

"We can make the same arrangements we have here. We don't have to all be in the same room."

He stepped away from her. "We need to talk about our living arrangements."

"What about them?" She knew him, knew his moods, his tones. This tone concerned her. It was as if a decision had already been made. But she had news for him, she was not leaving.

"I've decided to move out."

"Move out!" she yelled with hands on hips. She walked over and snatched his arm. "You are moving out on me and Sierra? The daughter you claim to love so much."

"No, she's going with me. You can have visitation rights."

"Like hell she is. That's my child, wherever she goes, I go."

He sat in his chair and stared at her. "Really?"

"Yes, really. Try me. I will take her and you will never find us."

Her threat did not faze him. He knew all her antics and had prepared for them. "Take her where Latoya, to CJ's place? Hell, he barely wants you there. Or maybe Little T's place? Surprised I know about them, you shouldn't be. You know how this business is, everyone knows who you blow. You taught me that." He turned his back on her and went back to his work. "You have one month to find a place to live. I'm putting the house on the market."

Surprise turned into anger, and then anger turned into rage, when he turned his back. She reached into the playpen and grabbed Sierra out. The child cried out. "If you value any portion of your life you will put her down." He said without looking her way.

"What you going to do if I don't? Huh? What you going do?"

Jason turned slowly in his chair and glared at her. "Do you really want to find out?"

Latoya thought to dare him, but changed her mind. There was something different about him, no one thing she could put her finger on, but something was different. There was a certain confidence about him, a more defined swagger. She had one month to find out why. She put the child on the floor and Sierra ran to him with crocodile tears in her eyes. "You know I would not hurt her."

Jason picked the child up and consoled her. "Apparently she doesn't know that. Look, you know I would not leave you high and dry. You are Sierra's mother and I want her to be in a good environment. Find a place for yourself and I'll handle the financial end. But you will not use my daughter against me again. I will always take care of her, but all financial assistance to you will cease to exist. Do we understand each other?"

"You will take care of me financially?" she questioned for clarity.

"As long as you take care of Sierra, as you should," he emphasized. "And as long as you do not try to keep her away from me."

"What kind of finances are we talking about here, a monthly allotment or a lump sum?"

The fact that she asked the question pissed him off to no end. She did not question the terms of his proposal, visitation arrangement or even where Sierra's primary residence would be. No, she wants to know about the money. "We will discuss that later. Find a place." Dismissing her and any further conversation, he sat back down, placed Sierra on his lap, and began working again.

Back at her end of the house, Latoya paced, wondering what was going on with Jason. There has been no word about another woman stepping on her turf. In fact, her sources swore that Jason had been solo for the last few months. Not so much as a one night stand. Nevertheless, something was going on she reasoned as she opened her cell and dialed a number. As she waited for an answer she wondered *how in the hell did he know about CJ and Lil T. Whatever it was, it was messing with her livelihood and she don't play that.* "Hey boo. What you into today?"

"Toya?" Stanley questioned. "What you want?"

"I haven't seen you in a minute and I miss you. Can we hook up?"

"The last time we hooked up you acted like a fool. Beating that girl down like that was wrong Toya, it was wrong."

"Stanley, she was stepping on my turf. You know how I am about Jason. I don't want no straight up ho in his grill, you know what I mean. I'm just looking out for the brother. After all he is my baby's daddy." Now that she had his attention she went in for the kill. "Since you know he ain't breaking a piece off on me, I need a little somethin'—somethin'."

"You need Big Daddy to take care of you girl?"

"Nobody can take care of it like you do Big Daddy."

"You know I got you covered. Come on over, I'll be home."

Latoya opened the double doors to her closet and walked in. She had to wear just the right outfit to get the info she needed and leave there untouched by that little thing he called big boy.

The house the Davies called home in the states was lit up with laughter as Miriam played with her granddaughter and sons. This was what she looked forward to whenever she came home from touring, spending time with her family, especially the bundle of joy named Sierra. "It's hard to believe she is three years old. It seems like yesterday when she came home from the hospital." Miriam smiled as she watched Sierra in the other room continuously hitting Eric in the head with her stuffed toy and he played like he was being knocked out.

"She amazes me every day, Mom. I can't imagine my life without her," Jason said with a beam of pride.

"That's exactly what that hoochie of a mother is betting on," his mother replied. Jason threw her a warning look. "Okay, I take it back. Where is she anyway?"

"She is not allowed here," Jason replied with a quirky smile.

"Why, what happened?"

"Eric had a get together for the band and I came with a date. Latoya showed her butt and cursed just about everybody out. Eric forcefully removed her from the house." Jason laughed. "It was a sight. It had snowed and I must have been taking too long to get her out after he told her to leave. All of a sudden Eric came over to where we stood at the door still arguing, put her over his shoulder and threw her out the front door in the snow. Then closed the door behind him and locked it. The whole place applauded as he walked back into the house picked up his glass of wine and continued his conversation. It was so damn funny."

"Good for him. Now if I could just get my other son to do the same, I would be a happy mother."

"Well get ready to smile. I gave her a month to find a place to live."

A scream of elation escaped her before she could think to control it. "Thank God!"

Sierra was shaken by the sudden scream and jumped in her Uncle Eric's arms. Curious what the fuss was all about, Eric picked her up and walked over to the sitting area where the two were talking. "What's going on?" He asked with a smile as he noticed his mother's joy.

"Not in front of Sierra." Jason said as he took his daughter from his brother. "Gabby," he called out. Gabby came in from the kitchen and took Sierra with her. Jason then turned back to his family. "I gave Latoya a month to find a place of her own."

"He said it again," Miriam said with tears in her eyes. "I can't believe you finally did it. She never wanted that child; just the financial security having your child gave her."

Eric took a seat across from them. "What did she say?"

"She asked about the financial arrangements."

"And?" Miriam raised her eyebrow.

"I told her to find a place and we will discuss it."

Miriam sat back in her seat and crossed her legs. "So you're buying her out of your life?"

Jason looked at his mother whom he considered a wise woman. "Do you know another way to keep my daughter and get Latoya out of my life?"

"Yes, a foolproof way."

"You can't have the woman killed Mom," Eric rationalized.

"Why not? People do it every day. And this way you won't have to worry about her meddling in any of your relationships." Jason and Eric glanced at each other and decided their mother was not serious. "Oh, I'm not serious, but you have to admit it would solve all your problems," she joked. Hitting Jason on the knee, "Okay, tell me about her."

Jason tilted his head and smiled at his mother. "What makes you think there is a *her*?"

"Men don't make major changes in their lives unless there is a *her* attached. So spill it."

Eric shrugged his shoulders and grinned. "I have my own deeds to tackle, I can't help you brother."

"Oh I'll get to yours. You have been preoccupied since I've been home. I know something is up with you, too. But Jason first." She picked up her glass of wine and sipped as she waited. Miriam, who could easily be Diane Carroll's younger sister, crossed he legs and waited.

Jason lowered his head and smiled. "I met this woman a little over a month ago in Virginia and we have been spending a lot of time getting to know each other."

"Mainly because Jason has not gotten rid of Latoya," Eric supplied.

"Smart girl, I like her already."

Jason glared at Eric. "Do you mind?"

"Not at all, go ahead."

"As I was saying, her name is TeKaya Kendrick. She's a photographer with a small studio of her own." He sat up.

"Mom, remember when you used to say, you will know when you meet that someone. Well, TeKaya is that someone for me. She's beautiful Mom, inside and out. She's intelligent, caring and she don't take no bull from me. Whether we're together or not, she is always foremost in my mind. She made me see that what I thought was a stable environment for Sierra, was a ruse, and as she grows older she will see it for exactly what is. It was at her urging that I consulted an attorney that specializes in custody cases to see exactly what rights I have as a father. I have known her for a short period of time, but she has had a huge impact on my life."

A stunned Miriam looked from one son to the other. She had never heard her son speak so passionately about a woman before, not this one. Eric, yes. He was the romantic, but not Jason. "He's not objective. Is she that beautiful?" she asked Eric.

"Yes, she is. She is very real, down to earth. I actually think she could whip Latoya's behind and ask what's next. Miriam and Jason laughed. "But she is not as beautiful as her sister," Eric added. Both stopped laughing and stared surprisingly at Eric. Looking back at the two he repeated, "She's not."

Jason grinned as his mother turned her attention slowly from Eric, back to Jason. "So when do I get to meet this woman?"

"We are trying to keep her a secret a while longer. When the media get wind off her, that will set off a whole chain of events and to be honest, I just want her to myself for a while before that happens."

"I understand that son. But I'm not the media, I'm your mother and when a woman has this type of influence on one of my sons I want to meet her in person and judge for myself. Set it up before I leave the country."

Jason looked to Eric for help. "You might as well get her blessing and move on. You are going to have enough to deal with when Latoya finds out. You might as well get Mom out of the way."

"Thank you, I think," Miriam replied.

Jason stood, pulled out his cell and looked at his brother as he placed his call. "You are going to need me one day soon, and I will repay your brotherly loyalty." He walked out of the room as his call connected.

Miriam's sights now went to her baby boy. This one she could read like a book. Yes, he was the quiet one, the one that never talked about himself, or his feelings. He just put them in a song and it told the story. "Tell me about *Heaven's Gate*." She watched his suppressed surprised expression and smiled. She had not lost her touch.

He sat forward and smiled. "I can't yet."

"It's a beautiful song."

"For a beautiful woman," Eric replied as he nodded his head. "She's the one, she just doesn't know it yet," he said in his quiet confident manner. He stood and walked over to the window of his family room that allowed a spectacular view of the back of his ten acre estate. Before Siri, the scene was the only thing that helped to create his music. "I purchased a small place in Richmond to be near her." He turned back to his mother, "She's dealing with a lot and I want to be there for her. When she's ready, I'll be there."

Miriam looked from one son to the other. She had to meet these two sisters that had completely captured her sons.

Jason walked back into the room as he closed his cell phone. "We have been invited to Sunday dinner tomorrow. Anyone up for a quick trip to Richmond?"

Chapter 8
Kerri and Miriam

Although they spoke every day, it had been two weeks since TK had seen Jason. After their last visit Eric had shows in New York, Washington, DC and Charlotte, North Carolina. Eric had requested shows only on the east coast for the next year and they were all limited engagements. For that TK was eternally grateful. Her studio was picking up business and spending time with Jason was next to impossible, unless it was in Richmond. However, this was not a usual visit. He was bringing his mother to meet her and her nerves were on edge. Normally she would not care, but this was Miriam Davies, one of the classiest vocalists there ever was. Her style was as legendary as her voice. Jason was clear on his mother's position in his life. He not only loved her but he respected and valued her judgment. A bad rating from her could end their relationship before it really got started.

They had an intimate relationship without being intimate, but that was her doing. Jason was gracious enough to accept her position on his situation and had not pressured her in any way. She knew sometimes when he visited he left in need and she felt guilty about it. However, the reality of it was, she did not truly know his situation at home, only what he told her. The role of a fool was not one she wanted to partake in again. Been there. Done that. Don't want to do it again.

"You okay?" Siri asked as she brought in her diamond earrings Carl had given her as a wedding gift.

TK reached for the box and dropped it. "Yes," she replied as she picked it up. "Why do you ask?"

"Oh, I don't know. Maybe the fact that you still have a big roller in the top of your head might have something to do with it."

TK turned back to the mirror and snatched the roller out. A thick strand of hair curled perfectly down the side of her face. The remainder was brushed sophisticatedly into a ball of curls that hung leisurely down her back stopping right at her shoulders. She stood and turned to her sister. "How do I look?"

"Stunning."

She looked in the mirror again as she put the earrings on, and then smiled brightly at Siri. A frown of fear creased her forehead. "Tell me this is going to work out, Siri."

Siri took her hand and smiled. "It's going to be fine TK. She is going to love you as much as Jason does."

"Do I really look okay?"

"Yes," Siri insisted.

"Oh, you don't know. You will say anything to make me feel better." The doorbell chimed and TK just about jumped out of her skin.

Siri smiled. It was good to see TK excited about a man. Squeezing her baby sister's hand to ease her fears Siri assured her. "You are right I would, but trust me on this you are stunning."

"Well they're here. I just have to work it."

"Oh, I know you will. Come on, I'll walk with you."

Kerri opened the door to great Jason, Eric and their mother. Jason embraced her, "Hello Mrs. Kendrick."

"Hi Jason, Eric."

Eric kissed her cheek. "Mrs. Kendrick, it's good to see you again."

"Mrs. Kerri Kendrick this is my mother Miriam Davies." Jason smiled.

"Miriam, it's wonderful to meet the mother of two of the finest men I know. Welcome to our home." She extended her hand.

"Thank you and I agree they did turn out rather well." She returned the warm smile that greeted her. She stopped and looked at Eric, who was making his way into the kitchen. "Where are you going?" Miriam asked.

"In the kitchen," he replied as if it was a foregone conclusion. "Don't you smell that food?"

"Boy, where are you manners? I taught you better than that," she scolded.

Kerri laughed and decided she liked Miriam. There was nothing pretentious about the woman and that pleased her. The girls coming down the steps captured everyone's attention. Kerri turned in the direction of everyone's eyes. "It took you long enough," she declared.

"It was well worth the wait," Eric murmured.

Miriam looked at Jason and noticed his eyes were glued to the first exquisite young woman coming down the stairs and from the look of things she was certain that was TeKaya. She then noticed Eric had not taken his eyes off of the second woman as she descended the stairs. *Interesting*, she thought. Jason stepped forward and took the young woman's hand as Eric stood his ground and watched the other's every move.

"Mother, this is TeKaya."

Miriam extended her hand. "Well, my son was not exaggerating. You are gorgeous."

"Thank you, it's nice to meet you Mrs. Davies," TeKaya said nervously.

"My name is Miriam. Is that band too tight on your head?"

TeKaya shoulders relaxed as she exhaled. "Yes."

"Take that thing off and relax your brain girl. We are just here for dinner."

Smiling brightly, TeKaya complied, releasing the curls to flow freely down her back. "Thank you."

Siri stood quietly in the background, as did Eric, both passing glances and smiling politely.

"This is my sister Siri."

Siri stepped forward and extended her hand. "Hello Mrs. Davies."

"Siri. What a beautiful name for a beautiful woman."

"Thank you," she blushed.

"Ahhh you are the bashful one," Miriam stated as she looked in Eric's direction.

"Guilty," Siri smiled. Would you all like to have a seat while I get some refreshments?"

Jason and TK walked into the family room hand in hand and took a seat on the couch. Miriam and Kerri followed.

"I'll help Siri," Eric offered and followed her to the bar.

Miriam and Kerri exchanged the all-knowing motherly glance at each other. "Miriam, dinner is going to be a few more minutes. Would you like to join me on the patio?"

"Yes, I would like that." The two women walked through the kitchen onto the patio and beyond. "You have a wonderful yard, Kerri."

"Thank you. I'm glad you could join us for dinner."

"Thank you for inviting us. Are we through with the niceties?" Miriam asked.

"I'm done. Mother to mother, do you see what's going on?" Kerri began.

"I do," Miriam sighed. So, it as I suspect. My sons are enamored with your daughters."

"TeKaya is very open and clear on her position. She is in love with your son and plans to spend the rest of her life with him, no questions asked."

"And Siri?"

"That's a hard one to call. She's very reserved and not one to speak openly about her feelings. However, something is there. I sensed it before I met your son."

"I sensed it yesterday when I was told about TeKaya. Eric made it a point to express his opinion of Siri, not by name of course."

"What do you think we should do about it?"

"Hmm--hard to say. But I think I'll stay around until both situations are resolved."

The women extended hands and shook on it. "Mothers unite."

"You got it sister. Let's eat dinner and watch. I don't know who they think they are fooling," Kerri exclaimed as she took Miriam's arm and marched into the kitchen.

Sunday dinner at the Kendrick house was more of a military surveillance then potential in-laws getting to know one another for the first time. The methods used by both mother's were a perfect combination of observation and bait. Kerri would introduce a seemingly innocent topic while Miriam watched for reactions. Every now and then you would hear one of the women go, "Mmm-hum." What was most noticeable was the quietness of Siri when TK was describing the first time she saw Jason at the concert. Siri's eyes glanced at Eric just for a moment, then looked away. Anyone not looking would have missed it, but not Miriam, who had a perfect view. She was sitting at one end of the table and Kerri sat at the other end. Jason sat to his mother's right and Eric on the left. TK sat next to Jason and Siri sat next to Eric. The mothers' ears belonged to Jason and TK, but their eyes were on Eric and Siri.

"That's a wonderful story," Miriam smiled as she pushed her now empty plate forward. Propping her elbows on the table, and then folding her hands under her chin she closed her eyes. "When your father and I met it was sparks from the beginning. And we knew just from that first moment that we were going to be together. However, there were obstacles in the way. He lived in Europe and I lived in Georgia. We did not have the luxury of a private jet to use at our disposal. To make matters worse, he was a wealthy foreigner whose skin was a whole lot lighter than mine." She smiled sadly, as if remembering her beloved Pierre. Everyone around the table listened intently to the story. "He came back stage to meet the performers and when I was introduced to him he kissed my hand and said, "Your mesmerizing beauty has captured my heart, mademoiselle." Her smile brightened. "We spent the most amazing week together. When it was time for me to leave, he said he was in love and wanted me as his wife. Of course that was in the sixties and at that time home was a battleground for civil rights. There was no way in hell I could take a Frenchman home and tell my daddy we were getting married. I told him that and walked away. I knew I was leaving my heart in Paris, but it was the only way I knew to protect my family from the bigotry of narrow-minded people. It's fortunate for the two of you that Pierre was a man that believed that love conquers all. He came to Georgia and refused to leave until I agreed to become his wife. It didn't matter that his skin was white and mine was brown. What mattered was love. It is my hope that we instilled that in our sons. Do not allow issues, people, or distances keep you away from true love. For it is that kind of love that will get you through any and all-rough times to come."

Most of the occupants at the table assumed Miriam told the story to encourage Jason and TeKaya to fight for the love they had found. But at the end of the story Miriam looked and smiled at Siri. The impact of the story caused a moment of self-examination for each of them. Silence ruminated through the room. "In 1976 no, no, ------"Kerri began.

"Arghhhhh," Siri and TeKaya threw their hands in the air as their mother began her story. The men began laughing until they noticed the look on their mother's face. They both cleared their throats and sat up straight.

Kerri stared at her daughters with the "watch yourself" mother look, then continued. "As I was saying, in 1976 or 78. I don't remember which, my mother told me the best way to know if you have the love of a man is if he will give you the last bite of strawberry shortcake. That's all I was saying."

The girls laughed as Siri stood. "I'll get dessert."

Eric stood. "I'll give you a hand with that." Siri hesitated for a moment; them being alone had proven to be sexually dangerous. Noticing her hesitation, he touched her arm, "It's in the kitchen right?"

Looking into his eyes was a mistake. The determination she had today to not be alone with him slipped away. "Yes," she replied then walked into the kitchen. Miriam and Kerri passed those knowing glances again.

Kerri then turned her attention to Jason. "There is something we need to discuss Jason before Siri's return. I made a mistake by not speaking up for Siri and she was hurt deeply. I'm not sure if she will ever believe in love again. I'm not making that mistake a second time. Please hear me out. Your living situation is a concern for me. The woman you have your arms around is my baby girl. She is in love with you and will readily accept what you tell her. Love does that. I like you but I'm not in love with you."

"Mommy!"

"Don't interrupt your mother TeKaya. She has a right to ask," Miriam commented.

"As I was saying, I don't like my daughter being involved with a man that is living with another woman, regardless of the technical details."

Jason moved his arm from around TeKaya, turned to Kerri and nodded his head. "I understand your concern. My situation is the result of a bad decision on my part. The woman that lives in my home is the mother of my child. It was a brief relationship that was over before I knew she was carrying my child. I felt it was important that I play not just a financial role in my child's life, but a paternal one as well. That was my reason for providing a home for her and my child. I realize my solution was not fair for either of us. It did not allow us an opportunity to move on with our lives. That fact did not affect me until I met TeKaya and saw what I was missing. But more importantly, the arrangement was not good for Sierra, my daughter. She needs to see what a loving relationship can be, and know that it does exist. I have taken steps to correct my situation. I'm in love with your daughter Mrs. Kendrick. I would never ask TeKaya to come into my life without eliminating the drama first."

Miriam held her breath. She liked TeKaya and believed she would be good for Jason. But she understood Kerri's position as a mother. No one wants to see their child in a potentially hurtful situation. Her silent prayer was that Jason's words would touch Kerri's heart.

"That's admirable of you Jason and it speaks to the kind of man you are. What I need to know is when?"

TeKaya looked nervously at Jason. She loved him and believed he would rectify the situation. But she knew her mother was concerned for her and was not going to let this go. As much as she wanted to step in, she knew Jason had to answer.

"I have a real estate agent looking for a new house as we speak. She has indicated there are several prospects available for viewing. I plan to meet with her this week." Siri and Eric returned with the dessert and place it in the center of the table as Jason added. "If TeKaya likes one I will purchase it."

"Your intention is to move my daughter to Georgia to live with you?" Kerri questioned.

"No. Mrs. Kendrick. If all goes according to plan, my intention is to ask your daughter to become my wife."

TeKaya slowly gazed in his direction amazed. This was the first time he had mentioned marriage and it took her a little by surprise. "I am my father's son. I refuse to allow love to pass me by. There is nothing I would not do to ensure she becomes a permanent part of my life."

Miriam lowered her head. "Hmm," she murmured. No words could explain the pride she felt at her son's words.

Kerri held Jason's eye as they became more intense as he continued to speak. Her heart swelled for the love the man was proclaiming for her daughter and truly believed he would go through hell or high water to have her. A smiled appeared. "Thank you, Jason." She looked to TeKaya who had not taken her eyes from him. He turned his head slightly in her direction and looked into her eyes. Taking her hand in his, he gently kissed her fingers.

"Mother would you mind if we skip dessert?" TeKaya asked without turning away.

"Not at all," Kerri replied knowingly. The couple rose and disappeared out the patio door.

The two mothers looked at each other and smiled. "You must be in heaven at this moment," Eric commented to his mother. "You're finally getting one of your son's married off."

"I'm betting for a hundred," she smiled then turned her attention back to Kerri. "Let's take a walk outside."

Kerri stood. "Sounds like a plan to me. Why don't you two have dessert while we talk?"

Eric and Siri watched the two women walk off as if they had known each other for years. "I don't know about your mother, but my mother is up to something," Siri commented as she reached for the strawberry shortcake.

"My mother's mind is definitely working. Are you sure they just met?" Eric replied as he took the dessert she offered.

"Yes, I'm sure. They may just be concerned with Jason's situation. If I know my mother, she wants to make sure TK doesn't get hurt like I did."

Eric tilted his head and looked at Siri. "I was disappointed with the news you gave me in the kitchen. A small part of me was a little excited with the idea of a baby."

Deep down Siri understood, because she to was a little disappointed. Yes, a baby at this time in her life would definitely have been a complication, but that didn't stop the perk of joy she felt with the possibility of bringing a little life into this world. "A child would have put you in the same position as your brother; tied to a woman you did not love for the rest of your life."

"I don't know if the thought of that is as frightening to me as it is to you. Do you realize how difficult it has been for me to not kiss you or touch you today?"

Did she? Hell yes, she was having the same internal battle. Her sexual attraction to him was understandable. Before him she hadn't had sex for almost two years and here he was the sexual healer for women around the world. "That's just lust Eric. As soon as you are back on the road there will be another woman that captures your attention."

"You think so?" he asked knowing she was wrong. But that was a reality she had to come to grips with. He was going to help her get there, but he wasn't going to force it. "If it's lust for me, what's your excuse?"

"I was lonely and needed to feel attractive, wanted. You took care of that need."

"So you used my body?"

"No." she replied quickly. "I would never use anyone. I hadn't had sex in a while and was needy."

"Oh, that explains the first time. What about the second?"

Getting a little frustrated with the conversation Siri, dropped her fork onto the crystal plate. "Look, you and I both wanted each other. I fulfilled your need and you fulfilled mine. Let's just leave it at that."

Eric stood, wiped his mouth with his napkin, braced his arms on the side of her chair and looked into her eyes. "Apparently I hit a nerve. Why is that?"

She sighed and looked away. "What do you want from me Eric?"

With a finger under her chin he brought her eyes back to his. "I want you to get over the past, look into your heart and be honest with yourself." His lips barely touched hers in a brushed kiss. He stepped back and exhaled. "What do you say we clean up the dishes for your mom?" He picked up several plates and walked into the kitchen.

Grateful he had stepped away and missing his closeness at the same time, Siri shook off the feeling his words left. *I am over the past, aren't I? It doesn't matter, there will be no repeat. I will not give my heart away again.* With that settled Siri picked up the remaining dishes and when into the kitchen determined to dismiss Eric's words.

Kerri and Miriam sat on the patio contemplating their children's dilemmas. "Children, they know it all and don't know anything," Kerri summarized.

"You got that right. So what are we going to do about it?" Miriam raised her eyebrow.

"I haven't known you long, but I get the feeling you are a very resourceful woman."

"I've been known to handle one or two situations in my day."

"Really, any of them have to do with a hip-hop hoochie trapping your son?"

"No, but I've been itching to get at that one."

Laughing Kerri replied, "I bet you have." She then became serious. "He has supplied her with the good life; she's not going down easy. The baby may be caught in the middle."

"I know Sierra is going to be used as a pawn against Jason, that's the kind of woman she is." Miriam watched Jason and TeKaya talking at the end of the yard. "I have never seen him so happy. With all that is about to explode around him, he is happy."

"You've been in the business for a long time and seem to live a pretty high society lifestyle. Can you get street?" Kerri asked with a raised eyebrow.

"My husband was six- two, dark hair with a trust fund that went back three generations. I've been known to give a few honeys a beat down. Besides, I was born and raised in Atlanta, Georgia, the street never leaves you."

"That's good to know. I think it's time to introduce girlfriend to an old school beat down."

Miriam shrugged her shoulders one side at a time. "I can handle that. Now what are we going to do about the other two fools?"

"That ones on me. Eric seems to be a strong willed young man. If it's Siri he wants, he will eventually get her."

"I don't know what happened, but that child has been hurt. You can it read it all over her. I think you are right, your daughter does not believe in love."

Shaking her head Kerri sighed, "She did once, but all of that was stripped from her, by a bitter, old, loveless woman trying to hold on to her only child."

"Maybe you ought to give her an old fashioned beat down," Miriam laughed.

Kerri looked over at Miriam, frowned, and then laughed. "I'm scared of you."

Chapter 9
Latoya

The last thing she wanted to do was have to indulge Stan, not the man. But it was the only way she could get the information she was looking for on Jason. Latoya sat on the side of the tub in Stan's master bathroom and waited for Gabby to answer the telephone. The last thing she needed was for Jason to know she had stayed out all night. "It's about time you answered," Latoya snapped when Gabby picked up. "What in the hell took you so long?"

"I was giving Sierra her bath, Ms. Wright."

"Where's Jason?"

"He left with his family early this morning and will be returning later tonight."

"He went somewhere with Eric?"

"And Ms. Miriam."

"Jason's mother is here! When did she come?" Latoya stood as she yelled into the phone.

"She arrived yesterday."

"Why in the hell didn't you tell me Jason's mother was here? Where did they go?"

"I don't know," Gabby replied.

"These are the things you are supposed to tell me Gabby. I ought to fire you for being so damn inefficient."

Latoya hung up the telephone and began to quickly dress. As hard as she tried, Jason's mother did not like her. Well, she was just going to have to try harder. According to Stan, she was about to be seriously replaced. So far she had been able to keep the hos away from Jason, but somehow this one slipped in. Well, if Jason thought for one minute he could just push her aside he was wrong. She had a sure fire weapon—Sierra. She sacrificed a year of her life to give birth to that child. Now it was time for the payoff. Looking in the mirror, she was thankful for the reflection that looked back. Her mother may not have been the best one in the world, but she did give her the good looks, the hair and the body of an angel. And her stuff was all natural, that's what the men loved about her, she was real. She knew what she was doing when she went after Eric, so what, if it was his brother that fell for her. Either way she got what she wanted, a ticket to the good life. "I will be damned if some country ho from Virginia is going to take that away."

Walking back into the master bedroom, Stan was still knocked out spread eagle on the bed. A repulsive act was needed to get him to talk, but once he started, he spilled it all. Leaving the house, she made a promise to herself—that was the last time. Someone was going to come out of their pockets with a few million or take care of her until Sierra turns eighteen. Driving home she devised a plan. First she had to play the adoring mother while Miriam was in town. That meant she would have to sit low for a minute, no extra-curriculum activity for a while. Actually, that could be a good thing. It would give her time to do a little research. The internet was a wonderful thing. She could use it to see who the woman was that was trying to put an end to her life of leisure. Damn, why did she have to get stuck with Jason, the street smart brother? Eric would have married her the moment she told him she was pregnant.

That was something she never understood back then. When she entered that room at the after party a few years back every man in the room stopped to check her out. Walking by them all she went straight to Eric, extended her hand, "Hello, I'm Latoya Wright", and flashed that dimpled smile that knocked most men to their knees. But not Eric, "Silk" Davies. He simply returned the smile. "It's nice to meet you. Jason, would you make sure Ms. Wright get an autographed CD," and walked away. The shock of the rejection lingered for a moment, until Jason took her hand and asked her to forgive his brother. He was in a zone with his music and nothing, no matter how beautiful the package, could get his attention. But she wasn't deterred, she looked at Jason and smiled, being a music executive, he was just as much of a catch as his brother, and just as rich. Smiling she remembered dropping the hint that Eric might be on the down low. It was no more then he deserved for brushing her off like he did. Nevertheless, she accomplished what she set out to do, capture a power broker in the music business to take care of her for the rest of her life. It helped that the brother wasn't half bad between the sheets, Lord knows Jason could work her body overtime. They had some good times, before things turned bad. A few months into the relationship she had to beat down a few honeys that were trying to move in on her turf and the reporter telling Eric who had planted the down low story didn't help. It seemed the brother bond was tighter then she thought. But then the ticket to paradise arrived, she found out she was pregnant. There was no way Jason Davies would turn his back on his child. Life had been good until now. How dare he tell her to find a place to live? He had to deal with her for at least fifteen more years whether he wanted to or not. Pulling into the garage, she turned the engine off and walked into the house. Let the games begin. "Sierra, baby. Mommy's home."

The fifty-eight year old grandmother of twelve, Gabby looked at the clock and made a note in her journal while shaking her head wondering why God gave children to some people. Standing, she closed the journal and put it inside the pillowcase on her bed. The bellow occurred again as she walked into the adjoining room to look in on Sierra, who was down for her nap. Seeing the angel was still asleep, she walked towards the suites that belong to Ms. Wright to get the woman to stop yelling through the house. In the twenty years she had been a governess, she had come across some trifling parents and this one was no different. But just like the others, she too shall reap what she sowed. "Ms. Wright, Sierra is taking her nap."

"Good," Latoya smiled. "I have some things I need to do. Let me know the minute she wakes up." She said while walking towards the other end of the house.

Gabby learned early on not to ask questions of this one. But she wondered where Ms. Wright was going. Mr. Davis did not like her in his part of the house and that was the only thing down that hallway. Mr. Davis paid her a rather nice salary to keep his home clean and daughter safe. A part of that was protecting his privacy, especially from Ms. Wright. Why was it always the good men that ended up with trifling conniving women? She shook her head as she entered the door right off the kitchen. In the security room Gabby watched the woman's movements on the monitor. When Latoya entered Jason's office, Gabby hit the record button and adjusted the camera to cover the entire room. She then walked out of the room and continued with her chores. Some women never seemed to have enough. Here the man had put her in a seven bedroom mansion with every amenity known to man and she still was not happy. One day she would learn. Gabby just hoped it was not at Sierra's expense.

Inside the office, Latoya wasn't sure what she was looking for but when she saw it she would know. The man was too organized. Everything was neatly in its place, so whatever she did she had to make sure it was put back in its place or he would notice. Sitting at his desk she opened the center draw, nothing. She tried the bottom two drawers, they were locked. Turning to the computer on the side she hit the enter button, just to see if he left it up—he didn't. Damn, there had to be something. She opened the planner on his desk and looked at his appointments. He had several with a realtor, she wrote down the person's name and number that might come in handy later. Turning the pages backwards, she read the appointments for the previous months. Nothing she did not know about. Going back another week she looked at each date and came across one that read: *Siri - Va. - Elementary School.* Hmm, I wonder what that could mean. She dialed a number on her cell phone and sat back in his chair. "Hey girl, what's up?"

"Toya? Hey girl. Long time no hear. You still beating people down in the ATL?'

Laughing Latoya replied, "Hey a girl got to protect her turf. That's why I'm calling."

"Oh hell. I just came from church and you got me up to no good already."

"It's all for a good cause and you know I'll look out for you."

"Yeah, yeah, what do you want and how much do I get?"

"A thousand for some information."

"Wow, Jason got you on that type of allowance for you to dish out a grand just for information?"

"If my plan works, it will be a whole lot more zeros behind that grand."

"You got my attention."

"Do your computer thing and see what you can find with this combination." She gave the information to her friend, but did not give any specifics, the fewer people that knew what she was up to the better. Money would keep some people's mouths shut, but not everyone's. "I need this, like now."

"I'll see what I can do as soon as I see half in my account."

"Done, call me today," she disconnected the call. Now phase two. She closed the book took a look around and made sure everything was back in place.

It was late when Jason walked into his home. The driver pulled off taking his mother and Eric home. All he wanted to do was see his daughter then dream about TeKaya. It was getting harder and harder to leave her. But he knew he was the one with baggage to clean up. Shaking his head and smiling, he had to admire the way TeKaya was handling the situation. She was not giving him an inch. *If you care enough about me to tell my mother you plan on making me your wife, then you will find a way to clean up your house before bringing me in.* The woman told him to clean up his act. He wondered if she had any idea how many women would not care about his situation, they would take whatever he had to give. Hell he was Jason Davies—music executive. TeKaya could care less. To her, he was the man who claimed to love her and she expected nothing less than his all. That was what he loved about her.

He froze at the door of Sierra's room. Latoya was there on the sofa with Sierra in her arms asleep. One would think it was normal for a mother to be holding her child, but not Latoya. He picked Sierra up to place her in her bed and Latoya woke up a little disoriented. Once Sierra was settled, he looked at Latoya, "What are you doing in here?"

Stretching she yawned, "She wasn't feeling well. I think she has a fever."

Jason turned and felt his daughter's head, she didn't feel warm, but she was still asleep. Usually she would wake up as soon as he touched her. "When did this start?"

"I don't know, around two this afternoon," she said as she stood to look over at the child.

"Why wasn't I called?"

"I didn't know where you were or how to contact you."

"Where's Gabby?"

"It's late. I'm sure she's asleep." She reached down and tucked the cover around her daughter. "I was a little worried for a minute. But she's sleeping soundly now."

He took off his suit jacket and placed it across the chair. I'll stay with her through the night."

"I don't mind staying."

"Since when?"

"You know Jason our child is not feeling well. It's not about you or me. It's about her. So I'm not going to argue with you tonight. If you want to stay, stay. I'll take the monitor with me and check on her in the morning." She picked up the monitor. "Good night." She walked out of the room. Upon entering her room, Latoya set the monitor on the night stand and placed the bottle of brandy she had tainted Sierra's Kool aide with inside the cabinet and then crawled back into bed she had vacated just a few minutes earlier, with a smile.

The next morning Gabby walked into Sierra's room and found it empty. Not seeing anything out of place other then the child missing, she took a look at her watch. It was a little after six. She began walking towards Jason's suite, for she knew Ms. Wright was not up this early. Tapping lightly on the door, she called out, "Mr. Davies, are you decent?"

"Yeah Gabby," he groggily replied. "Come on in."

She walked into the suite to find him in the sitting area of the room and Sierra asleep in his bed. "I came looking for our pumpkin. Did she con you into sleeping with you?"

Standing with just his pajama bottoms on he walked into the dressing room and returned while putting the top on. "What happened with Sierra last night?"

Frowning, Gabby looked at him confused. "What do you mean?"

"Latoya indicated Sierra wasn't feeling well. Why didn't you call me?"

"I have no idea what you are referring to. Sierra was fine when I put her down around nine last night." She went over to the child and touched her forehead, now quite concerned. "She doesn't feel warm or anything. Sierra, sweetie wake up for Gabby."

"Do you think we should wake her?"

"I need to know my pumpkin is okay," Gabby replied. When the little girl stretched in her arms, Jason released the breath he did not realize he was holding and Gabby smile. "Good morning pumpkin. Daddy said you don't feel well. Can you tell Gabby what hurts?"

Now Jason was standing next to the woman and his daughter close to the bed. "She seems groggy. By this time she would be all over the place." He picked up the cordless telephone next to his bed. "I'm calling the doctor's office to see if she can see her today."

"I'm sure it's nothing, but it's better to be safe than sorry. With a young child you never know."

Jason tenderly caressed dark curls on Sierra's head. Concern was etched so deeply in his face that Gabby had to try to ease his fears. "I'm sure she's fine."

"Hey pumpkin," Jason smiled down at his daughter as he listened to the recording from the doctor's office. Sierra smiled at him, closed her eyes and went back to sleep.

Gabby put the child in her father's arms. "I'll get some clothes to dress her," then left the room. Jason hung up the telephone and then dialed Eric's house. Before he had a chance to tell his mother Sierra's symptoms she had hung up the telephone. He was sure she would be there within the hour.

By seven thirty, Jason, Miriam and Gabby were all in the kitchen watching the very energetic child chasing her Uncle Eric around the island with her teddy bear. Eric stopped and turned suddenly scooping the giggling child up into his arms. "Eric don't toss her around like that," Jason said still concerned for his daughter.

"Jason, the child is fine. Who said she was sick in the first place?" Miriam asked as she smiled up at her granddaughter.

"Ms. Wright," Gabby replied with a little bit of sarcasm as she placed a cup of juice in front of Miriam.

"What would she know?" Miriam mumbled.

"She was not what you see now an hour ago. Gabby woke her and she went right back to sleep," Jason tried to defend his over protective actions.

"I must say, I was a little concerned at first. Sierra is usually waking me up in the morning. I can always hear her talking to her dolls through the monitor. But not this morning," Gabby offered as a defense.

"Good morning," Latoya said from the doorway. "Sierra," she smiled as she took her daughter from Eric ignoring everyone else. She brushed the curls back from her daughters face. "How are you feeling this morning?" She went through the motions of touching the child's face. "You don't seem too warm today. Are you feeling better this morning?"

To most people the scene would have appeared to be a mother's genuine concern for her child. But to Eric this was anything but. Latoya should have continued with her acting career, for she was putting on quite a show.

"Jason did you call the doctor's office?"

"I did, but mother doesn't think it's necessary now."

She looked up at Jason with such concern, and then looked over at Miriam. "Hello Mrs. Davies. I'm sorry I didn't notice you at first." She then turned to Eric, "Hello Eric." Before he could answer she turned back to Miriam. "Are you sure she doesn't need to be seen by the doctor. She had such a temperature last night."

"She didn't seem warm to me last night when I put her to bed," Gabby stated.

"Well she did to me when I checked in on her," Latoya replied with a little bit of an edge to her voice.

"What time was that Latoya?" Miriam asked as a look passed between Gabby and Eric. The two had seen similar performances from Latoya whenever she was trying to get Jason to purchase something she wanted.

"I'm sorry Miriam, what did you ask?"

"What time did you look in on Sierra?" Miriam repeated the question.

"Well, it was a little after eleven, I think. I was out with a girlfriend last night. Where were you Jason?"

"I was out with a girlfriend as well," he replied then took the child from her and reclaimed his seat.

Sierra began eating the fruit from his plate. "Grape Daddy," she held a grape up to his mouth as he shook his head.

Standing with her hands on her hips, the tears began to form in her eyes. "Why do you continue to do this Jason? Even if that was where you were, did you have to embarrass me in front of your family?" She did not raise her voice or sound angry, she sounded hurt. Looking around at the people in the room, she stopped at Miriam. "I'm sorry, excuse me," and ran from the room.

Sierra looked up at her father, "Mommy crying Daddy. You kiss her and make better."

He kissed her forehead, "Okay baby."

Eric gave Jason a curious look. "Do you have an appointment with the realtor today?"

"Yeah, why?"

He looked at the doorway Latoya made her exit then turned back to his brother. "Does she know?"

Jason never looked up from his baby girl feeding him fruit. "Apparently so."

Eric began to chuckle as Miriam looked stunned. "No. No."

Gabby looked and nodded her head, "Okay, now that makes sense." She put the plates in the dishwasher. "Excuse me folks. I have a roach to stomp."

"You go get her Gabby," Eric smiled as he took a seat at the breakfast bar next to Jason. "Let me have some of that fruit."

"No," Sierra turned and looked up. "It's for my Daddy."

Taking notes from the call, Latoya was pleased with the information being shared. She had a name, address and even knew where the woman worked. Now all she had to do is make the travel arrangements. Clap–clap–clap. She turned to the doorway and saw Gabby standing there giving her applause. "That was some performance you gave. You know you didn't fool anyone."

"I didn't have too. But I bet you this. The next time Jason leaves, I will know how to reach him. You see he's a caring father, whether he trust me or not. He will not leave here again without me knowing how to contact him, just in case his daughter gets sick."

"Mr. Davies, can take care of himself. Sierra however, is a child. If I find out you did anything and I do mean anything, to my pumpkin your ass is mine."

"Hmm, don't play me old woman. You're going to find yourself as the first casualty around here." She walked over to the door and slammed it in Gabby's face. She looked down at the notebook in her hand then made another call. "I need you to trail someone in Virginia. I want anything and everything you can get on her. I want pictures, I want dirt, and I want it now."

She hung up the telephone and looked at the notes again. "Okay, Siri Austin—your time is up."

Chapter 10
Siri

It was Friday afternoon, the end of the first week of school. The children had begun to settle down from the excitement of returning to school and Siri's system had adjusted to being back in the class room. Roscoe was still being a pain in the butt, following her around, and barking out demands. But none of it fazed her. She was happy. Her life resembled something it hadn't in a long time—she was living. After the divorce and all the publicity she walked around with her head down, ashamed of all that had taken place. Not any longer. Now, she woke up with a smile after a night of dreaming about Eric. Of course, she realized that all she could do was dream; they were safe. Neither he nor any other man could hurt her in her dreams.

She looked up from the stack of homework on her desk and decided to call it a day. Placing the papers in a folder, she decided to take them home and grade them over the weekend. She didn't have any other plans. TK and her mother were in Atlanta looking at houses with Jason, leaving her with the house to herself.

The September weather was still warm, so she drove with here windows down while listening to Eric's voice serenading her from the CD player. There was something about his voice that just did it for her. It healed all her wounds, or at least she thought it was his voice. It could be the memory of his hands on her body, or his lips touching hers, but whatever it was she was thankful for him. He made her want to live again, not just exist. It was a shame she could not allow herself to get close to him. Just the thought of going through the publicity of a relationship with him sent chills up her spine.

When she reached the front porch of her house, she heard the telephone ringing. "I'm coming, I'm coming." She repeated as she turned the key in the lock and ran into the kitchen. Breathlessly, she answered the call. "Hello."

"Hello, this is Maxine Long with Crimson Publishing. I'd like to speak with Siri Austin."

The briefcase Siri was holding fell to the floor with a thump as her mouth gaped open. "Hello is anyone there?"

"Yes," Siri voice finally answered. "I'm Siri Austin."

"Well, Ms. Austin, are you ready to meet the world?"

"No." Siri answered honestly but still a little shocked.

"Well lady, you better get ready, because I'm putting you on the map. *A Night of Seduction* is wonderful and I can't wait to meet you. I sent a letter by carrier that you should receive today with an offer. Get it to your agent and have a response ready for me by Monday evening. You are free to meet with me on Monday for dinner, aren't you?"

Not able to get a word in, Siri hesitated, then realized she had been asked a question. "Yes, of course I can meet with you. But I—I don't have an agent."

"You don't?"

"No."

"Hold on for a minute." As Siri held the telephone, she wondered, "*Will not having an agent lose the deal for me?* "Take down this number. I don't usually do this, but I want this project. The name is Kiki Simmons, that's K i k i Simmons with a S, Call her and tell her I referred you. If you like her, sign on with her as your agent. Give her the offer to review and I'll see you on Monday at six at TJ's in the Jefferson Hotel. I look forward to talking with you. Bye now."

Just like that the call ended. Siri still held the telephone in her hand as she glanced at the name and number she wrote on the message board on the wall. Slowly a smile appeared and excitement began to build. She quickly hung up the telephone to disconnect the previous call then immediately dialed the telephone number to Kiki Simmons.

"Kiki Simmons, may I help you."

"Um Ms. Simmons, my name is Siri Austin and I was referred to you by, she looked at the board for the name, Maxine Long."

"Maxine Long?"

"Yes, I need an agent and I was wondering if we could meet?"

"What's you name again?" Kiki asked

"Siri Austin."

"And Max referred you to me?"

"Yes, is that a problem?"

"No, not at all, I'm just a little surprised. Are you in Richmond?"

"Yes, I am."

"Alright, let's meet tomorrow; let's say around one at the Rendezvous Restaurant on Broad."

Writing down the information, Siri agreed, "Okay, I'll see you then."

"I look forward to meeting you Siri."

"Same here. Bye."

She wasn't sure how long, but Siri stood there bewildered, and then looked at the names on the board. Picking up her briefcase, she pulled out her laptop and immediately checked Crimson publishing site for the name of Maxine Long. There she was, listed as Senior Editor. "Oh my God....." She sat mindlessly on the stool at the breakfast bar in awe. A publishing company wants my book. She reached for her purse to get her cell phone out to call her mother, but the tune played indicating a call was coming through. "Hello."

"Hello Siri. Since your mother and sister are in Atlanta I thought I'd come to Richmond to spend some time with you. Do you have any plans for the weekend?"

"Eric, you will never believe what just happened." She told him step by step what just had happened.

He could hear the excitement in her voice. "Then, I'm right on time for a celebration dinner.

As ecstatic as she was, she knew she could not go out in public with Eric. Nor was it a good idea to be in the house alone with him. "I don't know Eric."

"I promise to be on my best behavior. Besides you are going to need advice on how to handle an agent and an editor." The line was silent. "Siri, I'm already in Richmond at the airport. Are you going to leave a brother hanging out here all alone, not knowing anyone here to call except you?" There was no need to tell her he was there to check out the condominium on the top floor of the James River building.

"That was a low guilt trip."

"I know. Did it work?"

"Yeah, it worked." She replied slowly, "Why don't you come over here for dinner? Just dinner, nothing more."

"I'll take whatever I can get. See you around six," he replied, then hung up before she could change her mind.

Siri looked at the clock on the wall in the kitchen, it was a little after four. That gave her time to shower and change before starting dinner. As she walked towards the steps she kept reminding herself this is just going to be dinner, no dessert or anything else is going to be happening in this house. The doorbell rang as she reached the second step. Then she remembered, a courier was dropping off the offer. Excited, she signed for the package, placed it on the stand near the door, ran to her purse and then tipped the runner. After closing the door, both hands went to her mouth as her eyes widened on the package. It wasn't just a simple white envelope that a rejection letter would be in—it was a brown envelope. It resembled the acceptance package she received from Spelman. She opened the package and tears sprang to her eyes as she read the letter from Maxine Long. Behind the letter were legal looking documents that she was not interested in reading. She placed the legal documents on the stand and just held the letter to her heart and closed her eyes. She looked at the letter and read it again, just to make sure nothing had changed from a moment ago. She sat down in the chair next to the stand and read it again. Her novel was going to be published. How cool is that? She thought. Then she let it out with a scream!

An hour later, Siri was in the kitchen dressed in a pair of jeans, a t-shirt and a pair of flip flops; checking the baked sweet potatoes she'd put in the oven. She was in the process of sautéing green peppers and onions for the steaks she planned to grill, when the door bell chimed again. "Eric's early," she said as she looked at the clock.

Walking, almost running to the door, she was giddy with excitement. She slowed her pace as she tried to determine why. Was it because of the news about her book or was it the man standing on the other side of the door. *It's the book*, she reasoned in her mind. Shaking the thought from her mind, she opened the door and knew immediately she had lied—it was the man.

Leaning against the doorframe stood the sexiest, most sensuous man she had ever laid eyes on, wearing a simple pair of jeans and an open collar shirt. Nothing about the outfit was outstanding; it was purely the essence of the man wearing it. She exhaled, knowing it was going to be hell resisting him.

"Are you going to let me in?"

Eric's smile was electrifying to her senses, as was the look of appreciation that shown through his eyes. Looking into them made her see herself differently. His eyes always seemed to gently caress her.

"You're early," she replied, still unable to move.

"I couldn't wait to see you." He walked into the house as she took a step back. "I brought wine and flowers to celebrate. Leaning forward, he kissed her cheek. "Congratulations on the book deal."

She took the flowers and savored the kiss. "Thank you," she exhaled with a smile. Looking away, she pointed to the kitchen. "There's a wonderful breeze this evening, so I thought we would eat on the patio. Come on back, while I find a vase to put these in."

Following her into the kitchen was not making his promise to behave easy. The jeans Siri was wearing revealed the luscious curve of her behind and the tiny waist that he remembered circling with his hands. Her walk was slow, sensuous, and tempting. All he could think about was holding the two globes in his hands. He stopped at the breakfast bar and watched as she continued to the cabinet under the sink, bent over and pulled out a vase. She stood slowly, stretching her body out lazily like a cat, joint by joint until she reached her full height. Reaching across the sink, she turned on the faucet and filled the vase with water. On anyone else, the movements would have had no effect on him whatsoever; however, with Siri the movement caused a rise in his already strained libido. "Siri."

She didn't have to look at him. The sound of her name on his lips was all the indication she needed to know his intent. "You promised," she said as she turned the faucet off and placed the flowers in the vase.

He walked up behind her and reached around her body, taking the vase from her hands with one hand and wrapping his other around her waist pulling her back against him. He set the vase on the cabinet, wrapped his other arm around her, and whispered in her ear. "Don't you feel it Siri? Don't you feel how thick the air is around us?" He kissed the area right below her right ear. "I feel it every time I'm within arms reach of you." He ran his hand down the front of her stomach to the top opening of her jeans and pressed his groin against her behind. His hand felt it when her abdomen contracted from his touch. "You can't fight it Siri and neither can I."

Siri held on tight to the edge of the cabinet, trying desperately not to sink into the warmth of his arms. But her body betrayed her as her head laid back against his chest, giving him more access to her neck. He kissed the crook of her neck and used his other hand to ease under her shirt and caress her nipples. Another contraction came in anticipation of more. "We're supposed to be celebrating," she whispered breathlessly.

"I can't think of a better way than to hold you and tell you how very proud I am of you accomplishing your dream." He turned her around in his arms and kissed her deeply, slowly, and passionately. Her body was trapped between him and the cabinet; there was no room for escape. She wrapped her arms around his neck, fleeing was the last thing on her mind. His hands traveled up her waistline to the side of her breast where his thumbs lingered and played with her nipples until she couldn't take any more. Suddenly he pulled away and literally crawled down her body with his tongue, dropping to his knees, and began kissing her navel. He pulled back, sat on his heels, and looked up into her eyes. "Let me make love to you Siri. No rushing, no hiding in the back yard, just you, knowing it's me, Eric, making love to you and you, Siri making love to me."

Her hands were braced on his shoulders and they tightened as he spoke. She wanted to do exactly what he asked, but she knew every other time they made love; he took a small piece of her heart. This was not a man she could be in a lasting relationship with. The publicity was not something she could go through again, if things did not work out. The only way to protect herself from public humiliation again was to stay away from men with a public persona to uphold. Could she make love to him this one last time, knowing self-preservation dictated she walk away?

"Look at me Siri." He saw the look of caution enter her eyes. "Don't think about anything else, but what you are feeling at this moment. I need you to make love to me."

The sincerity in his eyes touched her somewhere deep and she knew she could not deny him. "The food is going to get cold," she said so innocently.

He stood, looking down into her eyes and smiled as he ran a finger down her cheek. "We can always reheat the food."

She turned off the oven, took his hand in hers, walked out of the kitchen and up the stairs. They walked to her bedroom as she pulled her blouse over her head. With her back still to him, she slipped out of her jeans and panties then removed the hair band allowing it to flow around her shoulders.

Turing to face him, she witnessed the affect her naked body had on him, for he had disrobed completely and stood there with his need protruding extensively from his body. Mesmerized, she stepped closer, dropped to her knees and captured him in her hands, then gently kissed the tip of his manhood. Using her tongue, she circled him as if performing a taste test. Then her lips closed around him.

The moment she touched him, his body wanted to explode. This woman wreaked havoc on his senses in a way he could never explain to anyone for fear of being placed in an insane asylum. "Siri," escaped his lips. He pulled her up to him and carried her to the bed, for fear of losing all control. Lying beside each other, he ran his fingers through her hair, while exploring every inch of her face with his eyes. After covering himself with protection, he brought her lips close to his. "You are my heaven right here on earth." He kissed her with an intensity that literally made her toes curl. Without guidance from him, his manhood entered her. She welcomed him by wrapping her legs around his waist holding him securely in place. There were no further words spoken, but music played in his mind the same as it had the other times they were together. And she must have heard it too, for their bodies moved together in a rhythm of its own, neither missing a beat until the explosion that merged their souls together. Soon, they both fell peacefully asleep.

Later, Siri crawled out of bed, put on a nightshirt, and went down to the kitchen to put away the food that had been forgotten. While in the kitchen, Eric came up behind her, eased his arms around her waist, and kissed the area right behind her ear. "You left me alone in a vulnerable state. He said as he rubbed his growing need against her backside. She bent forward giving him a better feel and it was on again.

Running his fingers across her nipples, they hardened instantly; the cotton material was no match against the heat he was generating from his touch. Trailing her body with his hands, outlining her breasts, her waist and reaching her behind he cupped the two melons in his hands and squeezed. Siri braced herself against the table with a need to feel his natural heat on her skin. As if sensing her need, he raised the shirt over her behind and kissed her lower back. "You are beautiful all over," he whispered. "So smooth," he said gliding his hand to her front until he touched the heart of her heat. She lurched forward from the raw need that began to consume her with every stroke of his finger. "So hot, so wet." She felt one hand leave her body, but the other was causing so much havoc on her senses, she really didn't care. All she knew was she did not want him to stop the torture. She heard when his jeans hit the floor and smiled with anticipation of what was to come.

"Eric," she moaned.

"Yes baby," he replied still massaging her core. "Tell me what you want." He leaned further on her back and whispered while placing kissing between her shoulder blades. "Tell me Siri and it shall be yours." His hand ran down her back, while the other continued to ignite the fire between her legs."

"You, Eric. I want you inside me."

There was no sound sweeter to his ears. He pulled his hand away, bent her further at the waist and his lifeline entered her with a vengeance. From the first touch he was possessed. Nothing could deter him from giving her what she wanted, what he needed. Each thrust had a meaning, a purpose, a determination to please her. He pumped fiercely until he was on the verge of explosion, but this was not for him, this was for her. He reached around and stroked her bud with the same intensity of his thrusts. Her body tensed encouraging him to bring her full circle. She cried out his name as her inner lips began contracting around him causing him to lose all control releasing his seed into her body like a waterfall. They both collapsed on the table, neither able to speak or move.

"I'll never be able to sit at this table again." Siri said after moments of sheer ecstasy captured her body. He reached up and clasped his hands with hers. Still lodged inside of her, he could not believe his desire was building again. "I'm taking you back up stairs. I'm going to make love to you again and again and again." He kissed her shoulder. "Until you tell me to stop."

"Well I hope you brought your toothbrush." They laughed as he reluctantly pulled out and carried her back up stairs. They awakened a few hours later in each other arms. He stretched his leg across hers pulling her closer. Facing each other on the pillows, he smiled. "This is how you're supposed to wake up after making love."

Siri blushed and bit her bottom lip. "I have never celebrated like this before."

He sat up on his elbow and brushed her hair from her face. "Tell me about your book."

"Really? You want to know about my book?"

"I want to know everything. I want to know your success, your failures, what makes you happy, what makes you sad." He kissed the tip of her nose. "So tell me. Is it suspense, romance, or mystery?"

"Romance."

"Hmm."

"Unrequited love."

A slow smile creased his lips, "Really." He laid back with one hand behind his head looking at the ceiling and gathered her in his other arm. He was sure this was going to be a story about her first marriage. If it was, he wanted to be there to ease her through the rough spots. "Tell me the story."

She placed her head on his shoulder, a leg over his and her hand around his waist then began telling him the story. Neither thought about the patio door that was left open.

Jason, TK, Miriam, and Kerri stood in the foyer of what TK selected as their new home. As soon as they walked through the door, TK turned to the realtor and stated, "This is it. This is our new home." Jason immediately signed the papers and wrote a bank draft for the full cost of the house. He did not want any delays on taking control of the property. The agent, removed the "for sale sign" and sat in the first floor office of the house to complete the paper work.

Jason was very pleased with her choice because it was one of the six estates located in the same gated community as Eric's home. She wasn't aware of that yet, but he would tell her later. It was important to him that this be her decision without influence. She would be moving away from her family and he wanted her to be happy. He stood in the foyer and looked up at the spiral staircase leading to the second level where TK stood talking to his mother and smiled. He could see the house filled with her laughter and his children.

"She is a beautiful girl," Kerri said as she came to stand next to Jason.

Not taking his eyes from TK, he replied, "Yes she is. If anyone had asked me six months ago if I would be getting married I would have laughed them out of the room. But now, I can't imagine a time without her. It's the strangest thing."

"You truly love her. I can see it. And she is in love with you. She's going to fight you about moving here."

He laughed, "She already has. I had to promise to purchase a home in Virginia too. But it doesn't matter. Wherever she is, is home for me."

TK looked down over the banister. "Hey Jason, I think we have picked out Sierra's room and Gabby's too. She is coming with us isn't she?"

He looked up at her worried face. "I haven't asked her yet, but I'm sure she will."

"Oh good, I can't wait to meet her."

Miriam came around the corner. "TeKaya, come look at what I found in the master bedroom."

The two went running down the hallway as Jason laughed. "I don't know which one is the most adorable, TK or my mother."

Kerri sighed, "I can't believe I'm losing my baby."

Jason hugged his soon to be mother-in-law and replied, "You are not losing your baby; you are gaining a son, or two. Depending on how Eric is making out with Siri."

Kerri exhaled, "That is going to take time. She went through a lot."

"I know and so does Eric. But he is determined to make Siri his and I believe he will succeed. Now what can I do to get that worried look off your face?"

"Just make my daughter happy."

"That is a given. How about I take all of my favorite women out to dinner?"

"Why don't we go shopping for the house?"

TK and Miriam came walking down another hallway from the back of the house. "Jason and I are meeting with a decorator tomorrow."

"A decorator? Oh lord. Next she'll be calling me talking about, 'Mother, let's do lunch why don't we', and I'm not going to understand a thing she is saying."

"Now, Kerri, it's not that bad. The boys come to spend a month with me every year in Paris. I'm sure we can convince them to bring you along. "

Kerri's eyes widened with surprise. "Paris, you say. Mmm, add a trip to the Cannes Film Festival and you two have a deal."

"Done," Jason replied as they all laughed.

Later that evening, the mothers went shopping while Jason and TK sat at an upscale restaurant in the Buckhead area of Atlanta. When he saw a friend of Latoya's enter the restaurant, Jason knew there was going to be some drama. "A friend of Latoya is heading in this direction."

"Is that a problem?" TK asked as she looked up.

"Not for me, but I don't want it to be one for you."

She reached over and touched his hand. "Don't worry about me. I can take care of myself."

"Hello Jason," the flamboyantly dressed man pushed Jason's shoulder with a flick of his wrist. "It's so nice to see you about and everything," he said with sassiness to his voice.

"Hello Adrian."

"How's my girl doing?" he asked cranking his neck as he placed his hands on his hips

"Latoya was fine the last time I saw her," Jason coolly replied.

"Uh-huh. And who is this?" He asked placing one hand on his chest for emphasis.

Jason put his fork down and looked at TeKaya. "This is my fiancée, TeKaya Kendrick."

"Fiancée?" He twisted and turned. "My goodness Jason you can't be serious. Fiancée?" He walked away and retuned. "Do my girl know? I mean you do know she plans on you and her doing that marriage thing?"

"I don't know if she knows, Adrian. But you are welcome to ask her."

"For real—for real. I mean you're for real engaged?"

"Yes," Jason replied finding it hard to refrain from laughing.

Adrian walked away again, exhaled and returned to the table with the flair of most runway models. "I love that turn you just made. Do you do runway modeling?" TeKaya smiled warmly.

"Why yes, I do," Adrian replied impressed she had noticed.

"Do you do runway?"

"Oh goodness no. I don't have anywhere near the grace that you do. I would fall all over myself trying to walk like you."

"Girl it's nothing to it. I can have you moving like this in no time." Adrian walked a step then turned back with flair.

TeKaya pulled out a business card. "Here's my card, I'll be moving here to Atlanta soon. Please come by and allow me to do a portfolio for you."

"Aw, for real. For real. You would do that for me?"

"Of course I would."

"Wait until I tell my Mommy. Thank you girl. I'll be in touch." He started to walk away, but stopped. "Oh by the way, congratulations."

"Thank you," TeKaya replied with a smile. She looked at Jason, "I bet he doesn't make it to the car before he calls her."

"Baby, he's not going to make it to the door."

Jason was right. Before Adrian reached the door he was on his cell phone. "Toya where in the hell have you been. Your man is at Shea's with a gorgeous woman and when I say gorgeous I mean gorgeous. She is stunning! And get this, he introduced her to me as his fiancée'. Girl you better come down here and get your man..."

Less than twenty minutes later, Latoya was walking through the doors of Shea's restaurant. The elegant atmosphere was not a deterrent to stop her ridiculous behavior. She walked up to the table with hands on her hips and stared at TeKaya. To her amazement the woman at the table was a little more competition than she thought. She would be a fool not to acknowledge the truth. And her Mommy didn't raise no fools. She looked at Jason then back to the woman. "I don't know who you are but you need to leave." TeKaya looked around to see who the woman was talking to as Jason stood.

"Latoya, this is not the place."

Latoya swung her long hair back over her shoulder, bent down placing one hand on the table and the other on her hip and spoke to TeKaya, ignoring Jason. "You can move or I can move you. What will it be?"

Jason held up his hand signaling for security to come forward, but before they could reach the table Latoya was on the floor looking up dazed with TeKaya standing over her. "Hello Latoya. It's nice to put a face to all the tales I've heard about you. That is a beautiful dress you have on and girl I have to say you are wearing it—even on the floor." She had the most concerned look imaginable as she asked, "Are you okay down there?" She tucked her hair behind her ear and reached down to pull Latoya up by the dress collar. "Here let me help you up," she smoothed her dress down. "Would you like to join us for dessert?

"Get your hands off of me." Latoya pulled away.

"Mr. Davies, would you like for her to be removed?" The security officer asked.

"No. She can stay." He reached for TeKaya, "We're through."

"Please accept our apologies for this unpleasantness. We'll take care of the bill Mr. Davies," the Hostess stated.

"That's not necessary, this was not your doing." He pulled out his wallet and paid the bill then with TeKaya at his side walked out.

The owner stepped from the back room and met Latoya as she was stomping towards the door. "You are no longer welcome here, or at any of my establishments." He turned to security, "Please remove her."

Unknown to Latoya or Jason, one of the reporters from a popular morning show was present in the restaurant during the entire scene.

The car was quiet on the ride back to Eric's house. Neither spoke until Jason turned into the driveway and parked. "I'm worried about Sierra," TeKaya announced. "I don't know Latoya, but she is angry and the only way she can get back at you is through Sierra. I think you should make sure she's okay. Can you go check on her?"

Jason reached over, cupped her neck and brought her lips to his. The kiss that followed left no doubt how much he loved her and that was his intent. He released her, immediately turned the car around and drove to his house. When he pulled into the garage he knew immediately something was wrong. The door leading into the house was open. Then he heard the raised voices. TeKaya followed him in. He walked in through the mudroom, then the kitchen, down a hallway. The further they walked the louder the voices became. It was when he heard Sierra crying that Jason took off running. When they reached the child's room Latoya had Sierra under her arm like a football, screaming at the top of her lungs at Gabby.

Night of Seduction

"Daddy," Sierra cried out reaching for him. Jason walked over to take his daughter, but Latoya jerked her away.

"You come near her and I swear I will leave this house and you will never see her again."

Jason held his hands up. "Latoya, put Sierra down."

Latoya looked over Jason's shoulder and saw TeKaya standing in the hallway. "You have the nerve to bring your woman in this house. Either she leaves, or me and Sierra leave. What's its going to be Jason?"

"What do you want from me Latoya?" He yelled, "I take care of you and Sierra without question! I've found someone that makes me happy and you want me to choose between her and my child! Well I tell you what!. I will always love my daughter, but I refuse to allow you to continue to use her against me!. If you want to leave, okay, leave! But I have filed with the court to get full custody of Sierra! After I show the judge half of the evidence I have on you, you will be lucky to get visitation rights! Why do you think sleeping around with my boys was so easy? Did you forget who they work for? Did it ever cross your mind that I knew what you were doing or did you think I was that gullible?" Trying to control his temper, he calmed down. "I offered to put you in a house of your choosing. I didn't put any limitations on you. All I asked was that you did not come between me and my daughter. You didn't want me Toya, you never did. You wanted to live the good life. I am still willing to give you that and more. All I want in return is my daughter. Give me Sierra and you will not want for anything. You have my word on that."

His voice was a little too smooth, too cool for Latoya. She knew the calmer he was the angrier he was. If she were to give him Sierra now, he would go back on everything he said. Frustrated and feeling trapped, she lashed out. "Why did you do this Jason? We were fine, you me, and Sierra. You should have just been happy with that." She cried as she swung Sierra up into her arms. The child continued to cry for her Daddy. "I'm leaving here tonight with Sierra and I will call you when I feel like it." She walked towards the door. "Move" she said to Jason who was blocking her way.

"Mr. Davies, don't let her leave, we won't see our baby again," Gaby cautioned.

"Toya, you are not leaving with Sierra." Jason shook his head.

"How you going to stop me Jason? You put your hands on me and I will have you locked up for life. How do you think that will play out in the media? How would your brother handle that? Now, move the hell out of my way."

He hesitated for a moment then took a step back to let her by. She eased out of the room without turning her back on him. TeKaya stood further down the hallway waiting. When she saw Latoya she knew she could not let her leave with that child. "You've had a rough day haven't you Latoya? I mean I would be upset too if some woman came into my life and tried to replace me with my man and now with my child. If you leave Sierra here, I will walk out of Jason's life."

"TeKaya?" Jason called out.

She ignored him. "You have my word Latoya. I will leave and never come back if you give Sierra to Jason right now."

"Bitch please. I don't believe you!"

"Now I got to tell you," TeKaya shook her head, "I'm not going to be too many more bitches tonight. I'm willing to spend a night or two in jail just for the pleasure of whipping your ass for the way you are holding that child."

Sierra continued to call out to her daddy. "Shut up," Latoya yelled at the child then she looked back to TeKaya. "You know I would love the opportunity to kick your ass. But I have more business to handle. You are going to have to wait."

TeKaya kicked her shoes off and took her earrings off. "I'm here, you're here. Let's do it."

She walked over to Latoya and stood toe to toe. "But you are not leaving with that child." TeKaya put up her fist and begin bouncing on her toes. Latoya stepped back, but it wasn't far enough. The punch landed dead center on her nose just as Atlanta's finest officers in blue walked through the door.

Jason grabbed Sierra just as Latoya hit the floor. One of the officers grabbed TeKaya by the arms and wrestled her to the floor. The other officer went to assist Latoya who began putting on the performance of a lifetime. "This woman came into my home to attack me. She hit me with my child in my arms. Where is my child? Where is Sierra? Don't let that woman anywhere near my child."

Jason had left the room to take Sierra away from the scene. The last thing he wanted was for his daughter to see her mother being handcuffed by the police. When Gabby realized what was about to happen she ran down the hallway to inform Jason. "Mr. Davies. They are going to arrest your lady friend."

Sierra clung to her Daddy as she continued to whimper. "What?"

"Latoya just told them she is pressing charges against her. All they saw was your friend hit a woman with a child."

Jason placed Sierra in Gabby's arms and ran into the living room. Only one officer and Latoya was there. "Where is she? What did you say?" he asked angrily

"Aren't you even concerned about me? I'm the injured party here."

"You should thank your maker that it was TeKaya that hit you and not me. Come near me or my daughter again and I will kill you." He turned to the officer. "Did you get that?" He ran out the door to find TeKaya.

What hit him when he walked out was a living nightmare. Several media outlets were there filming the scene of TeKaya being placed in the police car in handcuffs. At the moment, he couldn't care less. He ran over to the car with cameramen running behind him and microphones thrust in his face. "TeKaya, I'll take care of this. Don't worry." He said as the police car pulled away. He pulled out his blackberry and turned to another officer. "Where is she being taken?" After pushing a button he heard it answered, and closed his eyes at the relief he felt in his chest. "Ty, I need you at the 16th percent now! TeKaya Kendrick is being charged with assault. Get her released ASAP. I'll meet you there."

He stormed back into the house and found the officer threatening to arrest Gabby if she did not release the child to her mother's care. When he attempted to approach them an officer grabbed his arm to stop his progress. Jason looked at the officer as if he had lost his mind. "That is my child you are blocking me from. I strongly suggest you move."

The officer looked at him. "It's my understanding that is the child's mother that your girlfriend just attacked in her own home. I would think you would show her a little more respect than bringing your latest conquest where you and she live together."

"Do you know who I am?" Jason asked in a threatening manner.

"I'm sure you're some hip hop music producer who thinks you can get away with bull like this and have people eating out your behind. But that's not going to be the case this time."

"Yes, it is." A man in a suit stood in the doorway.

"Chief," the officer spoke.

"Barry," Jason sighed and extended his hand while shaking his head. "I'm glad to see you."

"What's going on Jason?"

"Latoya tried to take Sierra from the house. I followed your instructions and backed off of her, but TeKaya wasn't having it," he said while shaking his head.

"Chief--," the officer attempted to interrupt. Both men, Jason and Chief Barry Goldman, gave him a look that told him where to go.

The chief looked at the officers in the room. "Who was first on the scene?"

"Casey and I, Chief," the female officer taking care of Latoya replied.

"Where is Casey?"

"I believe he took the perpetrator downtown to lockup."

"Did either of you check to see if an order of protection was in place for the child?"

"There really wasn't time. We walked in on the confrontation. Things went down pretty quickly."

The Chief looked towards Sierra and smiled. "Hello Gabrielle."

It was the first time in 3 years that Jason had ever seen Gabby flirt, but that was a flirtatious look if he had ever seen one. "Chief," she replied and looked away.

The chief walked over to Latoya and folded his arms across his chest. "I don't suppose you are willing to drop the charges against Ms. Kendrick." It was a statement, not a question.

"Why would I?" Latoya snarled.

"I didn't think so. And it would be a waste of my time to tell you it would be in your best interest if you did drop the charges." She simply rolled her eyes at him. "I didn't think so."

He stood and looked at Jason. "You're staying at your brother's and Sierra is going with you."

"Like hell she is," Latoya jumped up.

"Well, there is another option. You can leave," the Chief replied.

"I ain't going nowhere. I live here. I know my rights."

Jason turned to Gabby, "Pack a bag for Sierra and yourself. We'll be at Eric's until we close on the house."

"What house?" Latoya snapped.

Jason looked at her as if he was about to say something, but changed his mind and turned back to the Chief. "Would you make sure Gabby and Sierra make it to Eric's place? I have to meet Ty at the station."

Barry smiled. "I'll take Gabrielle.....and Sierra."

"How you just gonna take my baby? You can't just take her. I gave birth to her not you."

Jason lunged towards her, but Barry stopped him. "If TeKaya sheds one tear over this bull you created tonight, you are cut. Not a red cent and I will get full custody of Sierra. You better pray that TeKaya has a heart, I'm done." He turned and walked out of the door.

"Jason! Jason! Don't you walk out on me, Jason!"

Gabby walked back into the room with Sierra and an overnight bag. She looked at Latoya, shook her head, and then turned to the Chief. "I'm ready."

Eric and Siri had fallen asleep again after making love for the third, fourth or fifth time neither would have been able to answer the question, if it had been asked. The telephone, next to her bed, rung several times before she reached over and groggily answered. "Hello."

"Siri are you looking at the news?"

"What? Carl? Why are you calling me?"

"Turn on your television TK is on the local news."

Siri sat up, fully awake. "What?" She reached over for the remote and turned the television to the local news. A flash for the upcoming eleven o'clock news came across the screen. *Richmond native arrested tonight in Atlanta in the home of music producer Jason Davies. More at eleven."*

Eric got up looking for his pants, then pulled out his cell.

"I have to go Carl." Siri hung up before she heard him say, he was coming over. She dialed TK's cell, but only received a voicemail. She jumped out of bed and ran into the bathroom. She washed up quickly and put on her clothes. The two looked at each other, wondering what was going on. The first number Eric dialed was Jason, but he didn't get an answer. He then called Ty Pendleton, their friend and attorney. If anyone knew, what was going on it was Ty.

Relief appeared on his face as Ty answered. "What's going on Ty?" Eric anxiously asked.

As always, Ty was cool, calm, and in control—nothing seemed to ever faze the man. Which explained his success in court, even if he was losing; he never allowed the opposition to see him sweat. Ty looked over at Jason and TeKaya as they talked quietly in the corner of the police captain's office. "Everything is under control. Ms. Kendrick is being booked for battery, but she will be released on her own recognizance."

"Jason?"

"No. Latoya."

"I can't reach TeKaya. Are you talking to Jason?" Siri nervously asked.

"No. I'm talking to Ty, our attorney. TeKaya has been arrested." He replied, then returned back to the call.

"Arrested for what?" She asked while hurrying to put her shoes on and grabbing her purse.

"Hold on Siri. I'm trying to get the info from Ty."

"Siri?" Ty asked raising an eyebrow.

"Later Ty. Where is Jason?"

"He's here with TeKaya. Who is a beauty by the way."

"Not as beautiful as her sister."

Ty hesitated for a second thinking. "Siri?"

"Yeah. Let me talk to Jason."

Ty looked up to see Miriam and another woman walk through the door. "Your mother and a woman I'm pretty sure is TeKaya's mother just arrived and she is not happy."

"I'll be there in an hour. Put security in place at Jason's house. I am sure the press has that staked out. We will run everything from my place. Keep me posted." He ran behind Siri who was already running down the steps.

Siri ran into the kitchen to make sure everything was in order, when she noticed the patio door was open. She closed and locked it, checked the stove and ran toward the front door.

Eric had dressed and was running down the steps when the doorbell sounded.

"Siri, what's going on?" Carl stood at the door in a pair of jeans and polo shirt as they came out the door.

"I don't know," Siri replied as she turned to lock the door.

The look on Carl's face when Eric emerged from the house was completely lost on Siri, but not Eric, who was pulling his shirt over his head as he came out the door.

"My car. I'll call the pilot on the way."

Carl watched as the two jumped in the vehicle he did not recognize and pull off. With hands on his hips, he looked around confused. He looked at his watch. "What in the hell is he doing in your house?"

Chapter 11
The Paparazzi

This was unbelievable. Eric felt the air change between them as soon as they stepped off the plane. He wasn't sure how, but the press knew he was coming. The moment the first camera flash went off, he heard Siri gasp. He turned back up the steps, took off his jacket, and put it over her head, to hide her face from the cameras. His driver immediately opened the door to the sedan he had waiting and ushered the two inside.

"Mr. Davies, the family is at your place and so is the press." The driver explained as he pulled from the airport parking lot.

"Why is the press so interested in this? This isn't major."

The driver sighed, "It wasn't until that woman got in front of a camera and gave her side of what happened tonight. "

Eric closed his eyes and sighed. "What did she say?"

The driver hit the monitor on the console of the car and replayed the interview Latoya gave.

Before the camera, a distraught Latoya stood with tears streaming and an ugly bruise on her face describing a scene from her mind. She stated she returned home from a trip to find Jason and some woman attempting to take her daughter from their home. Of course, she fought, but the brute of a woman and Jason got the best of her. Then to add insult to injury, the police chief sided with Jason. She knew it would happen this way, she went on to explain. "I'm just a nobody without any money or influence. Jason Davies and his brother Eric have unlimited resources to influence the authorities. He used me and now wants to discard me like a piece of trash. And that's okay, because I still love him and I want him to be happy. But I can't let my baby go. I just can't do it." She broke down in the reporter's arms.

Eric and Siri just stared at the monitor. "You know, that girl missed her calling. She should be on somebody's screen." Siri turned to Eric who was sitting next to her on the back seat of the car. "If I didn't know the situation I would be calling Jason every kind of name in the book."

Eric shook his head. "I wish TeKaya would have knocked her ass out." The anger showing clearly on his face he asked, "Who's handling PR?"

"No one. Jason, has ordered everyone not to make any comments about this incident."

Eric glanced at Siri as she gazed out the window and knew the closeness they had shared earlier in the evening was slipping away. The progress he had made with her and the excitement surrounding her book were now replaced with concern for her sister. Today he had been given a glimpse of the free spirited Siri; the one who had shared her joys of reaching this milestone in her life. They laughed and joked about nothing and everything. Those few short hours, made him want her more than he already did. He was convinced the attraction between them was much more than just physical. It was mental, spiritual, and sensual. Now, an hour later, he could see her slipping away. He reached over and took her hand. "I'm sorry this is happening Siri. We will make it right."

She turned to him, with a look of fear. "The press is going to make TeKaya the bad person in all of this. I've been there. Not on this scale, but I know what it's like to be accused of something in the press and know it's not true. TeKaya is a professional and this is going to affect her business and her life. No one will be able to give her back this time in her life when she should be happy. There is no making it right with the media."

The tone of her words let him know the doors were being closed. The incident with TeKaya and the reaction of the press reminded her too much of what she had experienced with her ex-husband. He didn't miss the surprised look on Carl's face when he came out of the house. "Are you going to call him?"

"Call who?" Siri asked as she turned back to him.

"Your ex-husband."

"Carl? Why would I call Carl?"

"He seemed concern about you. He came right over after the call."

"I'll call him later," she replied then turned back to the window.

He had the strangest feeling he was going to lose her. If that was the case, there was no way he could let her go without tasting her one last time. Eric pushed a button on the door and two glass panels closed off the back seats. He then pulled her across the seat and sat her in his lap.

"No Eric," she said and tried to pull away.

"Yes, Siri," he said as his lips descended upon hers. He placed his hand on her face and used his finger to force her lips open. As soon as they parted, his tongue tasted what he had experienced all evening, her sweetness. The instant sexual pull they experienced each and every time they touched was there even under these circumstances. He knew it would never go away, but she had to learn that for herself. For now, he would concede, but he was going down fighting. His tongue entwined with the smooth silky feel of hers, as he plunged deeper with a hunger into the very essence of Siri. His hands held her tightly not allowing her to escape until he had enough to carry him through what he knew was going to be an exile from her. He knew enough about her to know she would not allow him into her life, at least not now. When he felt the fight diminish from her kiss, he eased into a sweet, loving embrace, hoping to calm her fears for her sister and to let her know when she was ready to accept his love, he would be there—waiting. She ran her fingers through his locs and moaned. That would have been his undoing, if the driver had not announced their arrival and the press.

Eric reluctantly ended the kiss, but did not release her—not yet. He held her gaze with a silent understanding that this was all there could be for now. He sat her back on the seat, pushed the button and the driver moved forward.

If Eric thought for one moment, they were going to avoid the press by going to his house—he was definitely wrong. Siri was shocked to see the number of TV trucks, cameramen and women, reporters, and police crowding the street leading to the gate that led to Eric's home. The press was in full force and it was ten times worse than the four network stations she had to contend with in Richmond.

The aftermath of the events on Friday night was relentless. Media coverage was widespread, from LA to NY and beyond. The stories mainly picked up Latoya's account of what took place. Saturday morning, Jason and TeKaya sat on the veranda of Eric's home. To everyone's astonishment, TeKaya wasn't the least bit concerned with the events or the news coverage of what had taken place. The two sat in a lounge chair watching the local news and their coverage of the incident. "I think I'll become one of the housewives of Atlanta. What do you think babe?"

Jason smiled down at her as he held her in his arms and kissed her forehead. "You can be anything you want as long as you are my wife." Her smiling up at him with beautiful brown eyes sent his body into overdrive and his mind back to the incredible night they had spent together.

He wasn't sure what to expect once he reached the police station, but he certainly did not expect to find TeKaya and Ty sitting laughing and talking as if they had known each other for years. In fact, this was the first time he had seen Ty crack a smile at a woman—his woman. He knew Ty never allowed anything to rattle him, but he was sure TeKaya would at least be upset.

"Hey sweetie," she smiled as she looked up at him. She walked right into his arms and kissed him. Not a cross look or angry word came from her mouth. He returned her hug then kissed her.

"Are you okay?" he asked with a concerned frown on his face.

"Oh sweetie, wipe that frown off your face. Tyrone has taken care of everything."

Jason looked over her shoulder. "Tyrone?" He had been through high school and undergrad with him and this was the first time he had ever heard anyone refer to his friend as Tyrone without him losing his cool.

"Yeah, I said it right, didn't I?" She looked back at the man that could have been a double for Morris Chestnut.

"You said it exactly the way it was meant to be spoken." Ty smiled back at TeKaya. He stood and continued. "In fact you said it so perfectly, I'm thinking of going to Virginia to find another woman just like you to call me Tyrone, for the rest of my life." He walked away while grinning at the angry frown on Jason's face. "I have to take this call."

Jason was stunned at his friend's words, but was not pleased with him flirting with his woman. Releasing an anxious chuckle, he held TeKaya close. "Are you sure you're okay?"

"Jason," she cupped his face, "I'm fine," and kissed him lightly on the lips.

"I'm so sorry TeKaya. If I had touched Latoya I would have killed her."

"If you had touched her, she would have gotten exactly what she wanted—a domestic abuse situation. That's why I did it for you. According to Tyrone, the most I will get is a battery misdemeanor, which might include a fine. After the way she was holding Sierra, I would gladly pay that fine. " She put her hands on her hips and began showing a little anger. "And if I ever see her or hear about her handling Sierra in that way I will whip her ass again."

"Ok, calm down Floyd Jr," Jason laughed.

"I'm serious."

Jason pulled her into his arms. "I'm sure you are." She put her arms around his neck and he reveled in the warmth of her embrace. "I love you TeKaya."

"I love you, too."

"Well, I don't love you very much at the moment," Kerri announced as she entered the room.

"Are you two alright?" Miriam asked as she reached out and pulled TeKaya to give her a once over. "Did that woman touch you? "

"No, Mrs. Davies. I didn't give her a chance."

"Good for you."

"TeKaya, what have I told you about handling yourself in public?" Kerri chastened.

"You told me to kick ass and ask questions later." TeKaya respectfully replied.

Jason and Miriam turned to Kerri with a quizzical look. "That's right. You hit them before they hit you. There's always plenty of time to ask questions later." She reached out and hugged her daughter. "Now tell me what happened."

"Yeah, and don't leave anything out," Miriam said as she pulled TeKaya to leave.

As they walked out, the media was in full force in front of the station. "We can exit out the back." Ty stated as he pulled out his black berry to call the driver.

"No." TeKaya shook her head. "Jason lives and works in this town. I am not going to run away from the media or anyone else. I did nothing any one of them would not have done in the same situation. I'm not going to allow the media to control my life the way they did Siri's. I'm going out this front door with my head held high. Tomorrow we will have a press conference and explain our side of the story. Let Latoya have her fifteen minutes of fame tonight. I'll have my day in court."

Miriam, Ty, and Kerri smiled as Jason took TeKaya's hand and walked out the door. Camera flashes went off in all directions. Questions were being thrown at Jason, but he did not give an inch. He placed TeKaya in the black SUV, as Ty secured the mothers. While in the car, Ty gave his phone to Jason. "I think you should take this call."

"Who is it?"

"Mitch Curry from the morning show."

"Man, I like Mitch, but I don't want to deal with the press right now."

"You do want to take this call." Ty said as he turned back in his seat up front.

"Mitch," Jason said, and then just listened. "You're joking," he smiled as he looked out the window contemplating his next move. "I think you just got an exclusive. Can you be at Eric's place by nine?" He listened to the reply. "I'll see you in the morning."

"Ty, get Sherri on the phone."

"She's already at Eric's."

"Cool," Jason replied and just smiled.

They were greeted at the gate with another media crowd, but the driver continued through the gate, which was closed immediately behind them. The grounds of Eric's estate created a safe haven for them all, the moment the latch clicked shut. When they entered the home, there was a sea of activity going on. A number of people were in the foyer on cell phones. Another group of people were in the media room watching different news outlets. A group of men that could only be security gathered in a corner taking directions from a woman that looked as fierce as any of the men. Ty went over to two men in suits and began talking. Miriam, Kerri, Jason, and TeKaya walked to the back of the house where they found Eric and Siri waiting. Siri was the first to reach out. "TK. Are you alright?" she hugged her sister then took a step back to look at her.

"Stop." TK said.

"What?" Siri asked.

"Stop trying to find a way to blame yourself for this. I know that look." TK looked over at Eric, "How many different ways has she claimed responsibility for this."

Eric had to smile, because TeKaya had nailed her sister to the wall. "At least three so far, but we've only been here about an hour. I'm sure if you give her more time, she'll have at least ten more."

Siri put her hands on her hips and frowned at Eric. He walked over to his brother. "Everything straight?"

"Better. Mitch Curry from the morning show will have an exclusive in the morning."

"He's syndicated radio. Why not television?"

"I'm sure Mitch will have a station or two interested in the exclusive before morning."

"Alright. What do you need from me?"

"Just be there with me."

"Always."

After checking in on Sierra, who was sound asleep in her room at Eric's house with Gabby next door, Jason finally had a moment alone with TeKaya. After all she went through today, he knew without a doubt this was the woman for him. He stood in the doorway of the room he used whenever he stayed at Eric's place. The room had always been a retreat away from home. But never had it been as beautiful as it was with TeKaya sitting on the bed against the headboard. Her hair was lose around her shoulders, and she wore a long, black night gown made of lace and silk. A pair of black stilettos, completed the heavenly vision. "I've been waiting for you." She said as she slipped off the bed and twirled halfway around the bedpost. Eric was kind enough to let me into your suite. I hope you don't mind."

Classic. That was the only word he could think of to describe her beauty. She had the classy look of Audrey Hepburn, the beauty of Lena Horne and the tenacity of Josephine Baker. The most amazing part of her standing in this place, at this time was simple—she was his. He closed the door behind him and walked towards her as she stood her ground. He stopped right in front of her and traced her face with his finger. "What could I have possibly done on this earth for God to favor me so? I will never know. But, I thank him for giving me you." She started to say something but he put his finger to her lips. "Just listen for a moment. Six months ago, I was ready to give up on finding someone to love or someone to love me. I'd stopped looking for you and then you appeared in the least expected place. But I knew, the moment I saw you, that you were the one. Since that day, I've thought of nothing else but making you mine. As much as I want you at this moment, and GOD knows I want you. You said you wanted to wait until we are married. The last thing I want is for you to regret our first time together."

TeKaya reached out and touched his chest. She ran her hand over his chest as if memorizing the feel of him. Taking a step closer she took his arms and placed them around her waist. "While I was in the back of the police car I promised myself I was going to make love to you as soon as time would allow. My heart has been married to you for a few months now. In a funny way, Latoya sealed the deal for me today. There is no way I would let that woman have one more moment with you. I love you Jason, from that funny lump on the back of your head, to that callus on the bottom of your foot. Before this week is out, I want to be your wife and moving into our new home. Before this year is over, I want to be carrying your child. Before this night is over I want you to claim me as yours." Her hands roamed down to his manhood and gently squeezed. "Make love to me Jason."

Taking her face into his hands, he kissed her, feeding a hunger so deep; it could have saved a small third world country from starving. Not another word was spoken between the two. They used their bodies to express their emotions. TeKaya pulled his t-shirt over his head and marveled at the wide shoulders, six pack stomach, and trim waistline. She begin kissing each shoulder, sucked each nipple, than used her tongue to trace from the center of his chest and circle his navel. Taking her time, she slipped her hands around his waist under his sweat pants and over his behind, pushing them down his thighs, allowing his manhood to spring free. With all the will power she had, she willed herself to continue until the pants hit the floor. Then slowly rising she started placing kisses up his legs, continuing up his thighs and finally the tip of him.

He grabbed her under her arms, pulling her up to him and took over the seduction beginning with her shoulders. He slipped the thin straps down her arms, trailing with his fingers on both arms. The gown slipped over her breasts and hung around her hips. Feeling the weight of each breast in his hands, he gathered one then the other, sucking until he felt her knees buckle, or was it his? He wasn't sure and didn't care. All he knew was the taste of her, the feel of her, and the very essence of her was calling him. Kneeling in front of her he gathered her tiny waist in his hands and pulled her core to his nose and he inhaled through the material. What he wanted, what he had longed for was beneath the piece of fabric that now hung on her hips. Placing his hands under the material he began to massage her behind with his fingers and pushed the fabric to the floor, revealing his most wanted desire. Nothing could have prepared him for her perfection. No imagination, no dreams he'd had over the last few months came close to what stood before him. He sat back on his heels and scanned her from her toes up to her eyes. Exquisite was the only word that came to mind. He reached out and touched the silky hair that was neatly trimmed at the V of her thighs. With his thumb, he stroked the bud of her love nest and her knees bent. Without warning he pulled her to his mouth, spread her thighs, and began to ravish her inner core. His hands supported her weight where she stood as she began to crumble from his all out assault. When she grabbed his shoulders and he heard her gasps, he smiled with the knowledge that he was the catalyst that caused her to scream. He waited for the sweet reward of her juices flowing, to quench his thirst. And he was just getting started.

    Standing he picked her up and gently placed her on the bed. He smiled down at her almost closed eyelids down to the stilettos that were still on her feet. She took that orgasm in her stilettos--now that's a woman. He went to the foot of the bed, removed her shoes, and threw them over his shoulder. She smiled and held her arms out to him. He shook his head no and gathered her feet in his hands, kissing the arch on each and sucking the big toe until she was squirming on the bed. He bent her knees up as he crawled between her thighs placing a kiss behind each one. Releasing her legs he laid snuggly in the junction of her thighs, slipped his hands over hers and entwined their fingers together. Looking into her eyes, his manhood continued to jerk to attention, with it's radar positioned for the target. But, this was one time he did not want to rush. He wanted to savor every minute, every feel, and every touch. Without guidance, he slowly began to enter her as if it knew exactly where it was suppose to go. The glorious feeling of her core enclosing so tightly around him, caused his eyes to close to the shear pleasure. He eased further into her enjoying the wonder of her until, he felt....no...it couldn't be. He opened his eyes and stared into her knowing eyes. She kissed him and smiled. Could this be? Could this beautiful woman have chosen him above all others? The look of contentment in her eyes answered the question, unequivocally, she had. He was now determined to prove himself worthy of such a gift. He kissed her eyes, her nose and finally her lips, gently probing his tongue and his manhood into her. Her fingers squeezed his as he broke through the barrier. He stilled until he felt her moving slowly, setting her own rhythm and then he followed until he could no longer stand the torture. Taking over he held her and moved within her like a man on a mission. He was not going to allow his explosion until he had drained her of all the sweet loving she had preserved just for him. It seemed this spirited woman, he had fallen in love with was not the lay back and take what you give. No, she was meeting him stroke for stroke, dip for dip and reaching up for more. It felt as if they were suspended in mid air. The deeper he plunged, the further up she came. The harder he plumbed the harder she slammed up to meet his body, until they both exploded and time stood still.

They both fell back onto the bed, hearts racing, and juices flowing. He lay to the side of her and pulled her on top of him. Pushing her hair back from her face, he kissed her deeply until their lungs dictated that they had to come up for air or die at that moment.

The next morning, the only thing on Jason's mind was the wonderful woman he was going to marry.

"Jason. Jason," TeKaya called out again bringing him back to the present. "Where did you go?" She smirked.

Looking down at her he couldn't help but return the look of love in her eyes. "It's six o'clock in the morning and I want to take you again."

TeKaya sat up' "Let's go."

Smiling at her, he shook his head. "No. You are going to be sore for a minute. And I don't want to cause you a minute of pain."

"Really?" She asked with this quirky expression on her face wearing nothing but his t-shirt.

"Really."

"So at this moment I can do anything that I want and get away with it?" She asked as she straddled him and kissed his chest.

Feeling the silkiness of her hair on his body, he closed his eyes and said, "Anything."

Suddenly he tensed as her hands reached down and pulled him free of his sweats. Before he could sit up her mouth had encircled him and he began to grow thicker. When she came up, she looked at him and said, "Tell me what to do."

He gave her a look that said you have to be kidding. "Girl if you do anything more, I'll die in this spot."

Her look grew serious as she held him in her hands. "I love you Jason Davies."

Reaching for her, he pulled her up by the waist and she positioned her center right over top of him and slowly eased down on him. "I love you, Jason Davies." When he was fully embedded inside of her, she laid on his chest and squeezed her insides, entrapping him in heaven. She began to move up and down on him repeating the words, "I love you Jason Davies." Each time she said it, he grew thicker inside of her. When the tension became too much she pushed against his chest and sat up as he held her by the waist. She began to ride him as if she were riding a stallion, pushing him deeper and deeper inside of her. Letting her head drop back she arched her back and begin bucking against him until they both called out the others name in total release. She fell forward on his chest and he held onto her like she was his lifeline. That's where they stayed until it was time for the press conference.

Latoya was in her bedroom quite pleased with herself. By the end of next week, not only would she own this house free and clear. She would also have at least seven digits in her bank account. All she had to do now was play it cool until the ink dried on the check Jason was going to sign over to her. She knew the truth was going to eventually come out, but the media didn't give a damn about the truth. They wanted scandals and for the next few days, until the arraignment, that's exactly what she was going to give them. Her cell phone chimed. She looked at the number and smiled. "What you got?"

"Seems like you had a busy night," the man on the other end replied.

"It's been interesting."

"Not as interesting as my night. Your place clear?"

"Yeah."

"Good, let me in. I'm at the back door."

Latoya walked down the hallway to the garage and opened the door. "This couldn't wait until the morning?"

Roy Kelly, the private investigator she used whenever she needed info on one of Jason's girls walked through the door with a silly smirk on his beet red face. "Show me where your DVD player is and I'll let you be the judge.

They went into the kitchen and used the player Jason had installed for Sierra to watch her Disney movies. He put the disk in and hit play. "I didn't get your boy, but I got his brother. Now, I figure this ought to be worth something to keep it from the media. What do you think?"

Engrossed in the homemade movie, Latoya didn't answer at first. "Damn, Eric got some moves," she mumbled.

"I rather enjoyed the woman. They were like rabbits in heat going at each other."

"How in the hell did you get this without them seeing you?"

"That was the easiest part of this job. They left the patio door open. I peeked in from the backyard and you could hear them all over the house. You want sound?"

Latoya laughed, "No I think I can translate this." They continued to watch, as the action on the screen began to heat up. "This could be a damn good movie."

Roy hit the stop on the remote, then ejected the disc. "Yeah it could, but it's going to cost you."

"I already pay you a healthy fee and it's not what I asked for."

"Alright," Roy tilted his head and put the disc in its case. I can take this to Silk, himself. It might be worth something to him."

"Eric will kick your ass for invading his privacy. You can forget your practice and anything else you may have planned. What's your price?"

"$100,000.00 cash."

Thank God for gullible people. "I can work that." She reached out to take the disc.

He pulled it out of her reach and dropped it down into his black bag. "You get this, when I get the cash."

Irritated, maybe he wasn't as gullible as she thought. She shrugged her shoulders, "Fair enough. Monday morning, your office. I want the original and don't make any copies."

"I won't make any copies. See you Monday." He walked out of the house pleased with himself. He didn't lie, he had no plans to make any more copies. He had what he wanted.

Jason and TeKaya sat on the veranda with Eric's gardens as their backdrop. During the night, while they were consummating their love, others were working diligently to bring the matter with Latoya to a close, before it literally took flight. And they succeeded. After the telephone call from Mitch, Ty sent a team out to interview others from the restaurant, gathering enough evidence to show Latoya was the aggressor in the situation between her and TeKaya. But Ty wasn't satisfied with just that. He wanted Sierra's fate settled once and for all.

Gabby had mentioned something about video cameras set up throughout Jason's home and he wondered if that could help with the custody battle that was sure to ignite. Sitting in the room next to the kitchen, Ty spent most of the night viewing tape after tape, until he came to the one that sealed the deal. When he was about to pack up and call it a night, he heard voices in the next room. He looked at the console to determine how to change the view of the camera in the kitchen. Searching he saw a button labeled rooms. He went down the list until he found the kitchen, then hit the button. One of the monitors switched to the kitchen where it picked up Latoya and a man watching something on the television monitor on the counter. He focused the camera on the monitor and was shocked to see Eric and a woman making love. "Shit. Where in the hell did that come from?" He tried to adjust the volume to hear what was being said between Latoya and the man, once he pulled the disc out and dropped it in his bag, but he couldn't pick up their voices. He pulled the tape. He'd get a still picture of the man and find out who he was. Once the way was clear, he left the same way he entered the house, through Jason's office.

With the tapes and the journal Gabby was keeping, he was sure Jason would be granted full custody of his daughter. Now, the issue was what to do about Latoya and this new situation.

Ty placed the evidence in his car and pulled away from Jason's home. Pulling out his cell phone, he searched for the telephone number to Latoya's cell phone and pushed the button to dial. When she finally answered the call, he could hear the music in the background. "Sounds like a celebration going on. I'm hurt, I wasn't invited."

"Oh, haven't you heard Ty, I'm about to get paid. I take it you are calling about a settlement. Don't bother to put anything less than seven figures on the table. Cause if you do Jason and his faggot brother can kiss my natural behind."

"Huh, you're right Latoya I am calling about a settlement. See I have several videotapes, but one in particular would really interest any juvenile court system. Imagine how they will react to a mother putting alcohol in a baby's kool-aid. Better yet, imagine Jason's reaction when I show him the tape." He heard her intake of breath, smiled and continued. "I know Jason. And I know he's going to give you something. Whatever it is--it would be in your best interest to accept with no questions asked. If it were up to me, you would get zip, nothing. Have your attorney contact me in the morning with a signed document releasing all parental rights to Sierra by 8:00 or you will be lucky to get supervised visitation. 8:01 and the deal is off." He hung up the telephone and smiled while imagining the words she was flinging at him.

As Mitch began his interview, he knew this was the break he had been looking for. Who would have thought Latoya would be the one to give it to him. Payback is a bitch. He was the one that gave Latoya the VIP pass to see Eric "Silk" Davies a few years ago after a night of mind blowing sex. As an entertainment reporter, he was the one with the connections and she played him better than Eric played that damn guitar. As soon as she had her in—she brushed him off and had been doing so ever since. Well, now it was his turn and he was going to put the last nail in her coffin. "Jason," he shook his hand when he walked out onto the veranda, "I want to thank you for giving me this opportunity. I know you could have chosen any one of the major networks to give this exclusive. I appreciate it."

"No man. I need to thank you. Last night with all that was happening, I wasn't thinking straight. The incident at the restaurant never crossed my mind, once we left. I owe you for coming forward with the information. You had my back and I will never forget that." He reached over and took TeKaya's hand. "Allow me to introduce my soon to be wife. TeKaya, meet Mitch Curry."

"Wow, you are breathtaking. There ought to be a law against that. Welcome to Atlanta."

"Thank you, Mitch. It's nice to meet you," she smiled. "Jason told me what you did. From what I've been told Latoya is not one to mess with in this town. It was brave of you to step forward."

"The only thing that gave her any power was her connection to Jason."

"That ended last night. I'm cutting her off."

TeKaya held his hand in hers. "No you're not." She gently kissed his lips and smiled. "Here's what you are going to do. You can sign the house over to her or purchase her a smaller one, pay her child support for Sierra, and call it a day."

"Why in the hell would I do that? Sierra will be living with us."

"Yes, she will. But Latoya is her mother and you will make sure that she lives at the same level that her daughter does. Because when Sierra visits her mom, we want her in a safe, loving environment."

"Who said I'm going to allow Sierra to visit her?"

TeKaya pulled away. "I did." She said and looked at Jason with those big brown eyes and he caved in to her request.

"I'll buy her another house." TeKaya gave him a kiss. "And maybe a monthly stipend or something," she kissed him again. "One of the cars."

She squeezed up close to him and put her arms around his neck. "See, you're getting the idea." Then rewarded him with a full kiss.

Clearing his throat, Mitch called out, "Let's get this interview started. I believe this man has better things to be doing."

Eric walked into the kitchen and found Siri sitting at the breakfast bar watching all the action taking place on the veranda. Mitch was interviewing Jason and TeKaya, with both mothers sitting next to them. A small crowd of photographers, camera men, light technicians, a make-up artist, and a few attorneys, all stood in the background listening. He had to admit, they made a beautiful couple. But he wondered why Siri sat in the kitchen alone, while everyone else was outside. He heard Sierra giggle in the background and before he turned to see what she was up to, he noticed Siri wiped a tear from her cheek. The thought of her being sad cut through him like a hot knife against butter.

She knew the moment that he was in the room. The fluttering in her stomach alerted her that he was somewhere near. It would have been easy to give in to the man behind her. The way he made her feel last night almost convinced her to let go of her fears and give in to him. But looking around, all she could she were news camera in the front, at the back of the house, and now inside the house. This was more than she could stand. The public life was not for her. A tear fell as she came to the realization that Eric and his lifestyle, were and always would, be off limits to her.

"Siri," his smooth voice called out to her as if it was a melody to a song.

Never looking around, she began talking. "They make a beautiful couple don't they?"

He was now standing right behind her. "Yes, they do."

"We can never have that Eric. I've been through the hurt of a public marriage, I barely survived. The life you lead is different from normal men; it's even different from Jason's. People want to be you, know you, touch, and love you. You belong to them. What you and I feel for each other is secondary. The media is a permanent part of your life."

"I would give it up for you."

"I wouldn't want you to. Music is a part of who you are. Hell, it was your music that drew me to you. Please don't ever change that. Would you do something else for me?"

The two never touched or looked at each other, but he knew this was the last time he was going to be alone like this with her. The reality hurt. "Anything."

She wiped another tear. "Don't ever kiss anyone the way you kiss me. You have a wicked tongue." She picked up her purse and stood. "Tell my mother and TeKaya I'll see them when they get home."

"I'll take you back to Richmond."

"No." She replied never looking at him. "I have a flight booked."

She began to walk away. "Siri,"

"Yes," she stopped but did not turn around.

"Send me a copy of your book."

She smiled, but did not trust herself to answer, so she just nodded and walked out of the kitchen.

He waited until he heard the outside door closed before he moved. He walked over to the door leading to the veranda. His heart had just been shattered into a million and one pieces, but his brother's heart had been healed. Eric wasn't sure if he should laugh or cry.

Ty stepped back into the kitchen to answer his cell phone. "The damn papers are signed. But this isn't over. Your boys will have to deal with me again," Latoya, said right before the other end of the line went dead.

Relived to know Jason could now begin his new life, Ty looked over at Eric solemnly looking out at the couple. It was clear the woman on the screen with Eric last night was Siri. From what he observed last night, there seemed to be tension between them and Ty wasn't sure what steps to take in regard to the tape. If this woman was the one for Eric, the one to make him smile like Jason, then it was his duty to keep anything from damaging their chances. And that tape would do more damage than they could imagine. His cell chimed and he answered the call. "I have your guy. He's a small time investigator, not sleazy, but not clean either. I have someone sitting on him. What do you want me to do?"

"Sit on him. I'll hit you back in fifteen."

The frown on Eric's face, told him things must have gone badly. He wondered, whether Eric had feelings for this woman—only one way to find out. "You were right, Siri is a beautiful woman." Ty said as he stood off to the side of the room. "Makes me wonder, how a man could let a woman like that go."

Eric turned to Ty with fury in his eyes. "I have no intention of letting her go. It's taking her a little time to realize it, but I know just like there is a heaven above she will be mine."

To Be Continued........

Book Two

Heaven's Gate

Chapter 1

On a flight from Atlanta, Georgia to Richmond, Virginia, the flight attendant approached Siri Austin as she stared out of the window. "Would you like any refreshments?"

Looking towards the attractive woman, Siri smiled. "No thank you."

Seeing the tears on her face the attendant asked, "Are you alright—may I be of any assistance to you?"

Wiping the tear away, Siri replied with a sad smile, "No, I'll be fine.'

The attendant acknowledged her response and moved on. Siri turned back to the window and wondered how she had allowed her life to be turned upside down again—by a man. A month ago, she was doing fine. After all the publicity surrounding her divorce from Carl Austin, she was finally getting her life back. She was teaching again, she had finished the book she had begun writing over a year ago and the book had been accepted for publication by Crimson Publishing. One of the most prestigious publishers in the business wanted her novel. The credit for the wonderful achievement did not belong to her and therein lie the problem. The completion of her novel could be attributed to one person, Eric "Silk" Davies.

A little over a month ago Siri's younger sister, TeKaya invited, or more like dragged her to the Friday at Sunset Concert series held in Richmond, Virginia every summer. That night's performer was soulful R&B singer Silk Davies. The man's music was known for being responsible for the conception of a number of children. Putting on one of his CD's was a sure thing for getting any woman in the mood for a good night of love making. Siri was no different. There was an instant attraction to the man that mesmerized her the moment he stepped on stage. All of the hurt she'd experienced from the devastating divorce began to dissolve the moment he began to sing. All the doubts she was left with, evaporated the first time they kissed. And all the shields she'd erected around her heart began to melt the last time they made love.

Siri arrived home with just enough time to shower and change to meet an agent name Kiki Simmons. She had set up the appointment before she went to Atlanta to be with her sister, and before she allowed Eric to claim her heart. Until Friday night, it was just a physical attraction, but now she just wasn't sure.

While dressing in her room, her eyes continuously roamed over her bed. The same bed that had not been changed or made up since she and Eric rushed to Atlanta. The temptation was so strong to go over and smell the pillow to see if his scent was still on it—but that would only make things worse. She immediately got up from her vanity, stripped the bed and ran downstairs to put everything into the washer. She was determined to get Eric "Silk" Davies out of her system. *I shouldn't have let him in, in the first place— right?* The thought crossed her mind minutes after the washer started. Standing in the middle of the laundry room, watching the machine was not going to answer that question for her. Somehow, she had to protect her heart from opening to him any further. The telephone rang and she jumped, startled by the sound. Thinking it might be her mother or sister TK, whom she'd, left in Atlanta, she ran into the kitchen to answer it. "Hello."

"Hi. I wanted to make sure you made it home okay," Eric's voice vibrated through the line.

"Yes," was all she could say, her heart wanted to say more, but her mind knew better.

Silence resonated around the room. "Be sure to have an attorney read over all those documents before you sign anything. That goes for your meeting with the agent as well. What was her name again?"

"Kiki Simmons," she replied as she cursed herself for being distant with him. Here he was trying to help her and she was being defensive.

"Well, that goes for Kiki Simmons and Maxine Long." He hesitated, "I'll be leaving for Paris in the morning."

"Will you be gone long?" Looking down at the floor she wanted to kick herself for asking.

"I'm not sure. I'll be back for Jason and TeKaya's wedding." Seconds ticked away before either spoke. He was happy for his big brother and Siri's little sister. They'd found each other and had not allowed others to interfere in their relationship. Siri was a little different from her sister. She had experienced hurt before and was not as willing to accept the love he was offering. For now, that was okay. But he had no intention of letting her go. He would give her time to come to terms with her feelings for him—then all bets were off. He planned to claim the woman that had captured his heart. "The media is a part of my life and that scares you. Your reasons are valid, but I need you to understand, I'm just a man that has fallen in love with a woman. Music is what I do—it's a part of who I am. When you are ready to accept the man and the musician—I'll be waiting. My heart is yours Siri, now and forever. Take care." He said before hanging up the telephone.

Siri sat at the breakfast bar with the telephone receiver still in her hand, closed her eyes and inhaled. "This is the right thing to do," she said. "This is the right thing."

The Rendezvous Restaurant on Broad Street was chic and elegant. You could almost see yourself through the shining hardwood floors. The long bar was to the left, covering the length of the wall and leather bound cushion seating lined the wall on the right, with a few tables in the middle for dining. The open area seemed more like a meeting place, than a restaurant. There were a few people seated at the bar, one couple at the table eating and two men standing in a doorway that apparently led to a VIP lounge. A young man dressed casually approached her. "Good afternoon, are you Siri Austin?"

The smile was immediate because he pronounced her name exactly right. "Yes. I am."

"Welcome to *The Rendezvous*. Your party has arrived. Just follow me. Is this your first time visiting with us?"

"Yes, it is."

"Then lunch is on us today," he said while pulling her seat out. "If you enjoy your meal, please tell others about our establishment."

"Thank you, I will."

"Wonderful, I'll let Ms. Simmons know you are here."

Waiting for Ms. Simmons to appear gave Siri a moment to close her eyes and think about her book. The story had changed so many times, but the night she met Eric, the ending was as clear as day. She remembered her laptop was literally attached to her body for almost three days as she added the finishing touches. After researching several publishers she had chosen to submit her manuscript to only one--Crimson Publishing. Their long history of gracing the world with love stories that enticed and entertained prompted her decision. Her story began as a way for her to put into words all the hurt, sadness, and betrayal she experienced during her divorce. But, after that first night with Eric, it changed—it began to heal the hurt, in a small way.

"Siri Austin, I presume."

Siri looked up at the heavy, almost masculine voice to find a very tall, slim female that might have been all of twenty. There was no way this child could be Kiki Simmons—the literary agent.

"Yes," Siri hesitantly replied.

Sure enough, the young woman extended her hand. "Kiki Simmons. It's nice to meet you."

Siri placed her tote bag on the floor, stood and took Kiki's hand. "It's—nice to meet you."

The two women sat as Kiki stared at Siri as if trying to figure something out. She folded her hands under her chin and smiled. "Well, you certainly are not what I expected."

Siri smiled. "Funny, I was just thinking the same thing about you. How old are you?"

"Twenty-six. But what I lack in years I have in determination and tenacity." She sat back. "At least that's what my mother tells me. Does my age bother you?"

"I don't know yet. Do you know much about the publishing industry?"

"Only to the extent that my father is an industry attorney/agent, my mother is a New York Times bestselling author—three times over. And my stepmother, Maxine Long, is a senior editor at Crimson, one of the longest running romance publishing houses in existence. My two older brothers own, Battle Publishing, which is where I worked during high school and have interned every semester during undergrad and law school. And unfortunately for them, the place I plan to resign if this manuscript of yours is as good as Max said." She paused long enough to thank the waitress that approached the table with her drink and allowed Siri to give her order. "Now tell me about you. And don't tell me about the stuff I read in the news. I want to know who Siri Austin is and why she wants to be published."

Siri reached down, pulled out her manuscript, and placed it on the table. "The why is because I have a few stories to tell that will—I want you to note—I said will, touch the heart of millions of people that have experienced a failed relationship and still believe in love. As for me," she sat forward and placed her hands under her chin, impersonating the young woman's previous pose. "I'm a simple school teacher that was born and breed right here in the good Old Dominion. I have simple wants, simple desires just like your average woman. Since it seems you have checked me out, you should know up front, I don't like publicity. I'm not flashy, and I refuse to settle for anything less than one hundred percent loyalty to this project. Is that something you can deal with?"

"Well, you certainly aren't the little prissy school teacher the media made you out to be. Yes, I can deal with that. However, can you deal with the fact that as an author only you can sell your product? That manuscript can be the second coming of Mark Twain and it won't matter if you are not willing to take center stage and tell people about your story. According to Max, this book has bestseller all over it. But it can't and won't stand alone. So make a decision Siri Austin. Are you willing to do the book signings, the publicity stops, and possible media coverage it's going to take to put this book where it is destined to be?"

Siri sat back and exhaled. "You read the articles. I'm sure you pulled up old news coverage of my divorce. The media and I aren't exactly on friendly terms."

Kiki sat up excitedly, "We won't be dealing on their terms. You had no control over how your divorce was covered by the media. Here, you are in total control, with the exception of what I'm going to insist you do. You choose who, when, and where your events are covered." She took the manuscript off the table. "Let's discuss financial terms while we eat. I'm starving."

The young man who had greeted her earlier, approached the table. "This is my youngest brother, Garland. He owns this place. Garland, this is Siri Austin and she is about to become my first client. So—we need to celebrate."

"Congratulations and good luck keeping up with this one."

Siri smiled, they seemed close. "Thank you. This is a very nice place you have."

"It's been a lifelong dream."

"Lifelong—boy you are barely twenty-two and still wet behind the ears. You haven't lived long enough to have a lifelong dream. Now go in the kitchen and put together one of those dishes you made for Max."

Garland looked at his sister, then bent down and whispered something in her ear that made her laugh aloud. "Ms. Austin, do you like seafood?"

"Yes, I do, but please call me Siri."

"Well, Siri I hope your mouth is ready for the culinary delight I'm about to prepare for you. Kiki will have to settle for something on the menu." He turned and walked away leaving Kiki's mouth wide open.

"I'm telling Mother." She said to his back.

"You know, I think we are going to work well together."

"I promise to give you my all, and then some, starting with the remainder of my weekend." Kiki said as she picked up the book. "*Night of Seduction*. Hmm, will I need to pull out my toys to make it through this book?"

"No, but it may help to have a live body next to you. A toy will not suffice," Siri replied as she picked up her drink and took a sip.

"Oh, I'm scared of you girl." The two women laughed.

The car was waiting at the side entrance to Eric "Silk" Davies' home when Tyrone "Ty" Pendleton parked his Mercedes. The driver was placing bags in the trunk, adding to numerous pieces of luggage already stored. "Who's leaving?" he asked.

"Mr. Eric," the driver replied and continued with his duties.

Ty walked through the door of the mini mansion, which led to the rear of the state of the art kitchen that was the heartbeat of the house. He walked across the room to the back staircase, taking them two at a time until he reached the second level. Smiling at the double platinum albums and pictures of Eric, Jason and himself with other celebrities that lined the walls, he proceeded down the hallway until he reached the double doors that were open. Walking through a sitting area, there was a sofa, table, and two recliners. On the wall was a flat screen television that covered it. To the left was a breezeway. Walking through, he entered the area of the room that actually held the bed, and nothing else. Eric stood near the window, dressed in a white long sleeve linen shirt, a pair of worn jeans and sandals, looking over some papers. With his locs hanging lose around his shoulder, he looked the role of a true musician. "Hey, what's going on?" Ty spoke.

Eric looked over his shoulder to see his attorney, and a man he considered to be a brother, standing in the doorway dressed, as always, in a stylish suit, tie and loafers. He gave Ty a half smile. "Man, it's Saturday afternoon, don't you ever dress down. Do you own a pair of jeans?"

"I work twenty-four seven, I don't have time to relax. And no, I don't." Ty walked into the room. "Where's Jason?"

"My, hopelessly in love, brother and his fiancée are out meeting with a decorator. Can you believe that, Jason is meeting with a decorator?"

"That is funny," Ty smiled. "Remember the first house Jason paid someone to decorate, giving no directions and he ended up with a space station theme with gray and black stripes." The two men laughed. "Afterwards, he had to pay to have it redone—twice. Maybe he learned his lesson. But, I'm not here to see them. I need to talk to you."

The hesitation in Ty's voice caught his attention. "Come on back." He said turning to walk into an adjoining room that was his office. He sat at the desk, still somewhat engrossed in the papers he was reading. "What's up?" he asked once Ty took a seat.

"Whew....where do I start?"

"The beginning is usually a good place. But if this is going to be a long story, we may have to put it off for a while."

"Where are you off to?"

Putting the papers down, Eric replied, "I decided to fly to Paris in the morning."

The decision surprised him. He'd met Siri Austin for the first time the night before, when she arrived from Richmond to see about her sister. TeKaya had had a little run in with Jason's ex-girlfriend and his daughter's mother that had landed her behind bars for a minute. From what he'd seen, there was a definite connection between Eric and Siri. "Really—so you are not going to fight for Siri?" The glare from Eric would have chilled most men, but Ty was used to the temperamental, kindhearted boy that he and Jason had spent most of their lives teasing about his sensitivity. Ty ignored the look. "I need to know if this woman means something to you before I threaten to take a man's life. Now, if what you stated yesterday, about not having any intentions of letting her go is not true, but was just your pride at being turned down talking, then I can let this situation drop."

Frustrated, Eric continued to glare at Ty. "What in the hell are you talking about?"

Ty bent forward, placed his elbow on his legs, and clasped his hands together. "Does this woman mean anything to you?"

Eric imitated his actions as his locs fell forward. "Do you realize you are getting on my nerves right now?" He stood and walked out of the room.

Ty sighed and followed Eric into his bedroom, but stopped at the doorway. "Eric."

"What?" He replied agitated.

"I'm the other big brother—not blood, but brother nonetheless. The women you and Jason choose to love become my sisters as well as your wives. Just like with you two, if their lives and or happiness are threatened in anyway, it becomes my job to eliminate the threat. You understand where I'm coming from?"

"I hear you and I love you, too."

Ty frowned. "Man don't be saying that. You know I don't deal with sensitive."

Eric smiled at the man, whose mother abandoned him when he was ten. One night he came to spend the night with Jason and never left. "Alright man. I don't love you—how's that?"

"Better."

"Good. I'm glad we could clear that up," Eric laughed. The only drama in their lives was and always had something to do with Jason's ex-girlfriend, Latoya Wright. He always kept his life simple and carefree. If he didn't, the media would eat him alive. They were always looking for a hot story when it came to him. But Eric always kept them at bay. Therefore, he was sure whatever Ty was talking about had nothing to do with him. "What is Latoya up to now? I would think she had learned her lesson after the punch she received from TeKaya." He said as he walked into his closet.

"Man, drop what you are doing and have a seat. I need you right here." He pointed two fingers towards Eric's eyes and then his own. Eric looked at the serious expression on

Ty's face, walked back into the office, and retook his seat. "Before you jump, know I have a solution to this issue."

"Why would I jump? Latoya means nothing to me. She's the mother of my brother's child—nothing more. You made sure of that."

Ty unbuttoned the button on his suit jacket, his tie swinging at the sudden freedom from confinement. He nervously ran a hand down his face and dropped his head. Eric was a serious type of man. Running from woman to woman, like he and Jason had been known to do, was not his MO. Between that and Eric's decision to leave for Paris, he understood Siri was not just another woman. Revealing what Latoya was up to was not going to be easy. "I'm afraid your friend Siri may be an innocent victim in Latoya's games."

Eric frowned and leaned forward in his seat. He shrugged his shoulder. "Latoya doesn't know Siri. They have never met."

Nodding his head, Ty agreed. "That's true; however, she stumbled across Siri while trying to get information on her sister, TeKaya."

"So."

This was harder than he thought it would be. "It seems Latoya hired a private investigator to get information on a Siri Austin from Richmond, Virginia. At the time, she thought Siri was the person Jason was seeing. On Friday, the investigator was in Richmond trailing Siri." Ty stopped, giving Eric a moment to analyze the information.

Eric sat back remembering the night before when he had reached and opened heaven's gates lying with Siri in his arms. "Okay..." he slowly replied.

Realizing Eric was not catching on; Ty stood and pulled a small compact disc from his pocket. He reached across Eric and placed it in the laptop sitting on the desk. He hit play then turned his back.

There was not a word or a movement in the room—only the sounds from the video that was playing. Seconds went by seeming like minutes before Eric could speak. "Who took this?" He asked calmly—too calmly.

"The aforementioned investigator."

Eric reached up and turned the video off. It was a video of him and Siri at her house making love on the kitchen table. From the angle of the picture, the person must have been in the window, or at the backdoor. *Was the door open?* He thought. Damn if he knew. He closed his eyes. "If this hit the media, it would kill her. Do you have the investigator's name and address?"

"Yes."

"Give it to me."

"No." Eric looked up with anger etched on his face. Ty almost took a step back, but then he remembered. Hell, *I'm six-two, two hundred and twenty pounds. Eric is all of six feet, one ninety at best. It's not like he could beat the information out of me.* But more importantly, he would not allow him to do anything that would damage his image.

"Give me the damn address." Eric commanded.

"Eric listen—this is something we can control."

This was something that could hurt Siri. He had waited all of his life for this woman. The one with the coal black eyes that looked straight through to his heart— the woman whose smile made him melt whenever he thought about it, the woman who put a song in his mind every time they made love. This is the woman he stood a chance of losing because the media would dig into the life of anyone they consider a celebrity, just to sell papers. Listening was the last thing he wanted to do. Eric stood and took the few steps that put him in Ty's face. "Did you have him killed?"

"Um, No," Ty replied looking down at Eric who was a few inches shorter than he.

"Why the hell not?" Eric yelled.

Ty released a nervous laugh. "Because it's against the law."

Eric gave him the most incredulous look imaginable. "What was that tape about? He trespassed on private property, and then violated our right to privacy. What about that law?"

Frowning at Eric's ridiculous comparison, Ty grabbed him by the shoulders. "Eric, invasion of privacy is not the same as murder."

Eric violently pushed into Ty's chest. "Get the hell out of my face. I'll find him." He said as he walked out of the room. "Latoya knows who he is—I'll find him, if I have to kill her to do it."

Ty ran out the door and into the hallway after him. "Eric—wait." Eric continued to walk down the stairs, through the kitchen, and out the door, toward the car that was waiting. Ty ran and grabbed him from behind. Eric came around with a fist high and hit him dead in the mouth. Ty fell backwards just as Eric's mother, Miriam, came out of the kitchen to see what was going on.

"Eric, what's wrong?" she asked seeing Ty on the ground.

Eric did not reply. "Take me to Jason's place!" He yelled at the driver, who stood a good distance away.

Ty jumped up, tackled Eric to the ground and a battle of the wills pursued.

"Stop it! Both of you! Stop it!" Miriam yelled to no avail. "Two grown ass men rolling around in the dirt like children." Miriam mumbled as she stomped to the side of the house, pulled out the water hose, and turned it on them full blast. It took her a moment to get the pressure high enough to get their attention. But when she did, she pointed the hose directly into Eric's face. When the struggle between the two stopped she yelled at her son. "Apparently you need to be cooled off!" She said as she lowered the hose.

Ty began to laugh. It had been many years since Miriam had had to pull them apart with the water hose. On the other hand, Eric did not find anything amusing about the situation and stood up just as angry as he was before. When Ty realized this, he stood and approached Eric, who roughly pushed him away.

Holding his hands up in a surrender posture, Ty spoke. "Man, I know how angry you are. But if we handle this right, we can get Latoya out of our lives for good."

"At Siri's expense. What is that? She did nothing—nothing but made love to me. And this is how she is rewarded. No, I don't think so."

"Eric," Ty calmly approached him. "Have I ever steered you wrong?" The look on Eric's face made him smile. "Okay, that one time, but—have I ever not had your back?" Eric didn't reply, but he knew Ty was always there for him and Jason. "Man, this is a way to get Latoya out of Jason's life, your life, and my life." He stepped closer. "I just need you to listen and follow my instructions and I promise you—I promise you man," he placed his hand on his chest, "I will protect Siri with my life."

Eric paced around in a circle in the yard—furious. He wanted to hit something, anything to release the anger. Wet from head to toe, he simply sat on the ground. Ty joined him, as did Miriam. "I know what I'm about to propose might seem a little risky to Siri, but it's a chance we have to take so this family can live without a person trying to destroy them for money."

Miriam sat on the ground beside Eric. The world known jazz singer whose home was in Paris was visiting her sons when she discovered they had both recently met the loves of their lives. Nothing could please her more, then to have both of her sons married and happy. It seemed her oldest son Jason, had won his battle for love and was about to marry TeKaya Kendrick, a beautiful, young photographer from Virginia. However, her son Eric was not as successful with

TeKaya's older sister, who seemed to have captured his heart. Whatever was happening was hurting her son deeply and whoever was responsible would pay dearly—she would make sure of that. "Eric, whatever we have to do, we will make this right."

Eric shook his head. "If this gets out, she won't survive the humiliation, Mother. Her reason for not giving into her feelings is because of the media surrounding me. There is no making it right. Her privacy is going to be violated and she will relive the nightmare of her divorce—all because of me." He stood up, held out his hand to help his mother up, and then reached out for Ty. Just as he stood, Eric kicked Ty's legs out from under him, which sent him back to the muddy ground. Eric stood over him with his arms folded across his chest. "Did you look at it?"

Ty, now quite pissed, looked up at Eric. "No."

"If you didn't look at it, how in the hell did you know what was on it?"

"Look, I'm not fighting with you anymore. Hell, I'm giving you a go on this."

"Don't curse in my presence," Miriam scolded.

"I'm sorry Mother" Ty said, then looked back at Eric. "I allowed you to do what you just did because I understand why you are upset. But don't let that go to your head. The next time you swing at me, it's going to be on."

A few moments passed, before Eric extended his hand again. Ty gave him a look of warning, then took his hand. Once he was standing they both wiped down their clothes. "Let's go set this trap to get rid of this woman once and for all," Ty said as they all walked back into the house.

Chapter 2
Eric and Latoya

The reality of the day began to take a toll on Eric. Friday, he was on top of the world and just as quickly, that world came crushing down. Nothing, not his family, his niece nor his music ever put him on a high the way Siri did; more so Friday night than the other times they were together. There was something about that night that took his feelings for her to an entirely different level. And now, the one thing she feared most was materializing and it would be his fault. There was a soft knock on the door as he sat in his solarium. This was the place where he went to think or work out problems. "Yes," he replied to the knock.

Kerri Kendrick, Siri' and TeKaya's mother slowly opened the door, then looked around. Eric was sitting on the loveseat of a beautifully crafted wicker furniture set, surrounded by plants of all kinds and a beautiful pond. "May I come in Eric?"

Smiling at the woman who gave birth to Siri, he nodded his head. "Of course you may."

"Oh my," she exclaimed as she ventured further into the room. "This is lovely. How many different plants do you have in here?"

Eric looked around the room he sometimes took for granted. "At least fifty. Half of them are from different places around the world. Something about their beauty captures me and I end up bringing them home," he smiled.

"You like beautiful things." It was a statement more than a question.

He softly raised his eyebrow and smiled. "I do."

She walked over, stood in front of him, and asked, "Is it my Siri's physical beauty or inner beauty that has you in a freefall?"

For a moment, he did not reply. Then he pointed to the single chair in front of him indicating she should take a seat, then sat forward as if he was about to reveal a deep secret. "Both," he replied with a knowing smile. "I'm in love with your daughter."

"I know," she smiled warmly. "And she is in love with you, but she doesn't know it yet." Taking his hands in hers, she looked into his eyes. It was so understandable how her daughter could fall in love with this quiet, sensual man. "The Siri we have with us now is very different from the Siri of before." She shook her head back and forth searching for the right words. "The love of another man took her from us. I'm hoping your love will bring her back."

How was he going to tell this woman, who was looking at him with so much hope and trust, that he might be the cause of more devastating hurt to her daughter? How was he supposed to protect her from her biggest fear when just being around him could be harmful? The more he thought about why Siri left this morning, the more he understood. The first time they were to step out as a couple, frenzy would begin with the media. They would want to know all about the woman who had captured the heart of the elusive Silk Davies. The way they were known to dig. He was certain that the incident in Richmond would come out, and so was Siri. That's why she walked away. But it may have been too late. "I'm afraid I will be the cause of more humiliation for her."

"Because you made love to my daughter and someone is greedy enough to try to exploit that moment. No, I think the responsibility for that humiliation belongs in the hands of the person destroying something so beautiful and private for personal gain. You shouldn't carry that guilt." She sat back. "However, Siri is not going to see it that way. The first thing she will think about is losing her teaching position. What she hasn't realized yet, is that she has outgrown that phase of her life. She's trying to recapture the past, and frankly, it can't be done. But she has to come to that realization on her own. Now as for you, here is my advice. Don't run away. Give her room to grow and find out what she wants for herself. Once she figures that out, she will be knocking at your door. Whatever you do, don't give up on her."

His heart stopped racing, his mind cleared and the anger of before dissipated. "You are an amazing woman. Here I thought my mother was the only one that could ease my fears." He smiled. "I want you to know, I will protect Siri no matter what it costs. I will not allow this to be used against her in any way." He stood and so did she. "I have to speak with Ty. Would you like to come along and see a grown man grovel?"

Pay day, what a sweet, sweet moment, was all Latoya could think about since eight this morning. She was now free of the brat and was 1.5 million dollars richer. Signing the papers giving custody of Sierra to Jason, was the cake, but what she had in store for Eric was the icing. The agreement was simple. She was to sign over custody, receive a cashier's check and the deed to the house once Jason had an opportunity to move his things. The packers were scheduled to be there by five that evening to begin the process. A week from Monday, the entire situation would be over. Jason certainly did not waste any time closing her out of his life.

Latoya thought as she held the check in her hand. Four years of her life, giving birth to his child and living with him, and it only took him twenty-four hours to end it.

Well, unfortunately, for the Davies, she wasn't through with them yet. Now, Eric would have to get down on his knees and apologize to her for the humiliation of turning her down. She looked at her reflection in the mirror, "That's right—no one turns me down without living to regret it." Even with the bruise on her face, courtesy of TeKaya, Jason's new girl, she still looked good and was 1.5 million dollars richer.

It wasn't enough. Eric would also have to pay, and double the amount she had received from Jason, to keep her from exposing the little love video. She picked up her cell phone and dialed Roy, the investigator. But his voicemail picked up. She left him a message. "Roy this is Latoya Wright. I want to complete that transaction today. Return this call within the hour or the deal is off." She hung up the telephone. "That should get him moving."

Roy listened to the message from Latoya along with two very big, intimidating men from Ty Pendleton's' firm. Lord knows, if he didn't have bad luck, he would have no luck at all. The moment he reached his office in the wee hours of Saturday morning, Ty Pendleton walked through his door, literally scaring the crap out of him.

The man didn't say much, just stared at him. He never gave his name, but Roy knew who he was. "Can I help you with something Mr. Pendleton?" He casually asked.

"Do you value your life Mr. Kelly?"

"I do," he replied while fumbling with the disc in his pocket. He knew it was not a coincidence that the attorney for the man he had a nude video of was standing in his office.

"Good," he replied and took a seat. "Let's negotiate."

Roy released a nervous laugh. "I'm not sure what we need to ..."

Ty held his hand up to stop what he was about to say. "If you are still standing by the time I reach inside my jacket, I will be pulling out a cell phone rather than a check book. Do you want to finish your statement or would you like to take a seat?" Roy was many things, but he was no fool. He slowly sat in the chair behind his desk. "Smart move," Ty pulled out his checkbook. "The item you have is more valuable than $100,000.00 and Latoya Wright knows that. She's going to make ten times that when she attempts to blackmail my client. You're going to help me stop her. As a reward, you will receive $500,000.00 and your freedom. If in a reasonable period of time, I feel you are trustworthy, I may send some work your way from time to time."

Thinking about the offer was not an issue, hell it was more than the woman was offering. But the prospect of working for Ty Pendleton would be beneficial. The man handled some of the top entertainers and athletes in the business. A few referrals from him could make him a rich man.

"What would I have to do to prove I'm trustworthy?"

"Turn over everything you have, from the disc in your pocket to the camera you took it on. And *never*," the word was emphasized, "let me see or hear one word about what you saw."

"I can do that. This didn't feel right to me from the beginning. I mean, those two looked like they were really into each other. It wasn't a booty call or anything like that. But it was my job."

"You saw an opportunity and you took it," Ty commented. "I'm not mad at that, but you need to seek better opportunities. Ruining someone's life only brings bad karma into yours." He stood and held his hand out for the items. Roy gave him the camera bag and the disc out of his pocket. "Is this everything Roy?"

"Yes. That's everything."

"This is your first test of trust, Roy." Two men walked in the door and stood there. Ty looked over his shoulder, then back to Roy. "However, just in case you have a change of heart, a few friends of mine, I like to refer to as The Towers, are going to be spending a little time with you. Before sunrise, I'll have a cashier's check delivered to you here. Don't feel intimidated by them; they're just here to keep your company." He took the bag and walked out.

Well, twenty-four hours later, the two towers were still with him. They were cordial. They talked sports, women, drinking, the normal things men talk about. But he wasn't fooled for a minute. He knew that if he made one wrong move, he would not live to see a dime of that $500.000.00 check Ty Pendleton had had delivered to him. Relief washed over him when the Wright woman called. He didn't expect to hear from her until Monday, but it seemed Ty knew she was going to call sooner. For a minute, he felt sorry for the woman, because apparently she did not know what she had coming her way. But then, he thought about his good fortune, and that moment of weakness disappeared.

"What do we do now?" he asked as he listened to the message again. Do I return the call?"

"Not yet," One of the towers replied.

"Do we need to call Pendleton and let him know she made contact?"

"He knows," the other tower replied.

Roy looked from one to the other. But before he could question them, tower number one cell phone buzzed.

"Yeah." He answered then listened for a minute and hung up. "We have to make a move." He stood, as did the other tower. They both looked at Roy.

The expressions on their face were not one to be questioned, so Roy stood. "I'm going with you."

"Glad you see it our way," tower number two replied and had the nerve to smile. They tapped Roy on the shoulder as they walked out of the door. "It's going to be fun breaking you in," tower number one said before turning off the lights and closing the door.

Twenty minutes later Roy found himself in the home of the man, he had just video taped and the tension in the room was thick. Eric and Jason Davies sat behind a desk in what appeared to be an office and then some, it was so expansive. Ty Pendleton and the towers stood behind him. He was center court. No one said anything when he was ushered through the mini castle and strategically placed in the center of the lion's den.

Eric didn't trust himself to speak or move. If he did the bastard, standing in front of him, would be dead in a matter of minutes. "Ty tells me you are not a bad person, Mr. Kelly. You are a man that was hired to do a job, and you did it very well." Jason spoke from the window where he sat, on the windowsill, beside his brother who was sitting in the chair behind a desk.

Roy knew an intimidation move when he saw one, and this one was good. Their weakness was that he knew not one of the men in that room would intentionally harm anyone. They were all decent people. Well, with the exception of the two towers. He was sure they would take your life out before you blinked an eye. But his concentration was on the man he was sure would have the final say on him. "Mr. Davies, this was not personal, it was a job. A job you made easy." Eric didn't flinch or bat an eye. That made Roy a little uncomfortable. "You and the little lady were reckless. I mean, I can understand why you were distracted. Cause the lady, well, she's a looker."

Before he could look up his eyes met Eric's fist. The next thing he knew Eric had came across the desk, and he was on the floor. "Eric," Jason and Ty called out, struggling to get Eric's hands from around Roy's throat. When they pulled them apart, the towers was holding Roy, and Jason had Eric.

Eric jerked away and calmly walked back around the desk and retook his seat. After everyone had settled down, Eric placed his arms on the desk and looked up at Roy. "It would be best Mr. Kelly if you refrain from referring to anything you saw during the timeframe when you were invading my privacy and trespassing on someone's property." The calmness of his voice was unsettling.

Jason took over, and his voice was just as chilling as his brother's was. "Ty tells me you have agreed to cooperate with us. Is that a fact or are you playing both sides against each other?"

Roy stood his ground. Whatever he might have thought about Eric "Silk" Davies before, was now completely erased. The man might be quiet and reserved, but he had a temper and could throw a decent punch. "Mr. Pendleton made me a very attractive offer that I have accepted. Whatever you might think of me, I don't slouch on my agreements."

"I'm glad to hear it. Here's what we are going to do."

Two hours later, Eric, Jason, and Miriam were seeing Kerri and TeKaya to the airport for the return flight to Richmond. "Well it's been quite an interesting weekend." Kerri smiled. "One daughter ends up in jail, the other on a scandalous video."

"Kerri, I can't tell you how sorry I am about all of this. I am so worried about Eric and Siri. I don't know if they can make it through this. But that tramp that started all of this is going down. That I promise you."

Kerri reached out and hugged Miriam. "Don't you worry about Siri; she is strong. Besides for the next week we have a wedding to plan. So there will be no worrying and no sad faces. Let the boys handle this and if they can't we will." They looked over at Jason and TeKaya talking to Eric. "Let's make a pact."

"Okay," Miriam replied.

"Come high or hell water, we are going to get Eric and Siri married before this year is out."

Miriam smiled. Kerri was indeed an amazing, forgiving woman. "Thank you for not blaming Eric in all of this." She sighed. "Eric isn't the player the media makes him out to be. To tell you the truth I think this is the first time he's been in love. I actually think he would kill Latoya over Siri, so that girl had better be careful. You can't mess with a man's heart."

"Okay ladies, it's time to go," Jason said as they walked to the steps of the plane. "We'll be in on Thursday." He hugged Kerri. "Thank you for everything."

Eric reached out and hugged her next. "I'll fix this," he whispered in her ear.

"Let's get on the plane while I still can," TeKaya said looking at Jason. "I'll call as soon as we land." She finally released his hand.

Jason, Eric, and Miriam watched as the plane taxied down the runway. "I have the name of a new reality show." Miriam announced. Jason and Eric looked at each other. "Eric and TK throw down. Yep, I think that's a good name." She turned and began walking back to the car and continued to talk. "I'm buying both of you punching bags for Christmas." Jason looked at his little brother. Shaking his head as they climbed into the car, "You know, I've never known you to be so violent, first Ty and then the investigator. I just don't know what's come over you."

Eric stared at his brother. "I've never known you to be so loving, first Latoya and now TeKaya."

"I never loved Latoya, but I do love TeKaya," Jason smiled.

Eric sighed. "I know the feeling."

Chapter 3
Siri

When TK and her mother returned on Sunday from Atlanta, Siri was so excited. She talked non-stop for hours telling them about the book deal and her new agent. Not much could spoil her good mood. They were sitting at the dining room table having a celebration dinner Siri had prepared, when the door bell sounded. Siri jumped up. "I'll get it," she sang out and left the room.

TK looked at her mother. "I don't know what all the tension was about yesterday at Eric's house, but I have a feeling it was about Siri."

Kerri sighed. "Why do you think it was about Siri?"

"Because Eric was upset, not Jason." She sat forward at the table and folded her arms on top. "Whatever it is, do not tell Siri now. Let her have this happy moment in her life without it being spoiled by anything or anyone."

"I'm not sure I can do that."

"Yes Mother, you can. If I can put up with Sierra's mother for the next eighteen years, we can certainly carry this burden for Siri for a little while. Call it selfishness or whatever, but I just don't want to see my sister unhappy while I'm beside myself with joy." She reached over and placed her hand on top of her mothers. "You understand—don't you?"

"Understand what?" Siri asked as she re-entered the dining room with Carl in tow.

"I don't understand why you would let the devil in the house on a Sunday?" TK smirked.

TeKaya, where are your manners?" Kerri scowled. "He is not the devil." *He's the devil's spawn*, she thought but did not say. She smiled instead. "Hello Carl. Would you like some dinner?"

"No thank you, Mrs. Kendrick." He looked at TeKaya who was shooting daggers at him. "I'm happy to see you are free and at home."

Before TK could respond and a have a full blown argument ensue. Siri interrupted. "Um, Carl needs to talk to me about something, so we're going to step out for a while."

"Siri we just got home and I have so much to talk to you about," TK exclaimed.

"That can wait until you get back. Go ahead," Kerri suggested.

Siri frowned; not wanting to choose Carl over her sister, she looked at TK. "Are you sure? If you really want to talk, I'll stay."

TK looked from her mother to Siri then up at Carl, who was scowling at her. "No, Mother's right. We can talk when you get back. You won't be long will you?"

"No," Siri replied smiling. "Not long at all."

"Let's go Siri," Carl said as he quickly took her hand. She pulled her hand away and walked in the direction they came from.

Once they were outside on the porch, Carl walked towards his car. "Where would you like to go," he asked as he pulled his keys out of his pocket.

Siri hesitated, then replied. "Let's just walk around the neighborhood."

He stopped and studied her. She had always been a beautiful woman, but today she looked radiant. A frown appeared on his face as the vision of Eric "Silk" Davies coming out of the house putting his shirt on came to mind. "It's not exactly what I had in mind. I was thinking something a little more intimate."

She stepped off the porch, took a few steps, and stopped in front of him. She took his hand and smiled. "You are and always have been a very handsome man. You know that?" She kissed his cheek. "Let walk and talk for a minute."

The sigh was loud and clear—he didn't want to have this conversation. But she pulled him forward and he reluctantly followed. "I'm not going to like this, am I?"

Putting her hand inside his arm, she walked beside him. "Probably not. But this conversation is long overdue."

"Siri," he closed his eyes and stopped.

She pulled him along, "Come on. You said you wanted to talk. So—we're going to talk, openly and honestly."

They began walking again, at first in silence, then Carl spoke. "I've totally lost you, haven't I?"

She smiled up at him as they continued to walk. "I'll always be your friend. This, is an improvement. A few weeks ago I could have cut your balls off, for making me think I was sexually inept," she raised an eyebrow. "Now, it's not important. I want to keep your friendship, even if only to make your mother mad."

Her smile was contagious—it had always been so for him. He knew, the moment Siri had agreed to marry him, he was a blessed man. But like most people, he did not appreciate the blessing until it was gone. "Are you sleeping with Silk Davies?"

They continued to walk until she was comfortable with her reply. "That's a complicated question. It's also not your business." She rubbed his arm to ease the bruised feelings she was sure he was experiencing. They stopped and she looked up at him. "You gave up the right to ask questions like that when you divorced me." He looked down at her and exhaled. "However, if you are asking as a friend," they began walking again, "I will say we have been intimate, however, we aren't any longer."

His sigh of relief could be heard across the street. He even chuckled a little, "Whew. I had no idea how I was going to compete with Silk Davies."

Stopping in front of him, she gathered his hands in hers and looked directly in his eyes. "There will be no repeat of you and I, Carl. The hurt cut too deep. I can forgive, but I will never forget what you and your mother took me through. I don't think I will ever get over the public humiliation. The problem is I have to find a way to at least come to terms with it and get past what happened. My first step is forgiving you and telling you a secret."

"Siri, I don't want to know a secret unless it's that you still love me," he sighed.

She pulled him forward to start walking again. "Yes, you do. I want you to think about something. Promise me you will think before you answer." He looked sideways at her. "Promise," she said again.

There was something so calming, so delightful about her, there always had been. Damn, he was a fool. "Okay, I promise."

"Alright, here's the question. Right at this moment is your body tingling with sexual excitement?" She pointed a finger. "Now think about it. Do you have an irresistible urge to pull me over to the back of the house and have your way with me?"

"I'm always ready for you, you know that."

"That's not what I asked you. You're playing the politician on me, and avoiding the question with nice words. Now, answer the question honestly or I'm not telling you my secret."

He laughed. "You are too much," he looked down at her and replied. "Okay, no, I'm not tingling with excitement.

But you just gave me a one two punch here. With the, there will be no repeat. What do you expect?"

"I don't expect anything. That's just it, we settled for each other. Both of us should have waited until that person came along that makes time stand still when they are around and leave you wanting when they are not; that wasn't us."

"Is that what Silk does for you?" He stopped and she looked away. This time he pulled her along. "If that's the case why are you walking away from him?"

"What make you think I'm the one walking away?"

"Because I saw the look in his eyes when he walked out the door and saw me. He was seeing me as his competition and I was seeing him the exact same way. Now, this time you think before you answer. I am asking you again. Why?"

She sighed long and deep. "Eric is a mega star. Everyone in the world wants a piece of him. I know that's an exaggeration, but that's what I feel. My being involved with him means dealing with the media and I just can't do it again."

Stopping he turned to her. It cut like a knife knowing he was responsible for her turning her back on something or someone that could make her happy. "Let's walk back." He took her hand and wrapped it around his arm. "I've never known you to be a coward, Siri. If Davies makes you happy and you are the person he wants in his life, don't let anything stop you from going for it. I made the mistake of allowing my mother to come between us. Now, I have no one."

"Well," she smiled up at him, "that's not exactly true."

"What part?"

"The part where you said you have no one. You do have someone and I think it's time for you two to give it a try."

"You dump me one minute and trying to hook me up the next, this is rich," he laughed.

"I know, I know. But it's time. Aren't you a little curious who I'm talking about?"

"No. I know who you are talking about."

She looked at him surprised, "Then what's stopping you from asking her out."

"You, Siri. You were stopping me."

"Well, that road block has been removed. So when are you going to ask her out?"

"Siri."

"Carl."

"Tell you what, I'll ask Cashmere out if you promise not to close your mind to Davies. I want to see you happy. If it can't be with me, then at least I'll know you have a decent brother."

"I'll think about it."

"Then I'll think about Cashmere." They smiled at each other and walked back to the house in silence.

TeKaya was waiting on the porch when they returned. She watched as Carl kissed Siri's cheek, got into his car and pulled away. How could she pick this man over Eric? Yes, Carl was tall, handsome, somewhat intelligent, but he was a momma's boy. Eric was all those things, but he was his own man. Besides, Carl had hurt Siri, hurt her so deeply she lost her big sister for a year and she would never forgive him, or that mother of his, for what they had done to her. And as soon as Siri reached the porch, she was going to tell her just what she thought.

"Hey, I'm glad you waited up for me. Have I told you how happy I am for you and Jason? The more I get to see him around you the more I like him. You glow when he's around and I can't think of anything in the world more wonderful than seeing my baby sister happy."

Damn, sometimes Siri really did get on her nerves. How was she going to fuss after that? "I'm scared Siri," she confessed.

"What?" Siri looked concerned.

"Siri, Jason is so worldly, so mature, so sure of who he is and what he wants."

"He sounds just like you," Siri smiled.

"No, she shook her head. "I'm so much younger than he is and when we made love my inexperience showed."

Surprised, but not allowing it to show, Siri sat down on the step next to her sister. "That was a big step for you. You want to talk about it?"

TK braced her hands behind her and began talking. "It was the most incredible experience of my life. I can still feel his hands on my body, the feel of his breath on my neck, his lips on mine." She closed her eyes and did not see Siri smile. "I could have stayed in his bed for the rest of my life and been happy. But we are not going to have the traditional 'happy ever after'. We are going to be together, I have no doubt about that. But we are going to have drama for the rest of our lives from Latoya."

"You know what I know for a fact?"

Looking over at her sister she shook her head, "No, what?"

Siri smiled. When they were little TK would answer just like that to her questions. "I know that true love, not the manufactured kind, or a forced love like Carl and I had, but true love will conquer all. What you and Jason have is a once in a lifetime love. Both of you recognized it as soon as you met and you refused to ignore it. That is awesome and brave."

"Siri, Jason paid Latoya 1.5 million dollars plus a multi-million dollar home to have me in his life. What do I have to give in return to equal that?"

"Love." No one said anything for a few minutes. "And of course a killer body, big booty, gorgeous eyes, and a wonderful, exceptional personality."

The two laughed like little girls. "I don't have a big booty, you do."

"Well, you got something he likes, giving up that kind of dough."

TK sobered. "I don't know if I'm worth it."

Siri put her arms around her sister's shoulders and pulled her close. "You are worth that and a whole lot more. Now, tell me about the wedding."

A huge smile replaced the somber look as TK began to tell her big sister about her plans.

Near the window in the living room, Kerri sat listening as her two daughters talked. They never realized that's how she always knew what was going on with them—the couch in the living room near the front porch. That's where they always sat to talk, just like tonight. The conversation eased her concerns about TeKaya, but Siri was another story altogether. She said a silent prayer that Eric would handle the situation with that woman in Atlanta so that it would not hurt her child. Siri would not survive another blow like the last one.

Monday had finally arrived. It was hard to believe it had only been three days since she received the call from Maxine Long about her book. Those few days were like a whirlwind—the call, making love to Eric, Atlanta, meeting Kiki, the talk with Carl. It was as if the Lord was clearing out old baggage to make a way for something better. At least that's the way Siri chose to look at it.

Walking into the school, she decided to go to Cashmere's class before her own. It was important to her to let her friend know it was okay for her to go out with Carl. She knew, Cashmere would feel uncomfortable seeing him because he was her ex and would not want to upset her. But it was the complete opposite. She wanted Carl happy and she was certain Cashmere was the woman that could turn his life upside down, if he allowed her to.

"Hey," she said while tapping lightly on the door to the classroom across the hall.

"Siri. How was your weekend?" Cashmere asked as she put reports on the children's desks.

"Hectic, but I did receive a call from Crimson Publishing. They want my book."

Cashmere turned with a surprise look. "Oh Siri, that is wonderful! Congratulations! You must be so excited," she said all in breath while giving her friend a hug.

"I am. I have a meeting this evening with the senior editor. And Saturday I met with and hired an agent."

"Oh my God, that sounds wonderful. Your mother must be beaming." She stopped and frowned. "How's TK? I saw the news. What happened?"

Siri sat her tote bag on a desk. "Baby mama drama. But she handled it, came home and is planning a small wedding for this Saturday."

"Oh my, happy news all the way around."

"There's more," Siri smiled.

Cashmere sat on the desk behind her. "Let me guess, you and Carl are getting back together."

"How would you feel about that?" Siri asked out of curiosity.

"If you were happy, then I would be happy for you."

Siri looked at her sideways. "But, you—won't be happy."

"Of course I would be happy for you," Cashmere replied, crushed by the insinuation.

"You would be happy for me even though you are in love with him?"

Cashmere stood, nervously looking for busy work. "I don't know what you are talking about."

Siri stopped her, pulled the papers out of her hand, and placed them on the desk. She looked directly into Cashmere's eyes. "I'm not getting back with Carl. I'm not in love with him and he is not in love with me. Personally, I think you and Carl would make a great couple. In fact, I have it on pretty good authority; he is going to ask you out." She saw the shocked look on Cashmere's face. "When he does, I don't want any of the nonsense about you not going out with him because he's my ex-husband. Understand. I want you to go out with him and as soon as you get a chance, rock his world." She picked up her tote bag and smiled at the still shocked Cashmere. "I have to get to class. Talk to you later."

Cashmere stood in the doorway, with her mouth still open, when Siri looked back. She held her hand up and motioned for her to close her mouth. Cashmere did so quickly and looked up and down the hallway to make sure no one saw her expression. Siri laughed and walked into her room. Before she could place her tote bag on the desk, Roscoe, the butt hole of a principal she had to endure, was at her door. "Mrs. Austin would like to see you in my office, now."

"Why, aren't you kissing her butt enough?"

"You are trying my patience with that smart mouth of yours. Just one word from her and your behind is out of here." He turned and walked out of the door.

For a moment, it crossed Siri's mind not to follow. Roscoe would have to grovel before queen bee—that was always amusing to see. Exhaling, she walked out of her classroom to the office. Inside sat the secretary, who was always pleasant, but never nice. It was rumored that Roscoe and his secretary were an item. But knowing how words or actions could be twisted into a world of untruths, Siri never engaged in those conversations. This morning, the woman looked uncomfortable, to say the least. "Good morning Siri," she said and held her eyes for a moment then looked away.

"Good morning. Should I just go in?"

"I wouldn't if I were you. But since you've been summoned I don't think you have much of a choice."

"That bad, huh?"

"Ms. Austin," Roscoe called out from the doorway, as he gave the woman a warning look.

Rolling her eyes, the secretary turned away.

Walking into the principal's office was never a good experience as a child and in some cases worse as an adult working in the school system. The sun was shining through the large window, behind the conference table and chairs that were placed near the door. To the right bookshelves lined the wall, two chairs were positioned in front of the large cherry oak desk and behind it, in the principal's chair sat the queen bee, Maybelline Austin. The secretary was right, she did not look pleased. "You wanted to see me?"

"Where are you manners Siri? It's customary to say good morning. But you never understood simple courtesy."

"Courtesy begets courtesy," she replied but continued to stand near the door.

"Close the door!" Mable demanded with a slam of her fist on the desk.

"It's customary to say please when you make a request of another person," Siri replied and made no move to comply with her request.

Never turning her eyes from Siri, Mabel spoke to Roscoe. "Leave us Roscoe and close the door behind you." Roscoe jumped up and did her bidding, leaving the two women in the room alone. "You continue to try my patience with your insolence, Siri. It's amazing the audacity you display time and time again."

"I realize you love to hear the sound of your own voice, but is this going to take very long. I have a class coming in soon."

It was beyond her as to what her son saw in this woman, Mabel thought. There was no denying she was a beautiful woman, standing there dressed in a red pants suit, with a white blouse and the right accessories, but her lack of respect for authority annoyed her to no end. "It's going to take as long as I want, that's how long it's going to be, if you value your job." When Siri did not reply, "Do I have your attention now? I thought that would work. You need to explain to me why you were seen walking hand in hand with my son yesterday?"

"I don't need to explain anything. If you want to know something about your son, I suggest you ask him." The pained look on her face took Siri a little off guard. "You did ask him." she almost smiled. "Didn't you? And he didn't tell you what you wanted to hear. Good for Carl. Could it be your baby boy is cutting the apron strings and becoming his own man?"

"You have always poisoned his mind against me. There were no problems between my son and I before he took up with you. Then everything I said was responded to with Siri said this, or Siri thinks that. You turned his head with that little body of yours and those dirty sex games you played." She stomped from behind the desk. "But I proved who had the power and I took him back from you. Don't you think for one moment I will allow you back into our lives?"

"You are talking like a jealous other woman rather than Carl's mother. There was only competition between you and I in your mind. I didn't take your son, he grew up like all children do, Maybelline. They grow up, leave home, start to lead their own lives, but they never, never leave their mother. I didn't poison Carl's mind. We fell in love, or at least we thought we did. It's a natural thing that happens between a man and a woman." She took a step towards the woman and put her hands on her hips to keep from smacking the stupid little woman that was once her mother-in-law. "Let me make this clear—you are no prize. I feel for the next woman Carl has feelings for, not because of him, but because she will have to deal with you. I never thought I would see the day that a mother did not want to see her child happy. It's all about you. What is it, exactly? Are you afraid your son will leave you alone with no one but yourself as company? That would scare me too."

Mabel reached out and smacked Siri across the face. "How dare you speak to me in that manner? You think because your sister is whoring herself to that record producer you no longer have to be concerned about your job."

After the initial sting of the contact wore off, Siri turned to walk away, but stopped and turned back to the woman. "I don't' want to be a part of your life. I'm a good educator, not even your slurs have convinced the school board otherwise. I'm tired of the threats. If you feel you can take this job away from me, give it your best shot." Standing there, with her hands on her hips, she exhaled, attempting to calm her nerves. "If you ever say anything in private or public regarding my sister again, I will forget that my mother raised me to respect my elders and give you the butt whipping you deserve." She turned and walked out of the door.

Outside the office door, several teachers had gathered, including Cashmere, who immediately went to her. "Siri," she took her arm, "come with me." She ushered her into the teacher's lounge ladies' room. Turning on the water, she wet a paper towel as Siri angrily paced the small area like a caged lion, needing to break free. Taking Siri's arm, Cashmere led her to a chair in the corner and placed the cool towel on her forehead. She witnessed the tears flowing from Siri's eyes, but never said a word. She retrieved another towel, wet it, and wiped the tears away. She then sat on the arm of the chair and held her friend's hand.

A few minutes later, the secretary came in, sat on the other arm, and took the other hand. "Don't you worry about that old bat. I have enough on her and Roscoe to cause them trouble for years to come. She'll be so busy trying to clean up the mess, she won't have time to get you fired."

Siri and Cashmere, with surprised expressions, looked at the woman, who never said much to any of them. Cashmere spoke first. "Roscoe and Maybelline?"

The woman nodded her head, "Mmm hmm—for years."

Cashmere and Siri looked at each other and burst out laughing. "Well, doesn't that beat all," Siri said as she sat up and took the cool towel off her face. "She condemns me for marrying her son, and the whole time she's sleeping around with a married man."

"Roscoe," Cashmere questioned, still not able to believe what she had heard.

"That's right. I have hotel rooms, dates, receipts, you name it. I've got it." the woman acknowledged. "If she tries anything with you, don't you worry I have your back." The woman stood, "Now both of you need to get to class." With that, the woman walked out of the door.

Siri took Cashmere's hand. "Don't allow Maybelline to keep you and Carl apart."

Looking at her friend Cashmere asked, "Are you sure you'll be okay with me seeing him?"

Siri reached out and hugged her. "I want him to be happy and yes, I'm very sure it's okay." The two smiled. "Let's go tackle those lovable rug rats we call children."

If the morning started bad, the evening was a paradox. Maxine Long was efficient, energetic, pleasant and to Siri's surprise, a Caucasian woman. Speaking to her and the fact that she was married to Kiki's father, led Siri to think she was a sister, but she was wrong. The great thing about it was, it didn't matter. The three women sat at the plush TJ's restaurant at the Jefferson Hotel and discussed what some would consider a very lucrative deal for a first timer. Apparently Kiki and Maxine had discussed everything from the book's release date, the distribution, book signings and the media blast that would "put the book on the map" in Kiki's words. That's where Siri had to speak out. "Ladies, I'm not sure I can do that."

"She's concerned about the bad press from her divorce," Kiki explained to Max while still reading the papers on the table. "After talking with her for hours, I believe she could handle the press, if questions were asked."

Max waived the statement off. "I'm not worried about that. It's public knowledge—history. We are dealing with the future. As long as there are no surprises lurking in the wood works, we're going to be fine."

"Well," Siri nervously spoke. "There is a situation that developed over the weekend."

"Oh, the thing with your sister and Jason Davies?" Maxine asked.

Siri nodded, surprise just how far the news traveled— Maxine was from New York.

"Wow, she knocked the hell out of the girl. Did you see the pictures?" Kiki asked Max.

Max nodded while pulling the fork from her mouth. "Girl, did I. Brought back memories."

Kiki laughed. "Yeah, I remember Mother smacking the crap out of you when she found out about you and Daddy. That was funny."

Siri tensed for a moment, until Max looked up with amusement in her eyes. The past was just that between these two, and the family seemed to have come to terms with whatever went down. She relaxed again. "So you two don't think it will be an issue?"

"No," Kiki replied. "Hell it might help to have Jason Davies and that fine brother of his, Silk, oh my God, Davies come by a book signing or two."

"Can we do that without your father knowing? He's kind of jealous of Silk Davies. He say's I spend too much time listening to his music."

"You're kidding?" Kiki laughed.

Siri sat and listened to the women talk about Eric. That was the reason why they could not be together. There were women all over the world having conversations about Silk

Davies and how he made them feel. The problem was, they really had no idea what that man was capable of doing with his hands, his tongue, his lips...Shaking the thoughts from her mind, she sat forward. "I don't think that's going to happen ladies. I'd like to do this on my own. I don't want my success to be based on my sister's new family."

"I understand, but let's not completely close that door," Max stated. "I'm getting hot just thinking about him." She took a moment. "Let's move on. This book is going to take the literary industry by storm."

"I agree. I'm just not sure of the most beneficial way to market it," Kiki said.

"It's a romance novel," Siri stated, but noticed the shocked expressions on her dinner mates faces. "I wrote this as therapy, to keep my mind sane while I was going through my divorce."

Max and Kiki looked at each other. "She doesn't have a clue," Kiki commented. "Shall I enlighten her or would you like the honor?" she asked Max.

"Oh please, allow me." Max put down her fork, as did Kiki, and turned her total attention to Siri. "What we have here is a how to manual that is told in a story. You have taken a romance story and turned it into an entertaining manual on how to deal with a bad relationship, find yourself, and in the process find the meaning of true love. You have it all, a good man, just not the right man, a conniving mother-in-law that means well for her son, and to top it all off, a once in a life time love. Reading this book for some women will change their lives. What we have is not your ordinary romance novel." She stopped and looked at Kiki. "That's the pitch." The two looked at each other and smiled as if they had discovered gold. "That's the pitch."

"This is not your ordinary romance novel," I like that, Kiki said as she tried it out. "I like it a lot."

By the time Siri made it home, she had a signed deal, a few suggestions for re-writes prior to it going for editorial review and a signing bonus check. Yes, the day started out rough, but it ended with Siri closing her eyes, allowing Eric's image to invade her mind and the memory of his touch to ease her into a sensuous sleep.

Chapter 4
Eric

The music world had been a part of Eric's life for as long as he could remember. There were so many nights his mother and father would sit them around the grand piano and make up songs for him and Jason to sing. He was always trying to outdo Jason, who, as quiet as it was kept, was just as musically talented as he. Jason just liked the business end of the industry better. Besides, he always said, "It's my way of protecting my little brother from all the vultures."

How he wished he could have protected Jason from Latoya. Maybe if he had been a little less short with her when she first approached him, she would have never set her sights on Jason. He shook his head while sitting in the studio, attempting to work on his sheet music. Somewhere along the line there could have been something he could have done to prevent this whole fiasco. One thing was certain, he was not going to fall short with Siri, the way he did with Jason. His attention now, was on one thing— protecting Siri.

If the trap that Ty was setting did not work, he was willing to pay whatever price Latoya asked to keep Siri's name out of the media. But he wasn't a fool. He would include a non-disclosure clause that would cost her twice the amount he would be paying her, if the video surfaced.

"Good morning," Miriam said from the doorway.

The reason his father fell in love with his mother and fought through segregation and prejudice to have her was clear; she had been and remained a beautiful woman. Even early in the morning. That's why he and Jason had been cursed with the taste for fine women. "Good morning Mother," he smiled and returned to his music.

"So, I take it the sabbatical to Paris is off."

Eric leaned back in the chair. "My plan was to give Siri some distance and get all of these songs, thoughts of her generated, out of my mind and on paper. But I can't leave things the way they are hoping Jason and Ty will handle this. I failed Jason, I can't fail Siri."

"How did you fail Jason?" Miriam asked a bit curious.

"Mother, I knew the moment Latoya entered the club the first night what she was about. That's why I steered away from her so quickly. If I had just given her the time of day, I could have prevented her going after Jason."

"Boy, please. That is nonsense and you know it. And if you don't know I'm telling you—its nonsense." She took a seat behind the music console next to him. "Jason is a grown man. He is responsible for his behavior, not you. I should have made you boys fight more or something when you were younger. You two always have this thing of being responsible when something bad happens to the other one. Even Ty is walking around blaming himself for the situation with you and Siri. He's crying that same song you are. 'There had to be something I could have done to prevent this from happening to Eric.' I swear all of you boys are getting on my nerves. Jason is in this fix because he thought with his lower head rather than his upper head by not protecting himself when he was having sex with Latoya. You were doing the same thing when you did not think to close the patio door before having sex with Siri in Kerri's kitchen. Which, by the way she is going to get you for." They both smiled. "There are people in this world that will use whatever tool they have at their disposal to live off of your fame. That's a part of the life we've chosen to live. You, Jason and Ty cannot walk around blaming yourselves for each other's unhappiness. You have to do exactly what Ty is doing—fight fire with bursting flames. He's not putting a band aide on the situation; he's creating a cure."

"Yes, but he's using Siri as the antidote and there in lies my concern."

Miriam sat back. "Well, I should have known once Jason fell you were not going to be far behind. I guess Ty will follow suit soon."

Eric smiled. "I can't imagine a woman that can deal with that arrogant man. Do you believe he said," Eric laughed at the memory, "that you saved me from him with the water hose the other day? He doesn't know the word defeat."

"He didn't realize your strength doubles when you are fighting with passion, with emotions. That could have been Jason and you still would have won that fight. You were angry because someone you've come to care deeply for was being hurt. I have never seen you react that way to anything. That's when I knew, I had to buy two wedding dresses."

Eric laughed and shook his head. "I don't know Mother. It's going to take an act of congress to win Siri over."

"Then I suggest you contact your congressman and have him put it on the floor for a vote. I just don't see you walking away from the love of your life. It's the life she's afraid of, not you."

"Well, she's going to have to get used to that once her book is published."

"What book?"

Proudly, Eric told her what he knew about the book deal. "If it's as good as the publisher thinks, she will be touring more than me next year."

"My, that little devil. I never would have thought she would write a romance novel. Is it juicy?

"I have no idea what you mean by juicy and I don't think I want to know," he laughed.

"I wonder if I could get an advance copy. Do you think she will let me read it?" Miriam asked excitedly.

"I don't know, but you can certainly ask her on Thursday."

"I'm glad you decided to stay around to see Jason get married. I know the thought of you leaving for Paris bothered him although he understood why."

"Yeah, I couldn't see missing that."

"Did you ever put a contract on the place in Richmond?"

"Yes, I did. The penthouse is being renovated to my specifications."

"Did you include a studio?"

He raised an eyebrow at the questions. "I did."

"You know what I think you should do?"

"I'm almost afraid to ask."

"I think you should go to Richmond and stay awhile. Think about it, you would be secluded. No one other than family would know you're there. Your staff could very well handle all the day-to-day things you would need. And you would be close to Siri. You could write and keep up with what's happening in her life."

Thinking about the suggestion, Eric thought it was a good idea, he saw the curious look on his mother's face. "What are you up to?"

"Nothing." She answered innocently. "You know, just because Siri is not willing to see you as her man, doesn't mean she couldn't use a friend. She is, after all, embarking on a new career that you have some knowledge of. I don't think she would refuse e-mails or a phone call here and there, just to say hello, how you doing? Do you?"

"No, I don't suppose she would have a problem with that."

"I think, tonight, after her meeting would be a perfect time for you to call just to see how things went."

He stared at his mother. Her mind was working over time. "I don't know what you are up to, but I will give your suggestion some thought."

"Good," she said as she stood. "I have a few errands to attend to. I'll talk to you later." She all but ran out the room.

The men had successfully put Latoya off until Monday, giving them time to put all they needed in place to trap her. Roy indicated after reviewing the tape again and doing a little research on it's value, he was raising his asking price to $250,000.00. At first, Latoya cursed and hung up the telephone on him, but later returned the call to accept his offer.

Early that morning Jason arrived at the house to meet with the movers. Ty and a police officer accompanied him to the house. Using his usual entrance, Jason walked into the kitchen and found Latoya there reading the paper and drinking coffee. "Well, well, well. Look what the cat dragged in." She held up the paper. "Look darling we made the front page of several publications. Aren't you pleased? I bet your brother loves all the publicity I got him over the weekend. Let's see, we were on most of the entertainment shows. And have you been listening to the radio this morning, every station is talking about the normally quiet life of Jason Davies exploding over the weekend." She laughed, "Man, your brother owes me—big time."

Jason smiled, not even Latoya could damage the inner peace he now had. Let her talk and have her moment, he remembered TeKaya saying. We will have our day. "Sierra's doing fine. It was good of you to ask. Unless the conversation is about our daughter, I have nothing to say to you."

He and Ty walked out of the room to Latoya yelling. "Don't think this is over!" She picked up one of the papers and smiled. "Just wait," she said.

While Jason dealt with the movers, Ty slipped into the security room behind the kitchen and positioned the monitors to ensure coverage over the entire house. Just in case Latoya insisted the meeting takes place here rather than at Roy's office. He locked the room and walked into the kitchen where Latoya was still seated. He looked at his watch. "I'm surprised you are not standing at the door of the bank waiting for it to open."

Flinging her hair over her shoulders, she smiled. "Thanks to your client, I don't have to wait in line for anything anymore. The banker is coming to me. I must say, you are always so loyal for an outsider."

"Better an outsider, than an outcast." Ty grinned. "How do you think you are going to be received at the few parties or social events you might get invited to, now. Do you honestly think they will welcome you with open arms? Tell me, have you talked to Stan or CJ, or any of the other men you've been pumping, and I do mean that literally, for information about Jason? Allow me to answer that for you— no. Would you like to know why?" He asked as he walked over to the table where she was sitting. "I'll tell you. It's because each of them have been meeting with my staff giving affidavits on you." He leaned on the table in front of her. "When this outsider finishes with you for what you have done to this family, you're not going to be able to find a rock far enough away for you to crawl under." He stood looking into the seething eyes of Latoya. "Enjoy your moment with the banker."

Latoya waited until he was out of the room then angrily threw the paper across the room. They would be eating her dirt by time she was done with the Davies. She had an ace up her sleeve and just as soon as she met with Roy, she was putting her cards into play. It was going to be a slow torturous death for Eric "Silk" Davies. It was all planned out. First, she was going to send out invitations to view the video using still pictures of Eric and his little friend. Then she was going to sell a copy of the video to the highest online bidder. All of this after she sold the original to Eric, to keep his reputation unmarred. Hell, personally she thought the video would help. She still wasn't sure if he was on the down low or not. Damn, now she believed her own lies. She started the rumor of his sexual preference because he turned down her advances. After seeing the man in action, she had to admit, she envied the woman in the video with him.

Later that afternoon Jason found Eric in the studio working on music. The sight of his little brother working diligently always made him proud. Whenever Eric released a successful CD, he was rewarded in many ways— monetarily, through public recognition, but most of all, his brotherly love, how very proud he was. There was nothing he would not do for Eric. The guilt from what Latoya was doing continued to eat at him. It was his fault this woman was in their lives wreaking havoc. In the past, he did all he could to keep her from touching Eric, publicly or personally. Now, she was about to do both. He closed his eyes and said a silent prayer that Ty's trap would work. But he knew Latoya like no other. She always had an ace in the hole. His problem was figuring it out before it exploded in all their faces. "You coming in or are you summoning the powers that be to come down to earth and destroy Latoya?"

He laughed at just how close Eric was to the truth. "Something like that," he said as he walked into the studio. "You looked busy—I don't want to disturb you. What you working on?"

"Man, this song is playing over and over in my head. As soon as I laid down the melody, the lyrics began to flow. It's awesome, man, it's awesome."

Pleased the anger from the weekend events seemed to have subsided; he reached over and took the notebook Eric was writing in. As he knew he would, Eric snatched the notebook back. "You can't see that. You know better."

"What? I just wanted to read what you wrote."

"You know you don't read it until it's finished."

"Well can I at least here the melody?"

Eric reached over and hit a button on the music console and a smooth blend of a piano, violin, percussions, and sax could be heard. "That is smooth," Jason said as he closed his eyes to feel the music. "Man, you should name that tune TeKaya. Listening to this is like hearing her voice right here." He put his hand on his heart.

Eric smiled at his reaction. "I know exactly what you mean."

"That's the tune you were playing on the plane the first night I went to meet TeKaya."

"At the time I was thinking about Siri. I just didn't know her name."

"I thought you said something about a call girl." Jason opened his eyes and frowned.

Eric smirked and turned away. "Siri was the woman from the hotel."

"Get the hell out of here."

"I'm serious. Remember when we went to the school to paint?"

"I remember you recognizing her, but I didn't think she was the woman you were running around in circles about." Jason laughed. "Both of us got caught on the same night."

"Yeah, the difference is you won your prize. I have yet to capture mine."

Jason sobered and sighed. "I've created a mess, haven't I?" Not expecting an answer to his question, he shook his head.

"No. You are not responsible for everything bad that happens in my life. You and I were thinking with the wrong part of our anatomy and now we are both paying the price."

"You are right about that."

"Glad you recognize my knowledge big brother." Jason didn't need to know he was just repeating what their mother had said to him a few hours ago."

"We are going to work this out. I promise you that."

"I know," Eric said as the music stopped. "It's called Heaven's Gate. That's what I feel like every time I touch Siri. I feel like heaven opened its gates to allow me to see the wonders inside. When I pull away she keeps a small part of me and leaves me longing for more."

Jason's brotherly instinct would normally kick in and tease him at this point in the conversation, but this time he could not—for he understood what Eric was experiencing. He'd found that someone that made the world right just for him. "Go get your woman, man."

Eric looked up at him and smiled. "I plan to do just that big brother, just as soon as this thing with Latoya is settled. Did you get everything out of the house?"

"The main things I needed from the office and studio. The tech people are at the new house setting up the computer and studio equipment. Depending on how much they get done, I might be staying there tonight. Gabby's over there now."

"The general will have you set by dinner," Eric smiled.

"I'm concerned about Sierra."

"Why, she's fine here. She certainly brightens up the house. I don't think Franco has stopped feeding her since she got here."

"I know she's good here, but Latoya is her mother. If this thing goes wrong, she could end up in prison."

Eric shook his head. "I know she gave birth to your child. But at some point, you've got to give up trying to make her into a mother. If she ends up in prison, it will be her doing, not yours. What she is about to do is called blackmail, pure and simple. It is a crime punishable by a stay behind bars. I know you—you have an offer already prepared to keep her out of jail. If she doesn't do this thing to Siri—wonderful. If she does, and refuses the terms you offer, then she goes to jail. Either way Sierra is better off with you. But know, if what she is doing harms Siri in any way, I will not physically kill her. But by the time I'm finished, she will pray for death."

"Have you talked to Siri today?"

"No, why?"

"You've got the hostile thing going on today. I think you need a fix."

Eric didn't respond for a minute. "She doesn't want to be with me." He slowly replied.

"Did she say that?" Jason asked.

Nodding his head, Eric replied, "Yes. Friday night was," he just shook his head, "unbelievable. Just the two of us talking, laughing, making love, then making love again." He sadly laughed, "It was the moment you wait a lifetime for. Then her ex-husband called about TeKaya. When we arrived at the airport, reporters were everywhere and Siri freaked. Saturday, while you and TeKaya were doing the interview, she said this was not for her and left."

Jason's cell phone buzzed. He looked at the number it was Ty. "Hey man, what's up?"

"Latoya is meeting with Roy six thirty at the house."

"That's less than an hour away. Is everything in place?"

"Yes, but here's the thing. She wants to view the tape in its entirety before making the exchange."

"Why in the hell would she want to do that?" Jason asked.

Ty exhaled, "I think she may have a deal brewing somewhere."

Jason stood, "Can we verify that?"

"I'm working on it."

"Ty, I'm barely keeping Eric sane as it is. Tell me this is under control."

"I'm doing my best man. I'll be back in touch."

Eric looked up at Jason's worried expression. "I trust Ty to work this out. Stop worrying. Everything is going to be all right. Come over here and listen to this."

Jason knew Eric was trying to get his mind off what was about to happen. He loved his brother for the effort. He exhaled and nervously sat back down, "Alright. I trust Ty too. So we will sit here, listen to music, and let him do his job."

"A job that he is damn good at." Eric added.

"If you think that, why did you try to beat the crap out of him the other day?"

"To make sure he understood the consequences if this trap doesn't work."

Chapter 5
Ty

A van was parked outside the gate of Jason's home with the towers and an off duty police officer inside. Earlier that day, the technicians sent to remove Jason's computer and studio equipment, were also there to adjust the surveillance system. The monitors were set to deliver the same feed to the van's system.

At the moment, they were listening to Latoya attempt to con Roy into reducing the price to the original agreed upon amount. So far, Roy was sticking to the plan. Ty had a good feeling about the man, but history had proven that men could be swayed by Latoya—case in point--Jason.

"This is actually my property. I commissioned you to follow Jason's girlfriend. The fact that you followed the wrong woman is on you."

"I followed the information you provided. In the end, I have a hot commodity here. If you don't want to pay my price," he shrugged his shoulder, "I'll take it somewhere else. I'm sure one viewing of the first five minutes will get me a deal." He put the disc back in the computer bag.

"Hold up. Now look Roy." Latoya said easing a little closer to him. "You and I have done a few jobs together. I've always been fair, right? So why are you giving me a hard time on this?" she asked while running a finger down his chest.

Damn, why did she pick this moment to come on to me, Roy thought. *Any other time, he would have jumped on that, but he knew they were being watched.* He took her hand from his chest and kissed it. "I'm not giving you a hard time, and I appreciate the offer, but this is business. You want to finish this deal or should I leave now?'

Ty liked Roy, more and more.

Latoya stepped back. "Let me see what you have," she surrendered. As he pulled the disc out and put it in the DVD player connected to the television in the kitchen. "You can't blame a girl for trying. I mean the price is a little steep."

Roy took a seat at the breakfast bar, as she pushed play on the remote. "The family you are dealing with has millions. You don't seem like the type to settle for less than all. So I figure you're willing to pay the middle man to stay out of your way. Two hundred and fifty thousand will keep me out of your way for good. I'm sure you will recover ten times that."

"So why not ask for more?"

"I didn't want to leave the impression that I was trying to take advantage of you." The video was hot from the beginning and he was getting a little aroused from watching. "You got something cold to drink in here?"

"Check the fridge," she replied still glued to the video.

Pulling the door open, Roy noticed a wire running along the back of the refrigerator. Following the wire, he saw another DVD player with a red button lit indicating it was recording. The bitch was doing a double take on him. The bad feeling of double crossing her with Ty ended. He reached over and hit the stop button. The recording light went off. "You want something?" he asked.

"Naw, I'm good." she replied still glued to the video.

Roy sat back down and watched the remainder of the video. "Well, does that meet your satisfaction?

"Mmm, it's not what I thought it was going to be. I don't know if it's worth it or not Roy."

"Really? I think it's good. You can see both of the participants clearly and man, that woman was off the chain. Hell, I'd buy that in a heartbeat and so would so many others."

"I don't know; let me think about it for another day Roy." She said as she hit the eject button.

Ty yelled, "What in the hell is going on?"

"You want us in there boss?" One of the towers asked.

"No," the officer replied. "Hold on for a minute."

Roy walked over, removed the disc, and placed it inside the case then into his computer bag. He turned back to Latoya. "Would it be worth it, if I told you I turned off the recorder behind the refrigerator?"

Latoya ran over and checked the box while Roy retook his seat. "Damn," she recovered quickly. She'd tried to record the DVD while it was playing, but he figured it out. Hell, she couldn't be mad, game knew game. She apparently underestimated Roy. "You caught me. Hell I didn't know if the dame thing was hooked up right or not." She shrugged her shoulders as she turned to him and smiled.

"No biggie. There is no honor amongst thieves—right. So here's what I'm going to do for you." He walked over and stood in front of her, then looked her up and down, from head to toe. "Just for you," he smiled down at her, "the price is still two fifty—for the next two minutes. In two minutes and one second, the price doubles to five hundred grand. So what you gonna do?"

"I don't suppose you would accept a check?" she rolled her eyes and walked away.

"You now have one minute and thirty seconds. The clock is ticking."

Latoya reached under the cabinet and pulled out the briefcase the banker left with her and placed it on the breakfast bar. "It's all there."

"I think I'll count it, you know the honor amongst....you know what I'm saying."

"I'm not sitting here while you count all that money."

Roy sat the bag he was carrying on the table and pulled out a money counting machine. He held the cord up to her. "Got a plug?"

Ty and the towers fell out laughing inside the van.

Roy plugged the machine in and placed stacks of bills in the top bind until the count was complete. He then placed the bills inside his bag and pulled out a disc. "It was nice doing business with you Ms. Wright. I hope our little issue a moment ago will not interfere with our future dealings," he smiled, "I don't have room in my bag to carry that," he pointed to the money counter. "You don't mind if I leave and collect it the next time—do you?"

If Latoya had had a gun, she would have pulled the trigger and shot his ass right between the eyes. But she had what she wanted and the money she'd just given him, wouldn't mean crap in a few days. "We're good Roy."

"Until the next time," Roy said and walked out of the door.

Roy drove off the property and outside the gate, then pulled over across the street from the van. He walked over and climbed inside to the men applauding. He took a well deserved bow. "Thank you, thank you. I'll have a repeat performance at ten. Thank you very much."

"Man, when you pulled out the counter, I thought I was going to die," tower number one laughed.

"A man's got to do what a man's got to do." He pulled the bag from his shoulder. "Here you go Mr. Pendleton."

Ty took the bag and pulled out the DVD, slipped it inside the player. "Close your eyes."

No one questioned the demand, they just complied. He needed to make sure he had the right disc. He then gave the bag back to a shocked Roy.

"I can't take that Mr. Pendleton. You did okay by me. You keep it."

"I don't' need it," Ty stated.

"Well, give it to Mr. Davies and tell him I apologize for my part in this."

"Eric doesn't need it," Ty said.

Tower number two reached out and grabbed the bag. "If you two going to fight over the bag, I'll take it."

Roy snatched the bag back and looked at Ty with grateful eyes and sighed, "I appreciate this Mr. Pendleton.

"Ty, will do. I believe in loyalty and trust from my employees. Clean up your act. Investigation is a career based on intelligence and dignity. The next time our path's cross I want to be able to say: "That's a good man. I trust him with my life."

Roy held out his hand, "Thank you for the opportunity to work with you." Ty shook his hand and stepped out of the van. The towers followed him. "Hey you guys not staying with me?"

"You're going to miss us aren't you?" Tower number two smiled.

"Hell no. Both of you are intimidating as hell."

"Good, then we did our job." Number one replied. "Listen if I were you I would use that money to close up shop and change your phone numbers."

"Yeah," tower number one added. "When girlfriend finds out you gave her a dummy DVD, she's going to be looking for you."

"Thanks for the advice," Roy stepped out of the van and shook both of their hands. "Take care."

Ty and the towers pulled off. The off duty officer drove away in the van and Roy climbed into his 1991 Ford, pulled off and drove straight to a car dealership.

When Ty placed the disc in Eric's hand, a profound sense of relief washed over his body. Taking a moment, he said a silent prayer thanking God this was no longer an issue. Now he had a personal dilemma—keep the disc as a reminder of that night or destroy it—guaranteeing Siri's protection. Normally the answer would be clear—destroy the disc. But what would happen if Siri never gave him another chance. "Are you sure this is the only copy?" he asked Ty.

"Yes. Latoya attempted to make a copy at the exchange, but Roy caught it, before it really got started."

Jason shook Ty's hand. "Man, you never cease to amaze me. You actually pulled this off."

"This part worked. When Latoya plays the DVD that she has, it will look like the real thing for the first five minutes. If she does the search thing, well, we're screwed on the next step. But if she doesn't and I don't think she will, then Eric you take center stage. No matter what she says, you can't lose your cool. You've got to play it through."

"I'll make Ossie Davis proud. How do I destroy this?"

Ty looked at Eric, "Are you sure you want to? There is nothing wrong with keeping the video of you and the woman you love."

"That night is etched in my mind. I don't need this."

Ty looked at Jason, who looked at Eric. "You could put it in your computer, select all and hit delete," Jason offered.

"No. That works, but it's no guarantee. To ensure the information is never restored, put it in the microwave." Eric and Jason looked at him with doubtful eyes. He laughed. "I'm telling you. Put it in the microwave for ten seconds, let it cool off, and then shred it. No information will be recovered from the disc." Still seeing doubt in their eyes, Ty took the disc from Eric, "You are sure about this?" Eric nodded. "Okay," Ty put the disc inside the microwave in the studio for ten seconds, and then opened the door. "Let it cool off and then we'll put it in the shredder. That disc will never be viewed again."

Eric smiled and nodded his appreciation. "Will you admit I kicked your butt the other day?"

"Never," Ty said as he sat down and laid his head back against the chair. "You two have taken five years off my life in just four days—all over women. How can you do this to a brother? Haven't I been good to you? Haven't I had your back no matter what? Why you got to take a brother through all of this over—women.?"

Jason who was sitting next to Eric at the console just shook his head. "He don't know. He has no idea what is in store for him. Now, we can sit here and try to explain it—but he won't get it until it happens to him."

"We should try. Here listen to this." Eric pulled a CD out and put it in the stereo. Luther Vandross' smooth voice came through the speakers singing, If This World Were Mine. Jason smiled and gave Eric a pound. "Just listen to the lyrics," Eric began singing.

From the doorway, Miriam and Gabby stood with Sierra in tow. Miriam walked in and began singing Cheryl Lynn's verse. Eric reached over and pushed the record button. Sierra quietly walked into her father's arms. Gabby took a seat near the door.

After the song was over, Sierra looked at her father and he nodded his head. She began clapping. "Thank you baby," Miriam smiled. "Why are men in here listening to Luther?"

"We were attempting to explain to Ty why he has spent the last four days dealing with us and our women."

"You are playing the wrong song and wrong duo." Gabby said as she crossed her legs.

Eric looked at her. "Who is better than Luther and Cheryl?"

"The original—Marvin and Tammi—Your Precious Love."

Jason sat Sierra in Gabby's lap. "I got this one." He began singing Marvin's part as Miriam did Tammi's verse.

When they finished, Ty stood, walked over to the CD collection, and pulled out a disc. He handed it over to Eric, who just looked up at him and shook his head. Ty removed his jacket and began singing and dancing to The Commodores, Brick House. Everyone laughed, but eventually got up and started dancing with him, including Sierra. Afterwards, they all sat down and began talking. "It doesn't matter what you use to explain it, he will not understand until it happens," Miriam stated.

"That's exactly what I just said." Jason laughed. "When you find the right woman, you will know. There is no amount of money, no bond with your boys, or love for your family that will keep you away."

"You should know, you just paid out a healthy sum," Ty joked.

"And would do it again to have TeKaya in my life."

Eric smiled. "If anyone came to me and offered Siri for every dime I have, I would gladly hand it over without a second thought. For I know my life will be richer with her in it, than without."

No one said anything for a few minutes. "What can I do to help?" Ty asked.

Eric shrugged his shoulders. "No one can do anything at this time. Siri has to come to the realization that she is running from her destiny."

Jason sighed, "You could do something for me."

"You got TeKaya, what more do you want?" Ty laughed.

"I want you to be at the wedding on Saturday—you too, Gabby."

Ty shook his head. "I don't do weddings."

"Well you're doing this one," Miriam said with a tone that left no room for debates.

"Yes ma'am." Ty replied as Jason and Eric laughed.

The house seemed big and empty now that most of Jason's things had been moved out. Latoya's telephone calls were not being returned as quickly as before from friends. The calls for interviews from the media were none existent now. Adrian had not retuned her calls, and for the first time in three years, her hairstylist cancelled her appointment. She had to use a C line stylist to get her hair done. Of course, she had her come to the house, there was no way she was going to be seen in that part of town.

This could all be her imagination, after all, it was just Wednesday, five days after the world was placed at her feet. Suddenly Ty's words came back at her. *Do you think they will welcome you with open arms?* Shaking it off, she said, "Maybe it's time to find out."

Going into her room, she opened the closet and walked through. "What do you wear to demand notice and respect at the same time?" She pulled out a black, jewel neckline, straight skirt, satin dress, which fell right above her knees with black, three-inch pumps. She smiled, quite pleased with her find. "This should do it."

Deciding to make her debut at one of Jason's favorite spots, she pulled into valet parking. The valet was immediately opening the door to her, straight off the showroom floor, Mercedes convertible. Of course, it was September, but the weather had not taken a drastic change. So the top being down with her hair blowing in the wind was not too dramatic. She thought as she walked over to the VIP door where she always entered and was immediately allowed access. She looked over her shoulder at the line of people waiting to enter and smirked.

The traditional, "yes I'm here," walk around was in order. So, she took her clutch bag from under her arms and took a leisurely stroll around the club. Yes, the men were looking, women were glaring—they were jealous. She waived at one or two people she recognized, but they were busy talking. After taking her stroll, Latoya walked over to the bar.

"Good evening. What can I get for you?" The bartender asked.

"Bacardi Cocktail—top shelf."

"Coming up."

Latoya smiled. "Thank you." She replied then turned her back to the bar and checked out who was in the place. A well dressed, well built man came from the far end of the bar and stood next to her.

"Ms. Wright," a man called out from behind the bar.

"Yes," she looked up.

"My name is Mario; I'm the owner of this establishment. While we appreciate your visits in the past, please accept this as a notice. You will no longer be welcomed here. Please accept this complimentary drink on the house and Phillip here," he pointed to the man standing next to her, "will be happy to escort you out. Have a good evening."

Before she could protest, he walked off. She looked at the bartender, who simply shrugged his shoulders and moved to the next customer, then she looked at the man named Phillip. "I just work here," he said to her unasked question.

"Well, I don't need your damned drink," she said with a wave of her hand and walked out of the club. Surprisingly, her car was waiting at the door when she arrived. Taking her keys, she got into her car and pulled away furious. Taking her cell phone out she pushed the first button, which was Adrian's number—he didn't pick up. She pushed a second button, for another friend still no answer. She threw the phone into the passenger seat. "Where in the hell is everybody?" she yelled. After talking a calming breath, she laughed at herself. "What did I expect; I went to one of Jason's spots." Turning around, she went in the direction of one of her favorite spots. "I'll hit my place. I'll find somebody to party with."

Sure enough, when she reached one of her favorite clubs, the music could be heard bumping outside. People waiting in line were jamming to the beat. "This is more like it."

"Hey Toya, what you doing here?" a girl she recognized, but could not remember her name called out.

"I'm here to party girl," she replied, glad someone had spoken to her. She walked over to the VIP door and just like before she was allowed in. Moments later, she wished they hadn't. "Adrian," she pushed his back. "Where the hell have you been? I called you three times today. What are you drinking?" She asked as she sat her purse on the table.

A dumfounded Adrian turned with his hands on his chest, "Girl you don't want to be here. Trust me, leave while you can."

"Stop it," she laughed. "I've been dying to party all week. It's time to celebrate my new freedom."

"Really?" A voice from behind her asked.

Turing her face went from glee, to what the ....? She came face to face with Ty Pendleton. "What in the hell are you doing here?"

"I tried to warn you girl," Adrian whispered in her ear.

Ty smiled, he loved catching people off guard. "Like you, we are celebrating."

"We who?"

"Oh, your friends didn't tell you. This is Jason's bachelor party. He's getting married this weekend. I made sure all your friends were invited," He pointed to a corner. CJ and Stan are over there. Your girl Candi is with your boy, John. I think they are hitting it off. And of course, Adrian here, who has been getting his drink on for about an hour now. I'm glad one of them called and told you about this. I'll let Jason know you're here to wish him well."

The heat from her anger was seeping through her skin. This was a set up to humiliate her, at her own spot. She turned to look at Adrian, who looked in another direction.

"I hope you are enjoying this moment Ty. Tomorrow you are going to be busy cleaning up your boys sh..."

"Don't do it, there is no cursing at this establishment tonight. Only happy people are allowed to stay and you don't look too happy. Now, I understand you were removed from another establishment earlier this evening. I would hate to see it happen to you again."

Her mouth gaped open, how could he know that? It just happened. As if reading her mind, he said. "People just call me and tell me things. What can I say, don't call me? I don't think that would be very nice. Oh, there's Eric. Hey Eric," he called out "come here man. You'll never guess who's here. I would have called Jason, but as you know, TeKaya was ordered to stay a hundred feet away from you. And since Jason and TeKaya are one, he can't come over."

Eric walked up and it seemed like the music volume got lower. For a moment, he wasn't sure if he could pull this off, but he promised an Ossie Davis performance and that's what he was going to give. "Are you here to cause problems for Jason?" he asked in the most cordial way he could. When she hesitated, a moment too long Eric snapped his fingers and the towers came into view. "I believe Ms. Wright has expressed a desire to leave."

Latoya looked around at the faces staring at her. Most of them she knew and considered friends. Not one of them acknowledged her, but Adrian. She turned to him, "I'll deal with you later." She then glared at Eric, almost smirking. "Are you sure you want to go up against me, Eric."

Taking a step put him so close to her, he could feel her breath on his face. "I've never been more sure of anything in my life," he whispered, then turned and walked away.

"Ms. Wright," tower number two said as he reached for her.

"Don't you dare touch me."

Tower number one stepped up and whispered, "You walk, or I carry you out—your choice."

Without looking back, she snatched her purse off the table and walked out shouting. "Your ass will pay, Jason and Eric! You will pay!"

Latoya reached the house in record time. She was beyond angry—she was livid. Going straight into her room, she took off her shoes and threw them in the closet, the purse landed on the floor and she flopped down on the bed. "I'll make them pay," she declared as she went into the safe and pulled out the video. Walking back into her room, she heard the chime of her cell phone. Looking at the number, she knew it was Adrian. "How could you let me walk into something like that?" she yelled. "You're supposed to be my friend—you're supposed to have my back!"

"Wait a minute girl..." he paused for emphasis. "I told you to get out of dodge. I wasn't like those other heifers that didn't even speak. So before you get your panties all up in a bunch you need to check yourself. Because I counted the number of friends you have right now and the count stopped at one—me. You get my drift?"

There was some truth to what he was saying, but she was still pissed. "Why didn't you tell me about this party?"

"I just got back in town today. The invitation was special delivered to me when I walked through the door. And you know I don't turn down free booze. You're mad at Jason and Eric, I'm not."

"Whatever happened to loyalty, Adrian?"

"He went out the damn door. Look girl, I got to go, the party is hopping." With that, he was gone.

Latoya looked at the phone in disbelief, then threw it across the room. "The party is hopping, okay. Let's see if we can get my party started." She put the DVD in the player and pushed the play button. When the video began to play, she smiled. "Party tonight boys, but I have a surprise waiting for you when you get home. She walked over and picked up her cell. She knew a little about computers but not enough to do what was needed with the video, she sat on the bed and called her tech person. "I need you, this time you set your price because I'm living large now."

"Tell me what you need."

"I have a video that I need stills from. Then I need to send them without the receiver knowing it came from me."

"Send me the DVD, I'll take care of it."

"No, not this time. I need you to walk me through it."

"That serious?"

"That serious," Latoya replied.

"Okay, is the DVD in your computer?"

"No," she replied as she looked over at the flat screen monitor, which was now black. Confused, she pushed the rewind button. "Let me call you back," she hung up the telephone without hearing the response. The video wasn't playing. She removed the disc and briskly walked into the kitchen and put the disc in that player. After five minutes, the screen went black again. "What the ...." She pushed the eject button and looked at the DVD, there weren't any scratches that she could detect. Something began to creep up her back. "Nope," she shook her head, "now is not the time to panic. She walked into the room and retrieved her cell phone and Roy's business card. She dialed the number as she walked back into the kitchen. "The number you have reached is no longer in service." She froze dead in her tracks. "The dirty mother....." she couldn't finish the statement she was so mad. She gave him two hundred and fifty thousand dollars and he double-crossed her. Quickly changing into a pair of jeans and a top, she grabbed the disc, and her keys. Roy was giving up her money or the real disc. She didn't expect him to be in the office at two o'clock in the morning, but something made her drive over anyway. Her nightmare was getting worse, the office space had a 'for rent' sign in the window. Still not willing to accept defeat, she got out of the car and took down the telephone number. She might not get an answer tonight, but she would call tomorrow to get some information. Her cell rang. "You didn't call me back," her tech friend stated.

"I'm going to need your help, but right now I have a problem. Can you get into bank accounts?"

"No, of course not," she hung up the phone. A minute later, a text came through. *Friday - your place.*

Walking back in the house, it was about three in the morning, she was tired, frustrated and mad as hell. How could she let a sucker like Roy get the best of her? Had she underestimated him that much? The more she thought about it, the more she knew there had to be other players in this game. Roy was not that slick. Latoya grabbed a bottle of wine out of the rack, took a glass down, popped open the bottle, and filled a glass. She drank nearly a half a glass, then poured a refill. Taking a seat at the bar she continued to go through the night of the exchange minute my minute. Then it hit her, she knew exactly when he made the exchange. Maybe she did underestimate Roy, she took another drink. But the feeling someone else was involved would not leave her. Roy wasn't that smooth, but Ty certainly was. "Damn it to hell. How did he find out about the video? She asked of the empty house. "Is it possible Roy was working for Ty?" No, she thought. The reason she hired Roy was because he had no connection to Jason or Eric, which automatically meant no connections to Ty. Something had gone very wrong on her end. Not one to give up easily, the thought hit her. Eric wouldn't know the tape is cut. There was a diffident way to find out if Ty was connected to this. But there was no way Eric would take a phone call from her. So how could she get a message to him? An answer came to mind, but it was not one she liked. Unfortunately, he was the only one stupid enough to do what she needed done. After draining the glass, she went into her bedroom to lay across the bed. She didn't remove her clothes or shoes. This had been a horrendous day. Tomorrow would be better. It had to be, was the last thought Latoya had before falling asleep.

The call Ty was waiting for came through around four in the morning. The towers gave the run down on Latoya's activities after leaving the club. She now knew that the tape was no good, and that Roy had disappeared. Now, she was more dangerous than before, every caged animal is more dangerous when they felt trapped. He looked at the clock sitting on the nightstand next to the bed. In three hours, they would be flying to Richmond for the wedding. He was pretty sure things would stay at a standstill until they returned, but just to be on the safe side, he left instructions for the towers to keep a close eye on Latoya. He looked out the window, over the skyline of Atlanta, that normally brought him some peace of mind, but tonight it didn't. He was too wound up from all the 'cloak and dagger' action. Doing a good job to protect his clients used to be enough, but lately, it was just a job. The only exception was with the people he considered family, Miriam, Jason and Eric.

He would protect them with his life if need be. Now, the family was growing, with the addition of Sierra, TeKaya, and now, Siri, who, at the moment was a mystery. Nevertheless, Eric was in love with her; therefore, she was now under his line of protection. Lying across the bed, he prayed, "Lord give me the strength," and promptly fell asleep.

Chapter 6
Jason and TeKaya

After arriving at Richmond International Airport, Jason and the family separated. Eric, Miriam, Ty, Gabby, and Sierra went to Eric's penthouse, while Jason went to meet TeKaya so they could pick up their marriage license. The building actually had two penthouse suites, one on the south facing the James River and the other on the north side of the building with downtown Richmond as a backdrop. Eric had purchased both. The renovations had not taken place, but the plans were in the making. Each penthouse consisted of a state of the art kitchen, three bedrooms, four baths, dining room, great room, office, four fireplaces, and a full length balcony. For the week Jason, Gabby, and Sierra took one penthouse while Eric, Miriam, and Ty stayed in the other.

"Man, I could live here," Ty, announced walking from the foyer into the great room.

"I can't believe the view," Gabby said as she walked in from the penthouse across the hall. "Did you see the river?"

"I like the city view better," Ty replied still walking through the rooms. "How big is this place?"

"I have no idea. You bought it," Eric laughed.

Ty stopped and stared at him, "I did?"

"You or one of your people."

"Well, they did a damn good job. I'll find out who did this and give them a bonus."

"Thank you. When they finish with the renovations we'll have four bedrooms, a studio, a game room, five baths a few offices and an indoor swimming pool. Should be nice."

Miriam walked out of one of the bedrooms. "By us I'm assuming you and Siri."

"If I'm lucky."

She walked over to him and kissed his cheek. "You're better than lucky—you are blessed."

"The furniture leaves a little to be desired," Ty mentioned.

"It's the model furniture. I asked for it to remain until the renovations are done."

"I'll call a maid service in for the week," Gabby stated. "Then I'll check for a good cook."

"You are here as a guest Gabby. We'll get that taken care of," Eric said as he took the telephone from her. Sierra ran into the room and straight into her uncle's arms. "Hey Pumpkin."

"Where's Daddy?"

"He went to see TeKaya."

"Where's Mommy?"

Eric hesitated then looked at his mother. "She's at home."

"Okay," she wiggled out of his arms and ran back across the hall with Gabby in tow.

Raising an eyebrow Eric smiled. "That was easy."

"Her father will have to explain things to her," Miriam said as she stepped out onto the balcony. "I have to agree with Ty. I love the city view."

Eric stepped out with her. "The master bedroom will have both views." He pointed towards the end of the building. "The renovated space will have the city view on the north end of the bedroom and the river on the south. Mornings are going to be breathtaking."

Miriam smiled at her son as he talked about his future. Though he didn't say it, she knew in his mind his future included Siri. Her prayer was that his dream would come true.

In the penthouse across the hall, Ty called his secretary. "Who handled the Eric Davies acquisition in Richmond, Virginia?"

"Let me check," she replied. "Um, that would be Rosa Sanchez. Is something wrong?"

"No, it's perfect. You should see this place. I could live here. There are renovations in the works, make sure she is included in on all decisions regarding this project. It looks as if he may be staying here for an extended period of time. He's going to need domestic service and a driver. I want her to handle all aspects of this project."

"Will do. We received the deed on Jason's new house and you received several calls from Latoya Wright this morning. I think she is a little upset."

"I'll get in touch with her. Is there anything else?"

"That's it for now."

"I'll be in touch." He hung up the telephone, sat back on the sofa that faced the windows and enjoyed the view of the historical James River.

Kerri had planned a family dinner in her home and the house was a buzz. TeKaya had invited her girlfriend Jasmine so that Tyrone would have a dinner partner and Siri came right home from work to help her mother prepare the meal and decorate the house. Unfortunately, her nerves were getting the best of her. Tonight would be the first time she would see Eric since the Saturday morning she left him. Seeing her daughter was distracted more than TeKaya, the one getting married, Kerri put Siri out of the kitchen and gave her decorating duties. The florist delivered several floral arrangements from Jason. Siri was placing them throughout the house. Every now and then, she would stop and inhale reminding herself this was a special time for TeKaya and it was important to keep her feelings of distress under control. They were adults, after all, and keeping their hormones in check should not be that difficult. She opened the French doors that led to the side porch to expand the room. The table was set with the lace tablecloth her nana brought with her, the best china and silverware, wineglasses, and water glasses. Standing back, Siri was examining the table.

"Child you can't put those candles in the center of the table, it will block people's views and I won't be able to watch their eyes."

Siri turned and smiled. "Nana why do you have to see everyone's eyes?"

"The truth is in the eyes honey child. The truth is in the eyes." She walked in and hugged her grandchild. "You know your daddy used to love flowers. That's where I think you got it from. You put together a beautiful table."

Siri hugged her. "Thank you, Nana."

"Now, what's got you so nervous child? You are shaking on the inside like a leaf."

Pulling away to move the candles as she requested, Siri shook her head, "I'm not nervous Nana. I'm just excited for TK."

"Umm hum," Nana replied never taking her eyes off Siri. "Where is TeKaya?" Not believing a word of what her granddaughter had said.

"She's with Jason." Siri looked at her watch. "They should be here soon. Why don't you have a seat? Would you like some tea?"

"No thank you dear, but a glass of wine would be nice. You get a glass and sit on the side porch with me."

Siri looked around to make sure everything was in place, then poured two glasses of wine and joined her Nana on the porch. There was still an hour before sunset. It was a little after six, the evening breeze was perfect, cool, but not cold, and traffic had slowed to a few cars here and there. The tranquility of the porch was a welcome comfort. Siri placed the glass of wine on the table next to the wicker chairs and sat across from her Nana.

"Thank you, baby."

"You're welcome, Nana."

"It always amazes me how you're able to hide your emotions. But I can see through you like a crystal ball. You're hurting and you're scared. Now you don't have to talk about whatever it is. Just know your Nana loves you and I'm going be here for you whenever you need me."

Siri looked away. "I know Nana."

"Where's that boy?"

"What boy?"

"That good looking one you married. What's he doing now?"

"Carl. He's a member of the City Council now. Doing very well with it."

"He was a nice boy. Nasty momma though."

"Yes, Nana, she was something."

"You still sulking for him?"

"No, Nana, I'm not sulking for anyone."

"You can lie to yourself child, but you can't lie to Nana." The doorbell rang and Siri nearly jumped out of her seat. Looking into her eyes, she could see the fear. "You going to get that?"

Reluctantly, Siri stood. "Sure." When she returned, she picked up her glass and took a long swallow. "The neighbor dropped off a cake."

"Umm hum," was all Nana said as she watched her grandchild relax. *Whoever has her tied up in knots is coming tonight. I'm going to get to the bottom of this.*

Well she didn't have to wait long. TeKaya and her burst of energy entered the house minutes later. Joining her was the entire Davies crew. While Miriam went into the kitchen with Kerri, TeKaya brought everyone else to the porch to meet Nana.

"Nana this is Jason," TeKaya beamed.

Jason reached down and kissed her cheek. "I've heard so much about you Mrs. Kendrick."

"Lord, boy, it's been a long time since a handsome man kissed me," she blushed.

"And these are Jason's brothers Eric and Tyrone." They both did the same.

"It's three of them in the same family," Nana laughed loving the attention.

Siri hoped she had blended far enough into the woodwork not to be noticed, but it wasn't to be. "Hello Siri." The same melody began to play in her stomach, no matter how much she tried to deny it.

"Hello Eric, Ty, Jason."

Eric could see her discomfort and it was the last thing he wanted. "Mrs. Kendrick," he sat beside her on the love seat, "TeKaya said you tell the most wonderful stories. Are you going to share one with us this evening?"

"Nana baby Nana." She looked into his eyes, then looked at Siri—the same sadness was in both sets of eyes. "Umm hum, I'm sure I can think of one or two to tell you. "Siri, why don't you offer our guests some refreshments?"

"I'm sorry, yes," she sat her glass down. "What can I get everyone?"

After taking everyone's order, she walked back into the house with TeKaya, leaving the men sitting around Nana. They walked into the kitchen. "Hello Mrs. Davies," Siri smiled.

"Siri," Miriam smiled and hugged her. "Eric tells me you are about to become a published author, congratulations."

"Thank you," Siri replied beaming.

"I don't suppose you have a manuscript you need me to read over for you. I'm sure I could give you a pointer or two," Miriam joked.

"I'm always open for pointers. I think I might be able to find a copy before you leave."

Miriam clapped, "Oh good. I love romance novels."

"Siri's is going to be a blockbuster," TeKaya added as they prepared the tray of drinks.

Kerri looked at the girls. "Dinner will be ready in about fifteen minutes."

"Okay Mom. Where's Sierra and Gabby?"

"Out back on the swings."

TeKaya beamed with joy. "You finally have a granddaughter to use that swing set."

"I knew it would be put to good use one day."

The girls walked back out on the porch that was filled with laughter. Nana was entertaining the men with one of her childhood stories. They passed out the drinks then TeKaya sat on the arm of the chair near Jason, Siri stood at the doorway. Ty motioned for her to take his seat, but she declined, preferring to stand so that Eric's back was to her and that was a small consolation. It didn't prevent the rhythm in her stomach, but it was something.

For Nana, it was the perfect view. She could see Siri's eyes and they were reading loud and clear. The doorbell rang, this time she didn't jump, but the opportunity to do something was appreciated. She came back with TK's friend, Jasmine.

"Hey Jazz," TK hugged her friend. "Let me introduce you around. This is Jason, Ty and Eric. You know my Nana."

"Hello everyone," Jasmine spoke, then looked at Jason. "Well, you're the one."

"I am," he stood.

"Thank you. I'm so glad you finally found this girl."

"Alright, stop," TK said. "You are about to say some things you shouldn't. So I'm stopping you before you get put out." They all laughed.

Jasmine walked over and extended her hand. "You're Tyrone,"

"Ty," he corrected.

"Ok, Ty, it's nice to meet you."

"Same here," Ty replied, but she was already turning to Eric.

"Silk Davies." She extended her hand. "I'm a huge fan."

Eric stood and offered his seat. "Thank you," he said then walked over and stood in the doorway next to Siri.

"Hello Nana," she leaned over and kissed her cheek.

"Would you like something to drink Jasmine?" Siri asked praying she would say yes.

"A glass of wine would be nice."

"I'll get that for you." Siri turned and walked back into the house. Eric watched and Nana watched him.

"Umm hum," she said, then continued her story.

Siri came back, gave Jasmine her glass of wine and announced that dinner was ready. They all went into the dining room and took their places at the table. Kerri sat at one end, with Nana at the opposite end. Jason, TeKaya, Miriam, and Eric sat on one side, with Jasmine, Ty, Gabby, Sierra, and Siri on the other. The conversation flowed easily, with TeKaya sharing information about the wedding and Jason teasing about the honeymoon. Sierra giving a mumbling here and there, capturing everyone's heart. Jasmine kept Eric and Ty engaged in conversation and Siri sat quietly listening, smiling and doing all she could to avoid Eric's eyes. The dynamics at the table transformed the house. This was family, but it was TeKaya's family, not hers. The thought hit her just as the doorbell sounded. "I'll get it," she said quickly jumping up.

"I'm sitting right here, I'll get it." Kerri began to stand.

Siri was already up. "No Mother you slaved over this meal. You're not lifting a finger to do anything else." She almost ran out of the room.

Nana looked at Eric. "Umm hum," she said. "Send that baby down here to me." Sierra climbed down and ran with open arms to the lady with a big lap. "Yes, you sit right here and tell Nana what you are talking about down there." Sierra pointed to the sweet potatoes still on Nana's plate and everyone laughed.

"Sierra," Jason laughed.

She looked up smiling and clapped, "Daddy."

Siri walked back into the room followed by Kiki. "Everyone this is my agent Kiki Simmons. Kiki, everyone."

"Hello. I apologize for interrupting your dinner but I need Siri for a few minutes."

"You're working this late," Kerri said.

"Twenty-four seven," she replied. Jason, Eric Miriam, and Gabby all turned to Ty. He would have never noticed because his eyes were glued to Kiki Simmons.

"Nonsense," Miriam said. "Come sit down and have some dinner."

"I don't want to impose."

Ty stood. "It's not an imposition, please take my seat."

Kiki stared at the Morris Chestnut look alike. "Hmm,"

Siri heard the appreciative moan. "I'll get an extra chair and a plate." The conversation resumed around the table as Ty helped with the chair and Siri set up another place setting. "Quick introductions." She pointed, Jason, TeKaya, Miriam, Eric, Nana, little Sierra, Ty, Jasmine, and you know my mom. Here's your plate grab some food and Ty can catch you up on the conversation."

Kiki took a seat between Ty and Nana who had Sierra in her lap. "Pretty," Sierra said.

"Thank you," Kiki smiled as people began passing dishes of food her way.

Siri sat back down with a slight gleam in her eyes. Nana looked between Ty and Kiki, Jason and TeKaya, Eric and Siri, then she looked down the table to her daughter-in-law and smiled. "You know, I've been a blessed woman. To sit here at a table where there is evidence of God's existence." Everyone quieted down and listened. "Any time you have a room full of love you know God is working his magic. I look at TeKaya who has always been a burst of energy, just like this child in my arms, and I wondered if she would find a man who could appreciate her energy and not try to stifle it. Well, it appears she has. I look into your eyes son and I see you love my grandbaby and I want all of you to look at the way they accepted God's gift of love and learn from their example. Many people live a lifetime and don't get that gift. I don't want any of you to be foolish," she looked dead at Siri, "enough to think you will get a second chance at a gift of love."

Miriam held up her glass. "Here, here,"

Kerri smiled lifting her glass. "Words of wisdom, well spoken."

"To Jason and TeKaya," Eric said lifting his glass.

Everyone else joined, "Jason and TeKaya." They all drank from their glasses and cheered.

After dinner the mothers, Nana, Gabby and Sierra retired to the family room as the younger guests cleared the table. Eric approached Siri and Kiki as they were taking plates to the dishwasher. "Why don't you two go take care of business?" he said taking the plates from their hands, "We'll pitch in, and get this done."

"No," Siri said. "It's too much."

"He's right, handle your business," Ty said as he smiled at Kiki. "By the time you are finished, we will be done and then we can all go out dancing or something." He took the plates from her hands and followed the path Eric had taken to the kitchen.

Jason and Eric were waiting when he entered the kitchen, both with arms folded across their chest. "Dancing, you dance now," Jason asked.

"What?" Ty asked as if he was confused.

"Umm hmm," Eric said.

Jason laughed. "Nana's been saying that all evening."

"Nana's been saying what?" TeKaya asked as she and Jasmine walked around the corner.

"Nothing babe. How do you feel about going dancing tonight?'

"Dancing!" Jasmine, exclaimed. "That sounds wonderful. But will it be an issue for you to go to a club Eric. I mean what about crowd control?"

"Most of the time, people don't notice unless someone makes a big deal out of it," he replied.

"Then it's settled. A few drinks and dancing," Ty smiled then left the kitchen to get more plates. Jason and Eric just stared at each other, over Ty's sudden interest in dancing.

The moment Siri and Kiki reached her bedroom the door was slammed shut. "Who in the hell is that?" Kiki demanded.

A surprised Siri took a step back. "Who?"

Kiki shook her head. "Girl don't play with me. Who is that man with the eyes, the body? Didn't you feel it? The pull the tension, didn't you feel it?'

"Okay, slow down. Are you asking about Ty?"

She ran over to the laptop on the desk and pulled up the internet. "What's his full name?"

Siri did all she could to suppress her laughter. She put her hand on Kiki's to stop her from keying. "Look at me." When she did, Siri continued. "His name is Tyrone Pendleton, he is an attorney from Atlanta and he is also Jason and Eric's adopted brother. Yes, he is single and a really nice guy, that's as much as I know. But I'm sure TK knows more."

"Get her up here," Kiki demanded.

"No. If you are interested in Ty—you find out what you need to know from him. Don't let the internet taint your mind one way or another. Get to know the man, yourself."

"Okay." She hesitated, "How?"

Siri frowned at her. "By going out, talking, asking questions. The normal way a girl gets to know a guy."

Kiki stood up. "Alright. Let's go"

"Where?"

Kiki pulled her by the arm and opened the door. "Dancing."

Calling ahead, Kiki cleared the way for the Davies party to be allowed entrance to the VIP lounge at the Rendezvous Restaurant. The music was pumping, the crowd was lively, and everyone seemed to be having a good time. Jason and TeKaya hit the floor when they first arrived and hadn't stopped dancing for more than five minutes since. Ty and Kiki sat at the table talking and sharing law school stories, while Jasmine stayed close to Eric. She had too much class to ask him to dance, so she kept sending subtle hints until he finally gave in and asked her to dance. His only reason was because Siri seemed to get a little more uncomfortable with him around. It seemed every time he said something or came near her she would squirm. To give Ty and Kiki some privacy, Siri strolled over to the bar and took a seat. A few minutes later, Garland, Kiki's brother stopped by.

"Please explain why a beautiful woman would be sitting at a bar alone when the music is off the chain and the men are plentiful?"

Siri smiled. "Hello Garland."

"Hi yourself. You don't appear to be having a good time."

"No, everything's good. The lounge is really nice."

"So, why the long face?"

"Been a busy day."

"You want to be alone, I won't push. If you need anything let me know."

"I will. Thanks." Siri smiled until he walked away then relaxed. "Whew."

Eric stood in the corner and watched Siri at the bar as Garland walked by. "You need something, Mr. Davies?"

"This is a nice place. If you ever need a performer let me know."

"If you're serious, I can set you up now," Garland offered.

"Not tonight. But, I'll stop by one night and do a number or two."

"I'll take you up on that." He watched as Eric eyes continuously roamed to Siri. "I'm about to change up the play list. Any requests?"

Eric looked at him and smiled. "Since you asked, I have a request or two."

"Name it."

A few minutes later Eric walked over and sat next to Siri. The moment he was near her, she knew. "It cuts deep to know I make you so uncomfortable. Anything that I can do to make the next few days easier, just say the word and I'll do it."

Tears began to form in her eyes. "It hurts to see you, be around you, and know we can never be." She looked sideways at him. "You are wearing that white linen shirt with those locs, the sensuous smile, and that smooth voice. All of it is driving my body crazy. And I'm trying so hard to control my senses. I'm failing miserably."

Moving a curl from her face, he smiled. "Me too." He exhaled. "Why did you have to wear that red dress with your skin glistering and calling out to me? My lower region is screaming freed me, feed me." He laughed.

She put her elbow on the bar, placed her chin in her hand then turned towards him. "We are adults, why can't we control this thing?"

Leaning closer he looked into her eyes and when he spoke, she could feel his breath on her lips. "We're fighting against the inevitable; forces much stronger than us. For you, Siri Austin, are my destiny. It has been said, it shall be written." Smiling she was lost in the web of sensuality he was weaving. The music changed to Eric Benet, I Wanna Be Loved. "Dance with me?" He stood and held his hand out. For a moment, he thought she would say no, but then she put her hand in his and he led her to the dance floor. Placing her hand over his heart, he eased the other around her waist and pulled her close. For now, this moment, she let go, placed her arm around his neck, placed her head next to his, and moved with his body. Everything and everyone in the room disappeared to them. It was just them, just the music, just their hearts beating as one.

"Wow," Kiki whispered, "look at that." Ty reluctantly pulled his eyes from her and looked on the dance floor where Jason and TeKaya and Eric and Siri were. The love could be felt throughout the room.

He held out his hand. "Shall we join them?"

Kiki smiled up at him. "Tyrone—you know if we hold each other at this moment it may lead to something more."

"Say may name like that again and there is no maybe about it, it will lead to something more. Can you handle that?"

Reaching out she took his hand and joined the other couples on the dance floor. As their bodies touched, she moaned in his ear. "Tyrone."

He quietly laughed and pulled her closer. "This is so on."

Jasmine stood in the doorway watching the couples dancing. When Garland walked up he smiled. "Looks like love is in the air."

"Umm hmm," she replied. "Now, I know about Jason and TK. Was suspicious about Eric and Siri. But when did Ty and Kiki happen?"

Garland stood a little straighter and searched for his sister. When he found her he frowned, then replied, "I don't know. But it does look like its happening."

The ride home had dwindled down to Jason, TeKaya, Eric, and Siri. Ty stated Kiki was dropping him back at the condo. Jasmine caught a ride home with a friend, leaving just the two couples. Jason and TeKaya went into the condo while Eric rode back to the house with Siri. His plan was to see her home, say good night and have the driver take him home. "We are going to make it though this night without making love," Siri stated on the ride home.

Eric raised an eyebrow, as he sat across from her. "You're sure about that?"

"Yes," she replied. "I will never get you out of my system if we keep igniting the flame every time we are within five feet of each other."

"Siri you are never going to get me out of your system. Just like you will never be out of mine."

"I have to, Eric. Don't you understand, I have to," she emphatically replied.

"Okay, Okay," he sighed as he reached out and pulled her into his arms. Wrapping his arms around her, he kissed her forehead. "I'm sorry. I didn't mean to upset you." When she didn't pull away, he felt all was forgiven. "Will you at least allow me to be your friend? I can't stand no contact with you."

Closing her eyes and leaning into his chest, she wrapped her arms around his waist. "You mean like telephone calls, emails, cards every now and then."

He smiled, she sound so serious as she thought it through. "Yeah, something like that."

She looked up at him. "I'd like that."

"You would?" he asked looking down into those wonderful black eyes. She nodded. He gently kissed her lips. "Deal."

When they pulled up in front of the house Siri didn't move. He watched as she bit her bottom lip. She wasn't ready for him to leave. "Do you think my new friend will come in and talk with me for a while?" she asked

"You're playing with fire girl," he laughed.

"Friends can talk, right," she said as she sat up.

"Let's go," he said as he opened the door and helped her out. He told the driver to call it a night.

Walking in the house there was one light on in the living room. "Mommy and Nana must be in bed. Would you like some wine?"

"Sure," he said as he pulled off his jacket and placed it over the back of the chair.

Siri went into the kitchen, pulled down a couple of glasses and returned to find Eric on the side porch. He stood and took the wine bottle from her. She placed the glasses on the table and sat on the loveseat with him. He sat back, put his feet up on the table, and relaxed. She pulled off her heels and put her feet under her. "Tonight was nice," she smiled as she sipped her wine.

"Was? This is the best part. Sitting here talking with my friend, controlling the raging hormones."

She laughed. "You're not funny."

"Okay, I'm sorry. I had to say that." He put the glass on the table and took her glass and did the same.

"Eric?" she warned.

"Nothing is going to happen. I just want to hold you while we talk." She did enjoy laying in his arms. Giving in, she laid on his chest as he adjusted them on the loveseat. "Okay, tell me what's happening at school."

"It's funny you should ask about that." She looked up while she laid on his chest and told him about her talk with Carl and then about her encounter with Carl's mother. When she told him about Roscoe and Mable, Eric laughed so hard she thought he was going to wake up the house. "Shh, shh," she put her hands on his lips.

"I just got a visual of that."

"I know. That was more of a shock then when she smacked me."

Eric sat up. "When she what?"

Seeing the anger in his eyes, she reassured him. "Oh it was nothing," she moved a lock from his face. "Lay back down. It was nothing."

He eased back down and pulled her closer. Then she told him about the meeting with Max and Kiki."I've told Ty to take a close look at those contracts, just to make sure everything is on the up and up."

"I'm sure everything is fine with the contracts," she said.

"I'm sure they are, too. I just want us to be certain. This is business; you don't take people at their word unless it's written."

"After tonight I'm not sure Tyrone will be very objective."

"Why do you say that?"

"By morning I'm pretty sure Ty and Kiki will be an item."

"Really? Did I miss something?"

"Where were you tonight?"

"I was a little preoccupied. Just like I am now. But I promised nothing is going to happen and I'm sticking to my word friend." She kissed his neck. "You're tempting fate woman. Stop that and go to sleep." He held her with his hand covering hers and placed it over his heart. This is how he wanted to fall asleep every night.

TeKaya stood in the window at the condo amazed at the twilight view of the James River. Being a Richmond native, she never took the time to appreciate the tranquility of the river or its beauty. When they arrived, she had been surprised by the size of the condo and the fact that Eric owned it. Those same insecurities she had talked to Siri about began to creep into her system again. Jason was such an established man; he was older, wiser and came with a readymade family. How was she going to keep him? Sex was not the way to keep a man, there had to be more.

Whenever she had moments of doubt, like now, she would reach for the one thing she knew she was good at, and that gave her so much confidence—her camera. Adjusting the lens, she captured the bank of the James River as the water splashed against the rocks. Then another shot of the houses in the distance. She became so engrossed in what she was doing that she did not hear when Jason walked into the room.

The vision that caught him when he walked into the bedroom would forever be etched in his mind. TeKaya was in his shirt, with her hair down, standing before a window that expand across the room, curtains pulled all the way back, taking pictures of the most magnificent backdrop. In that moment, he wished he had half her talent, her confidence, and her ability to see beauty in everything and everyone. God she was a sight to behold, and to think in the next forty-eight hours she would be his wife. On Sunday morning before they left for their honeymoon, he was going to church to officially give thanks for having been given such a gift. What had he done to be so highly favored by the God? Something made her turn and she saw him standing in the door way. A flash of worry crossed her face, but was gone just as quickly.

"Is Sierra asleep?" she asked as she began clicking pictures of him leaning against the door. He looked so good with his bare chest and pajama bottoms hanging low on his hips.

"Yes," he replied as he walked slowly towards her bare chest. She continued to click frame after frame until the raw masculinity of him forced her to stop. Reaching her, he took the camera, stepped back, and began clicking pictures of her. It's amazing what you can be seen through the lens of a camera that can be missed by the naked eye. Through the lens, he could see her vulnerability, her innocence, her unyielding love for him. At that thought, he stopped and held the camera down. "I'm scared, too." Instantly, her concern was no longer with her own fears, but instead turned to his. "You took me by surprise. I didn't expect it, wasn't looking for it, no longer believed in it. But, there you were walking towards the stage with your hair flowing and a smile a mile long. And I knew love had just walked into my life." He placed the camera on the dresser, then held his hand out to her.

She walked towards him. "It was your lips that held me mesmerized. Each time you spoke, I was glued to your lips. I'm not afraid of my love for you or your love for me. I'm afraid of my youth, my inexperience, and sometimes my immaturity." When she reached him, he picked her up and she wrapped her arms around his neck and her legs around his waist. He carried her over to the bed and laid her down. "Most of all I'm afraid you'll get tired of teaching me how to make love."

He could feel her center pulsating against his skin and almost laughed at the impossibility of her statement. "I know the physical, but it's you that's teaching me the emotion." He pushed her hair back. "Like the way you're looking at me right now; it's wreaking havoc on my senses. The way you're rubbing your leg against the back of my thigh, and the way you're always touching and kissing me; all are ways you demonstrate your love for me. It will take me a life time to learn how to love from you."

She kissed his throat, his nipples, his chin, and then pulled on his bottom lip with her teeth. He placed a kiss in the crook of her neck. "TeKaya." He kissed her shoulder, pulled the shirt open, popping buttons, and covered her bare breast with his mouth. She caressed the back of his head, holding him securely to her as sensation after sensation began to flow through her. Switching to the other breast to pay equal homage, he feared he might hurt her; he wanted to ravage, her so taking her slowly was no longer an option. Apparently, her need was just as great, for she was using her feet to slide his pajama pants down his legs. Taking her by the waist, with her legs still around him, he entered her with one powerful stroke. "Jason," she moaned as her nails dug into his skin. He slowly pulled out, pushed forward again, and held. "Again", she cried and he complied. "Ah. Again, again, again." Soon her mind was reeling so fast, she could no longer form the word. He was now a man possessed with the determination to bring her nothing but pleasure. Slowing his pace, he reveled in the warmth of her surrounding him and moaned at the pure ecstasy of them being together. "Come with me TeKaya, come with me." He pulled out and reentered to an explosion so strong, so powerful they both screamed out. After a moment, he rolled onto his back and pulled her with him. "I love you, TeKaya."

"I love you, Jason."

Tyrone and Kiki strolled along the canal walk as if they had all the time in the world. The fact that it was three in the morning did not faze either of them. They were enjoying each other's company and neither wanted their time together to end. "How many girlfriends?" she asked.

"I don't have time for girlfriends," he smiled down at her as they walked.

"You're going to make me hurt you. I answered honestly, when you asked me. Now you are backing up on me."

"No, seriously. In my business I barely have time to get a decent night's sleep and when I do, I take full advantage, because I'm never sure when it's going to happen again."

She stopped and looked up at him. "You're trying to tell me a fine brother like you doesn't have a steady place to get his grove on."

He stopped in front of her and grinned. "Now, I didn't say that."

"Mmm-hmm. That's what I thought," she nodded her head and began walking again.

"That's not the question you asked me. I answered the question you asked."

"Now you're playing lawyer on me."

"That's the first prep instruction from any good attorney,"

"Only answer what is asked, yeah I know."

He stopped in front of her. "Ask what you want to know." He looked down into her eyes. "We've talked about everything under the sun and the one thing I have learned about you is you don't pull punches. So stop beating around the bush and ask it."

"All right. Are you married, in a one-on-one relationship, have a significant other, a friend with benefits or anywhere close to being on the down low?"

He chuckled standing there with his hands in his pockets looking sexier than sin. "No, no, no, no, and hell no." He smiled down at her as if memorizing every aspect of her face. "Yes. To your next question."

Unable to look away she stepped forward. "What's my next question?"

He touched the tip of his nose to hers. "If I'm going to kiss you?" he said against her lips.

"Yes," she said. "I'm going to kiss you back."

His smile generated pure sexuality as his lips descended on hers. She stepped closer as she parted her lips to the pressure of his tongue. He kept his hands in his pockets, because he knew if he held her again tonight he would not let her go. This was to be savored and enjoyed. Ending the kiss, he never thought he could be affected by a first kiss. But that is exactly what entered his mind. This was his last first kiss. Still within inches of her lips, he said. "You are a dangerous woman." He took her hand and walked over to a seat and they sat and talked until the sun rose.

The next morning, Ty walked in the door to find Miriam sitting out on the balcony. He walked out and sat in a chair next to her. "Good morning Tyrone."

"Good morning, Mother."

She took a sip of her coffee then sat the cup down. "Still want to listen to Brick House?"

Ty smiled and looked out over the city. "No—I think I need to listen a little closer to some Luther."

"Mmm-hmm."

Siri stretched and smiled at the masculine fragrance that touched her nostrils. Slowly opening her eyes, her first sight was Eric's sleeping face with his lips only inches from hers. The temptation to kiss them was so strong she didn't try to resist.

The moment her lips touched his, his arms tightened around her and he whispered "Good morning friend," with a smile.

A soft giggle escaped her lips. "Good morning," Siri replied, then began to sit up and froze.

Feeling the change in her body Eric looked over his shoulder to see Nana sitting in the seat across from them.

"Umm hum," was all she said before standing and walking back into the house.

At six thirty on Saturday evening, Jason and TeKaya were pronounced husband and wife. The ceremony was short, sweet, and so elegant. The sanctuary of the church could have easily fit a thousand people, but less than ten attended. There were no flash or flair, just two people in love holding hands and exchanging vows in a candle lit church with fresh white roses, the minister, and their families surrounding them. Eric was the best man, and Siri was the maid of honor with Sierra as the flower girl. Jasmine was there as the official photographer.

Afterwards, Jason and TeKaya took their guests to Seducciόns, the place where they had had their first date, a little over a month ago. The top floor had been reserved for the wedding party and Eric serenaded them once again. This time, however, his words were meant for not only his brother's bride, but also for his new found friend, as well as for Ty's date.

Kerri, Miriam, Nana and Gabby sat at a table in the corner and watched the three couples. Miriam touched Kerri's arm. "Well, we got one straight. How long are we giving the next one?"

Kerri watched Eric and Siri near the buffet table talking. The uneasiness she'd witnessed between them on Thursday was now a thing of the past. "Oh, I don't know. The end of the year maybe?"

"Um," Gabby chimed in, "I'm thinking December, a Christmas wedding."

"Nope, got to be sooner than that?" Nana said as if it were a foregone conclusion.

"Why do you say that?" Kerri asked confused.

"Cause, she's with child." All the women at the table turned and looked at her with mouths gaped wide open.

"Did Siri tell you that?" Kerri found the words to ask.

"Didn't have to," Nana replied and continued to eat.

"Then how do you know?" Miriam asked.

"It's in the eyes. The truth is always in the eyes," Nana replied.

The women then turned to stare at Siri, and then turned back to Nana.

Nana looked at them then nodded her head, "Umm hmm."

Chapter 7
Ty and Kiki

The week after the wedding Ty was restless. Work was still demanding, but going home to his empty condo was beginning to eat away at him. He invited Kiki to come to Atlanta for a visit and she agreed. He glanced at the clock on the wall; it seemed to be stuck on three o'clock. Her plane was scheduled to leave Richmond at four fifteen. But the minutes were not ticking by fast enough for him. He wanted to see her again and would have flown to Richmond if she couldn't make it here. Both of them were dedicated to their jobs, so coordinating schedules was going to take some work, but he was willing. "Mr. Pendleton,"

"Yes, Wendy. There is a Ms. Simmons here to see you. She does not have an appointment..."

Ty was at the door before she finished her statement with a smile on his face. There she stood, all five feet eight inches of her slim, gorgeous body, with that sassy haircut. "Hi," she smiled. The grin on his face must have spoken volumes. She walked over, kissed him. "I'm glad to see you, too. Is this your office?" she asked as she walked by him through the door. He looked still shocked that she was there, and then turned back to Wendy.

"Hold all your calls," she offered.

"Yes," he said and closed the door behind him. Kiki had placed her purse on his desk and sat on the edge. He walked over, took her in his arms, and gave her a proper hello kiss. Every kiss they had shared since meeting had been like the first time. Slow, exploring and deep. "When did you get here? Your flight wasn't until four fifteen."

Still holding on to him she kissed his neck, loosened his tie, and replied. "I couldn't sleep after we talked last night, so around five this morning I gave up, threw an overnight bag into the car and hit interstate 95. And you know what happened?"

He was kissing her neck and savoring the feel of her body. "What?"

"It brought me to you."

He stopped and pulled away. "You drove," he thought for a moment, "ten hours to see me?"

"Yes," she pushed his jacket off his shoulders.

"Why didn't you call me? I would have sent the jet. I don't know where it is at the moment, but I would have found it."

"I wanted to surprise you," she said while pulling his shirt from his pants. She then threw her hands up. "Surprise!"

He began laughing as she threw her arms around his neck and they fell to the floor. She was kissing his neck, his chin, anywhere she could touch his skin and he was doing the same. Then he reached her lips and his body filled with need. He positioned his body over hers placing the object of her desire snug within the junction between her legs and they both moaned at the contact.

Every day since the night they met, they had talked until the early morning hours. They'd shared their wants, their needs, their desires. And now, they were together and the need to touch each other was overwhelming. He pushed her arms over her head, intertwined their fingers, and deepened the kiss. She moved in rhythm with his body merging the point of his need with hers until their breathing was out of control. Lifting his head up for air, he puffed two times and returned to her lips. She began to giggle and so did he. "This brother is glad to see you." He smiled down at her and sobered. She had the most amazing eyes; he could see the world in them. "I want you, but not like this." She touched the side of his face. "I have this really nice condo with a really comfortable big bed that no one has ever been in but me. We never discussed it, but stay with me. If you want a hotel room, I'll get you one. But it'll be a waste of money and time. So you might as well just stay with me."

She reached under her into her back pocket, pulled something out and held it up. "I brought my toothbrush."

He laughed as he held out a hand to pull her up. "You are a crazy woman."

She put her hands in her back pockets and shrugged her shoulders. "I don't know any other way to be."

They stood there smiling at each other. "Let's get out of here." He grabbed his jacket off the floor and her purse off the desk. Walking out the door, he turned to Wendy.

She waved her hand. "All meetings have been cancelled for the weekend and all emergencies will be reassigned."

"Thank you," he smiled, took Kiki's hand, and walked towards the elevator. Kiki looked over her shoulder at the woman and mouthed, "Thank you."

Wendy returned the smile.

Walking into Ty's condo would have been a wonderful moment if they had taken the time to appreciate the structure of the place, the elegant interior design that had cost him a small fortune, or the magnificent view of Atlanta. But it was all lost on them. Their only interests were each other, nothing more, nothing less. The clothing was discarded from the front door, through the foyer and up the spiral staircase that was in the center of the first floor. Hands roamed over every inch of both bodies relentlessly exploring and discovering until they reached the bedroom. They stood facing each other as naked as the day they were born and as breathless as marathon runners crossing the finish line, but they were just getting started.

    Ty took her hand and walked her over to the bed. He sat on the edge and she stood between his legs. Gathering her waist in his hands, he pulled her close and kissed her navel. He reached around and cupped her rear end squeezing as if his life deepened on them being there. She slid her hands across his shoulders, down his muscle bound arms, around to his back, touching, feeling, and needing. He reached into his nightstand and pulled out a condom. She took the packet from him. "Let me." She bent down on her knees and was pleased with the sight that greeted her. Kissing his inner thigh on one leg, his member jumped at the touch of her breath near it. She switched and kissed the other thigh sending surges of sensations through his body. "Kiki. He dropped his head to touch hers.

    "I know baby. I'm admiring." He moaned as a response. She opened the package, held the latex in her hand, and took his member in her mouth. Ty nearly leaped off the bed at her touch but she held on to his thighs. This was a new experience for her, but it was there, and so tempting, she just had to feel it on her tongue. He withdrew from her mouth, took the latex, and covered himself with the protection. Seizing her waist, he lifted her, kissed her, and entered her in one smooth motion. They both groaned at the onslaught, and begin moving to a rhythm as old as time. Two humans--becoming one with a need and hunger so deep they could not have stopped if their lives depended on it. Nothing could have quenched the passion of their two spirits as he drove deeper and deeper into her throne, searching and finding that glory that only, he could touch and expose. Holding on to the feeling of total ecstasy, she screamed out her orgasm. Her inner walls contracted against him, pulling everything from him rhythmically squeezing his member from its base to the tip, demanding his release. He cursed when the release came, but reveled in the feel of it at the same time. It was too soon, he was not ready for it to end. Holding her, he turned onto his back bringing her to lie on top of him, never breaking their intimate contact.

They laid there holding, caressing, and kissing each other until he began to grow hard inside her again. Kissing his neck, his chest, his nipples, she slid down his body then sat up, and began slowly moving her body against him. The power and control of the position was what she loved. She controlled how deep he would go and she wanted him deep, as deep as her body would allow. Taking her waist in his hands he raised his legs behind her as her body bucked wildly, attempting to fulfill its need. Her release came first. He pumped deeper and harder until he screamed her name. They both collapsed and eased into a peaceful sleep; neither knowing that their moment of peace was about to be shattered.

The night was so quiet Siri could hear the crickets outside the window. It was well after two in the morning, but sleep had eluded her. Her prayer to get through the night without thinking about Eric went unanswered. Of course, it didn't help that the radio station was playing his music and his silky, smooth voice was touching her senses—all of them. Nor the fact that he had sent her the sweetest email that morning just to say hi. Neither the call right before she went to bed to say good night. She turned over and pulled the pillow over her eyes.

She sighed. A minute later, she pushed the pillow aside and gave up the hope of sleep. Walking over to her desk, she eased into her chair and pushed the power button on her laptop. Waiting for it to power up, she picked up the Essence magazine that had a picture of Jason and TeKaya on the front cover with several other couples. The caption read, 'Our Future'. The computer beeped and she placed the magazine back on the nightstand and opened her emails. One message had come through since she logged off earlier. Clicking the message, she put her elbow on the desk and her hand under her chin contemplating which task from Kiki she was going to complete first--the interview questions or the acknowledgment page of the book. Looking up at the monitor, she saw the message addressed to her and Eric. It must be a picture from TeKaya, she thought as she clicked it open and anxiously awaited the exposure.

She gasped at a picture of her and Eric in an intimate embrace. Printed at the bottom was one simple statement—I have more! Siri stood so quickly the chair rolled back. She went to sit back down but ended up falling on the floor. She jumped up and retrieved the chair then stared intently at the picture. "Oh my God—Oh my God." No other words seemed to come to mind. The picture was taken in her kitchen the last time the two of them made love. But if she and Eric were together, who took the picture?

"Carl!" She thought. Is that why he showed up so quickly the night TeKaya was arrested? She stood and began to pace. Would he have taken the picture? And if he did why?

She sat on the bed with her face in her hands. "Oh God, the book. Negative publicity was the last thing she needed. If this hit the media, it would bring up the divorce scandal. Max said as long as nothing came out of the woodwork we would be fine—this isn't fine. Her cell phone chimed and she picked it up recognizing Eric's number. "Eric. Did you see this?" She cried losing control at this point. "Did you see what was on the computer? Eric this is on the computer. Anyone can see this!" She screamed into the phone. "How did this happen? How did they....How did...."

She was not pulling in air. She touched her chest but couldn't call for help, she couldn't do anything, then darkness descended and she collapsed.

"Siri!" Eric kept calling out. "Siri baby! I'm sorry! I'm so sorry! I'll be right there. Siri!" he called out again. But there was no reply. When he reached the house, emergency vehicles were parked out front with lights flashing. He ran in just as they were bringing her down the steps. Kerri was in the living room dressed and shoes in hand. Eric panicked, seeing her so still with oxygen tubing in her nose. "Siri, baby, please open your eyes."

The attendant touched his shoulder. "Sir, please let us get her to the emergency room."

Kerri touched his arm. "You ride with her, I'll follow."

"No, no, you go with her I'll follow." Eric walked to the waiting vehicle talking to her along the way. "It's going to be alright Siri. I promise you, it's going to be alright."

An officer came over to him. "Follow behind me sir. I'll get you to the hospital."

Eric did not know his way around Richmond so he had no choice but to follow the officer. Along the way, he called Ty's cell phone number again, with no answer. He hung up the call and dialed his house number. He answered on the third ring.

Not fully awake, Ty listened but did not understand what Eric was saying, but he did hear the urgency in his voice. "Hold up Eric," he said into the receiver. He sat up and in the process woke Kiki. "Eric man, please calm down and tell me what's going on."

As he listened, he stood and searched for his cell. Remembering they undressed coming up the steps he pulled out a pair of shorts. "I got you. What hospital?" I'll be there in an hour." He hung up the house phone, threw it on the bed, then ran down the steps.

"What's wrong Ty?" Kiki asked concerned with his actions. "Was that Eric?" she asked as he came back up the steps with his cell phone. "Yes, baby, it was Eric." He spoke into his cell phone. "Have the plane fueled and ready to fly to Virginia in fifteen minutes." He disconnected the call and dialed another number. "Get me a run down on Latoya Wright's actions for the last week. Then tap into Eric's PC and see what was received. No, you don't have his permission just do it or find another damn job." He disconnected that call.

Seeing he was getting dressed in a hurry. Kiki began doing the same. "Did something happen to Siri?" she asked.

He grabbed a shirt and his blackberry chimed. "What?"

"I'm sending you a copy now," the technician on the other end stated.

"I'm receiving it now." He held the phone until the picture popped up. He sat down on the bed not believing what he was seeing. "Track it." he said a little too calmly for Kiki."

"What is it Ty?" she asked.

He looked at her, wanting to share, but couldn't. "I can't tell you," he said shaking his head. "I'm sorry. I can't tell."

Seeing the look of despair on his face, she went to him. "Okay babe. I understand." She hugged him and he held her tight putting his head in the crook of her neck.

As if realizing what he was doing, he stood up straight. "We got to go." He grabbed her hand and ran down the steps. Two of the biggest men she had ever seen met them at the door. "The car is rolling." One man said and gave him a folder.

"Kiki Simmons--Jake Turner, and Peace Newman." The two men stopped: shocked that he had told this stranger their real names. Walking down the hallway he looked over his shoulder. "I don't have time for this," he said and the two men walked double time to the elevator. Reviewing the paper work in the file, he pulled out a picture of a woman entering a house. "Who is this?"

"Tina Melton. An IT specialist."

He looked at the date on the picture. "When did we lose inside surveillance?"

"Friday."

He hit the man in the chest with the picture. "When did she enter the house?"

The big man looked at the picture and looked at the other big man. Kiki didn't have to see the picture to know the answer was Friday.

"Why wasn't I told?" he asked as they climbed off the elevator into an SUV that pulled off as soon as the last set of feet was in, even though the door was still open.

"You were in Virginia at the time."

He put his head down struggling to control his emotions. "You still do your job regardless of where I am." His cell chimed. "Speak."

He listened as Kiki sat back and watched him in action. At one time, she thought she was a mover and shaker, but this man was in an entirely different league. The two big men looked nervous as she smiled to try to ease their anxiety. But it didn't work, whatever was breaking was not good. Ty hung up the cell phone, then pulled his blackberry out to wait for something else to come through. When it did he hit the ceiling of the SUV just as they reached the airport. After checking through security, they boarded the plane and were in the air en route to Virginia.

Once they were in the air, Ty looked over at Kiki. Not once had she complained about the sudden change of plans, or asked any questions, or even if Siri was alright. He never answered her. Unbuckling his seatbelt, he moved to sit in front of her. For a moment, the emotions of the day played across his face. She unbuckled her seatbelt and sat in his lap, she kissed his temple. "What ever it is, you will handle it. Just take a breath. You think better when oxygen is flowing through that beautiful brain of yours." She smiled sweetly.

Pulling her close, he kissed her neck and hugged her tight. "Thank you for being here."

"You're welcome."

"Siri was rushed to the emergency room, unconscious. Eric and her mother are there with her. But no word on her condition."

Kiki sat back in her seat and stared at him. "What caused her to lose consciousness?"

He stared back at her, realizing they were on opposite sides of the table on this. She was Siri's agent. He was Siri's attorney. There were certain things he could not discuss with her. "I can't say."

"This is where we are going to clash. You're citing client privilege?"

He nodded. "Client privilege."

"Whew." She closed her eyes; certain she was not going to like his reply. "Siri or Eric?"

"Both." he sat forward. "However, my brother's best interests take priority."

Chapter 8
Eric and Latoya

The emergency room was quiet, a little too quiet for Eric. However, he remained calm as he sat beside Kerri waiting for some kind of report on Siri's condition. It was four o'clock in the morning and they had been there for almost two hours. Surely, someone should have an answer by now. Reaching over he took Kerri's hand and kissed the back of it. "Have I ever said thank you for giving birth to Siri?"

Kerri looked over at the young man that was sitting beside her more worried than she was about her daughter. His hair hung to his shoulders and covered the side of his face as he hung his head. She squeezed his hand. "You know when you have active girls like mine you'll spend a good amount of time in emergency rooms with broken bones or sprained ankles. The first few times you worry because it takes them so damn long to tell you anything. After a few visits you learn, before the doctors come out to talk to you they are busy running every kind of test imaginable to ensure their finding are correct. So you learn to have a little more patience. You still worry, but you breathe a little better."

Still looking down at the floor with Kerri's hand in his, Eric smiled. "I don't think you answered my question, but your words were relaxing."

"Eric," Ty called out as he walked towards him with Kiki. "How is she—any word yet?"

Eric stood, "Nothing man." He said shaking his head.

Kiki went to Kerri. "Hello Mrs. Kendrick," she hugged her. "Can I get you some coffee or anything?"

"No, thank you. I'm fine. We're just waiting."

"What happened?" Kiki asked looking at both, Eric and Kerri. Eric looked to Ty, who shook his head indicating no, to his unasked question. "Look, professional differences aside," Kiki stated, "we are talking about someone I consider a friend. All I want to know is what happened to her. She didn't just wake up in the middle of the night and fall out. So what happened?"

"A loud voice awakened me around two or three this morning." Kerri explained. "When I got up, I realized it was Siri sounding very upset talking to someone on the phone. As I walked through the door, she fell, hitting the back of her head on the footboard of her bed. There was no bleeding or anything, but I couldn't wake her up. That's when I called the ambulance."

"I was on the telephone with her," Eric added. "She was so upset, devastated. I tried to calm her down, but then she couldn't talk. It was as if she was gasping for air. That's when I jumped in the car and drove over. The emergency personnel were there when I arrived bringing her out. We've been here ever since."

"Sounds like she was hyperventilating, but why? What would upset her to that point?"

Ty interrupted. "Eric, we need to talk." Walking a distance down the hallway, Ty looked over his shoulder. He could see Kiki, the woman that had just turned his world upside down a few hours ago was not happy. Pulling out his blackberry, he turned his back to Kerri and Kiki and looked at Eric. "A second picture was sent to your computer about an hour ago." He displayed the picture and the demand.

Eric looked at the display. "Whew," he sighed. "Pay it."

Ty shook his head. "No. If you pay this it will not stop. This is Latoya. She wants to destroy you and Jason. Even if we pay this, she will still expose these photographs."

Eric looked back at Kerri and Kiki, then looked Ty up and down. Then he looked him in the eyes. "If that was Kiki in those pictures what would you do?"

"Post them proudly on every billboard I could find. There is nothing shameful about a man and a woman expressing their love for each other."

"If posting them meant losing the woman you love, would you still do it?"

Ty looked down the hallway at Kiki and shook his head. "I don't know."

"You don't know, but that's what you're asking me to do?" Eric calmly replied. "I can't take that chance." Just then a doctor walked over to Kerri. Eric and Ty walked back over.

"Mrs. Kendrick's there's a few things. Nothing major, no broken bones, heart's good, lungs are good. So nothing major, however, we had a little bit of a hiccup. We ran some blood tests which show that she's pregnant which complicated our next steps. We ensured she was well protected and ran x-rays and a CT scan that revealed that she suffered a slight concussion from a blow to the back of her head, probably occurred during the fall. There is some swelling on the brain, but with a few days rest, no stressful situations, she should be as good as new."

"Did you say she's pregnant?" Eric asked.

The doctor looked at him and then back to Kerri. "It's alright, he's her fiancé."

While Eric did not blink at the statement, Ty and Kiki looked surprised.

"Yes, not very far along, I would say maybe a few weeks not a month. But her gynecologist could give a better diagnosis on that."

"Is she awake?" Eric asked. "Can I see her?"

"She has not regained consciousness. We'll be moving her to a room. You'll be able to see her then." The doctor touched Eric's shoulder. "She's going to be fine and congratulations," then walked away.

For a good minute or two, no one said anything. They all just stood there shocked. Then Ty turned to Eric and smiled. "You're going to be a daddy."

"In every tragedy, there is a silver lining," Kiki smiled.

Kerri sat down and exhaled. "Nana was right." She shook her head and began laughing. "Nana told us at the restaurant after the wedding that Siri was pregnant."

"Eric?" Ty said, "You still here man?" he laughed.

"Are you all right Eric?" Kerri reached up and touched his arm.

He sat down on the closest chair and looked at her. "May I have your daughters hand in marriage?"

"I would think so," Kerri replied.

"I promise to protect and love her and all our children with my life."

Smiling Kerri replied, "I know you will."

Kiki began laughing. "I wish I had a video camera. You should see the expression on your face."

Eric, Ty and Kerri all turned an angry expression her way. "No," Ty shook his head, "You really don't wish that."

Looking at Ty, Eric smiled. "Phase two. I want her behind bars before I get married."

Raising a questioning eyebrow. "Any idea when that will be?" Ty asked.

"As soon as I can convince Siri to say yes," Eric replied.

"I'll set things up." Ty turned to Kiki. "Are you with me?" The realization that she could say no had his heart racing. In a short period of time, she'd stolen a piece of his heart. And he wanted her to say yes. But there were going to be times when their professional lives would interfere with their personal lives. This was one of those times. The question she had to answer was could she deal with that? He extended his hand hoping she would take it.

"Damn?" she exclaimed as she took his hand. "I can see now you are going to get on my nerves." He wrapped his arms around her and smiled. "I'm not going back for you. My car is in Atlanta."

Eric and Kerri smiled at each other as they watched the couple walk down the hallway. "Mmm-hum." Kerri laughed.

By noon that day, Ty had gathered all parties needed to bring the Latoya Wright situation to and end. Back at the condo, he and Kiki barely had a chance to shower and change clothes before the meeting was set to start. Because Siri had not given him permission to discuss anything with Kiki, she sat outside the office with Wendy as the men filed into the office. Once the door was closed Tyrone Pendleton laid out his plan and ended the meeting with one statement. "Make no mistake in my meaning. One way or another the Latoya Wright situation ends now."

With that directive given, the meeting was adjourned. Kiki walked into the office. "You really don't waste any time do you?"

"Wasting time gives the other side an advantage. It gives them time to plan, to strategize. I like to strike when they don't see me coming."

"Hmm, I'm scared of you," Kiki replied with a smile.

He walked over to her. "No need to be. I'm putting you on notice," he pulled her by the waist to him. "I'm coming after you KiKi Simmons, with guns loaded."

Wrapping her arms around his neck, she grinned, "I think I like that."

"Good," he kissed her. "Now, how would you like to go to lunch and be my secret weapon?

She pulled back. "What do I have to do?"

"Be your sassy self."

"I can do that."

Thirty minutes later, they were seated at one of the most exclusive restaurants in downtown Atlanta when two women approached the table. "Well, well, well, if it isn't the one and only Tyrone Pendleton. I would think you wouldn't have time to entertain a female."

Kiki took an immediate dislike to the woman addressing her man in front of her. Ty didn't stand or look at Latoya and the woman he knew from the picture to be Tina Melton, the technician. "Latoya it didn't take long after Jason for you to venture to the other side, did it?" The flash in her eyes revealed she had taken a direct hit.

"That's funny coming from you. Still bending over for Eric?"

"Whoa, hold up my sister?" Kiki began.

"I don't recall speaking to you?'

"You didn't, however, you invaded my space. Therefore, I have the legal right to address you."

"Latoya," Ty interrupted. "How many places have you been escorted from in the last week? If you don't want to add this one to the list, I suggest you get the hell away from my table."

"I'll leave. But I strongly suggest, you have your client contact me before the day's end or his business will be all over the internet."

"My client instructed me to meet your terms, I just choose not to."

"Yeah," she replied with hands on her hips and head twisting. "I suggest you rethink your position."

"We'll discuss this at a later time. My office in an hour."

"After what you and Roy did, I'm not coming to your office."

"Then there will be no discussion." He raised his hand to get the waiter's attention.

"You don't want to play with me Ty," Latoya stated getting angrier by the minute.

"Do I look like I play games?" The waiter reached the table. "May I see the manager please?"

"Is there something wrong, Mr. Pendleton?" Ty looked around the waiter and raised an eyebrow at Latoya.

"All right."

"May we have a bottle of champagne? Thank you."

Latoya waited until the waiter was gone then turned back to Ty. "I'll accept a meeting, but not with you, and definitely not at your office. I want to meet directly with Eric."

"Girl, do you value your life?" Kiki asked.

Latoya looked her up and down. "A-B conversation." She said turning back to Ty. "I set the place and time. There is no negotiation on the terms. If they are not met by midnight, Sunday morning will be the beginning of an up close and personal look into the life of Eric "Silk" Davies." She smiled, thinking she had scored, and then walked away.

"Did you get all of that?" Ty asked.

"Yes, I did. But, this is circumstantial. There was no mention of the exchange of pictures for money. Therefore, extortion does not exist."

"True, however, she did threaten to reveal an up close and personal look into Eric's life if he does not meet her terms."

"It's still iffy. It will have to be up to Eric to get her to say, pay me or I will reveal. Now, that's good old fashioned blackmail."

Ty smiled. She might be young and feisty, but she knows a little something about the law. "You, I'm going to like having around."

Siri was moved to a room sometime after seven in the morning. Eric and Kerri remained at the hospital waiting for her to wake up. The doctor indicated it was good for her to sleep, but waiting was killing him. Not only was he concerned about Siri, but the baby as well. His telephone buzzed and he stepped outside the room.

"She wants to meet with you—one on one—tonight. At midnight the pictures go live."

"I'll be there."

"Eric!" Kerri called out.

"Got to go," Eric ran into the room to see Siri's eyes open. He ran to the side of her bed and smiled. "Hey."

She stretched and smiled back. "Hey," she whispered as she took his hand, placed it under her chin, and went right back to sleep. He laughed out of sheer relief and looked up at Kerri who was smiling right back. "She's going to be okay," he said more to himself than anyone else. Nodding his head, he pulled the chair up and sat beside the bed. "She's going to be okay."

Kerri smiled knowing her daughter was in good hands. Now all he had to do was convince Siri. She sighed. "I'm going home to get some sleep and I'll return in a little while."

"I have a meeting later tonight in Atlanta," he said as he laid his head on the back of the chair and closed his eyes. "After that, I'm not going anywhere."

The jerking motion of his hand awakened him from fretful sleep. Opening his eyes he saw Siri turning over. "Siri," he called out as he stood over the bed.

"Mmm," he heard her say.

"Siri wake up babe." He kissed her forehead, "Open your eyes for me please."

"Okay," she groggily replied, blinking a few times as if trying to come fully awake. She smiled and reached out and touched his face. "Hey."

Smiling like a Cheshire cat he replied, "Hey you." He gently kissed her lips."

"Mmm," she moaned.

"What are you doing here?" she asked, still not quite awake.

Rubbing her temple he replied, "I'm here because you're here."

She stretched again and looked around. A puzzled look appeared on her face. Eric pushed the button to call the nurse in. "Where are we?" she asked looking confused.

"You're at the Medical College of Virginia Hospital. One of the best hospitals in the nation." A perky—almost too perky, short, red-headed nurse announced as she walked through the door. "How are you feeling there, Ms. Austin?"

Siri looked at Eric, who had now stepped away while the nurse checked the monitors. "I have a headache and I'm hungry."

"All normal signs for a woman in your condition. Now you're going to have a bit of a headache for the remainder of the day and you might be a little nauseated, but all in all you should be able to go home tomorrow. For now, the doctor prescribed something for your headache and we'll see if we can get you some food—how's that?" She patted Siri's foot and left the room, before she could respond.

Siri and Eric both began to laugh. "Ouch, Siri said holding her head. "Whatever that was that just came through the door, may it not return."

Leaning back over her, Eric smiled and rubbed her temple. "I'll do my best." He kissed her lips and held the kiss for a moment, just to assure himself she was indeed alright. "I'm so sorry," he placed his head against hers.

"For what?" Siri asked.

Eric stared down at her, wondering if she remembered what had upset her. He started to say something then he saw the look of fear enter her eyes. She sat up quickly. "Eric, the pictures!"

She pushed the blanket covering her aside and attempted to stand.

"No Siri." Eric held her as she began to get upset again. "Siri, it's alright. It's alright baby I promise." He kissed her and held her tight. "It's being taken care of. We are doing everything in our power to get rid of them. Please baby, don't cry." He pushed her hair aside and kissed her face. It'll be alright. I promise."

She began to settle down just as the nurse came back in. Eric shook his head indicating not to enter the room. The nurse stepped back out and Eric laid Siri back down and crawled in beside her. He held her as she cried and told him about the picture. "I know. Ty thinks they took stills of the video," he told her.

"What video?"

He exhaled pulled her tightly into his arms and told her everything, as he knew it.

"Eric if that video or those pictures get out, I will lose my job, maybe even the book deal. My life will be ruined again. It happened before because I fell in love with a man whose mother was jealous and possessive. It's happening this time because I fell in love with a man, who is associated with a woman out there that is greedy and vindictive. Have I been that much of a bad person to deserve this?"

Eric held her with her back to him. He kissed the back of her head and placed his head on her. "No, Siri. You are not responsible for what Carl's mother did nor are you responsible for Latoya's actions. Both of them will have to answer to God for their actions against you. I can't speak for Carl, but for me, I love you with all my heart and will use everything at my disposal to protect and shield you from harm." He kissed the back of her neck. "I need you to trust that I will handle this. Can you do that?" He could feel her body relax against his as she nodded her head. "Thank you." His body began to relax and he smiled. "You know what you said a minute ago?" She shook her head. "You said you love me."

"I did not," she sniffed.

"Yes, you did."

"I said I fell in love with a man. I can fall in love and not like you very much. Like right now. I'm not liking you very much because I'm hungry and you haven't fed me."

He laughed and she joined in, that's the way the nurse found them. "Well, shall I get another bed put in this room?"

"No," Eric replied quite comfortable where he was. "But you can close the door." Once the nurse was gone and the door was closed. Eric began singing. "*I've lived a good life, I've made bad choices but God blessed me with a precious gift, the love of a wife. I've had times of joy, I've had times of pain, but he found his favor and gave me you. Now, we've had rough days, we've had loving nights, now he's granted us a newborn's life.*"

Siri kissed his arm. "That's pretty did you write that?"

"Those words filled my heart when the doctor said you were pregnant."

Her body tensed. She sat up and looked down at him lying on the pillow. "What?"

He smiled up at her, "The doctor said you are carrying my child."

The look of joy filled her eyes, but she frowned. "How do you know it's yours?"

Eric sat up and kissed her lips then looked into her eyes. "Cause I popped that thang girl. I had that kitchen table rocking!" Her mouth fell open and she covered it with her hand. "Ain't no need in you acting all shocked, you were there rocking right with me." He grabbed her, fell back on the bed and they both laughed uncontrollably for a few minutes. Gathering her back into his arms, they settled into the same position. "You know you have to marry me now, right?" He said then held his breath.

"No I don't have to marry you." He smiled at the tone in her voice. "I'll marry you because I want to and I'm tired of fighting you."

"Tomorrow?" he asked.

"No. but soon," her eyes began to close.

"Hmm, I would hope so," he replied closing his eyes.

Eric landed in Atlanta a little after nine that night. There was a different determination about him. Life was no longer just about him and his music. It was now about his soon-to-be wife and child. Walking through the house was even different; it didn't seem like home anymore. All his favorite things were there and would remain, but home was now in Richmond.

The only thing jeopardizing his peaceful existence was Latoya Wright. There was no way in hell he would allow her to destroy what he's waited a lifetime for. When he reached the solarium, he sat in his favorite chair with a bottle of beer and a little music, then allowed the memory of the first time he'd seen Siri to soothe his fears. Funny, how quickly life changes, it'd only been two months since that August concert. He made a mental note to tell Jason to make that a regular stop on his future tours. Hell, he'd do that one for free. After all they'd introduced him to Siri.

"Hey baby boy," Miriam strolled into the room, taking a seat across from him. "You thinking about Siri?"

"She stays on my mind. I swear, I don't get it. Music is pouring out of me right now. There are lyrics, instruments I have at least three CDs of music already down on paper and more is still up there," he said, pointing to his temple. At the hospital, I was holding her and words just jumped in my head for my child."

"What child?"

He looked over at his mother and smiled. "Siri's pregnant."

"Awe, no!" Miriam exclaimed.

"I haven't stopped smiling since the doctor told us. She finally agreed to marry me—not because she has to, because she wants to—her words. "

Miriam ran over and hugged him. "My word, Nana was right."

"Yeah, Kerri told me about that conversation. Is that freaky or what?"

"Well you know old folk aren't usually wrong about these things."

He took a swig of his beer. "Oh, wait, it gets better. Your other child has fallen in love and from all appearances he's fallen just as hard as me and Jason."

"Tyrone? That Kiki girl from the dinner table—my word. We're going to have some babies popping up all around us, soon."

"I thought that would make you happy."

"Happy—I'm ecstatic. So I take it Ty will be buying the floor of condo's under yours?"

"You'll have to ask him. He'll be here in a few minutes. We have a meeting with Latoya tonight."

"I'm glad Jason is still on his honeymoon. He was always too soft on her."

"He wasn't soft; Jason was and still is a loving father. I didn't understand that before—I do now. She knows that child means the world to him. Just like the child Siri is carrying means the world to me. I would do anything and put up with anything to see my child brought into this world. That's all Jason did."

Eric's cell phone chimed. He pulled it out. "Eric, this is Latoya. I've decided to change the time and location of our meeting."

"You should talk to Ty about that," he started to hang up.

"You hang up and the next email goes to Maybelline Austin. You know who she is, don't you. She's your girl Siri's, or whatever the hell her name is, arch enemy. What do you think she will do with the picture? You think your girl will still be teaching come Monday morning?"

Eric stood up; the anger was clear on his face. "Okay Latoya, you got my attention." He mouthed to his mother to call Ty. She picked up the house phone and dialed his number.

"Good. Now, here's what you are going to do. You are going to write a letter indicating the five million you are giving me is to settle your brother's obligation. I want it notarized. I want the letter and the cashiers check made out to me and delivered to the Marriott Marquis room 1211 personally, within the hour, by you." She disconnected the call.

On the other telephone, Ty was taking notes and dispatching one of his agents over to check out the room. Eric took the phone from his mother. "Did you get that?"

"I got it. I have someone on their way to the Marriott. There's no way you're walking into that room alone."

"How do we get the damn pictures Ty?"

"Eric, don't ask me questions you don't want to know. I'll meet you on the lower level of the hotel in thirty minutes."

Eric closed his eyes and said a prayer. "This is a nightmare and Ty is right. It's not going to stop even if we pay her what she asks." He hung up the telephone, and then dialed Jason's new number. "Hello Gabby, I need to call your friend— it's time to take Latoya Wright out of her misery."

The office was almost fully staffed on a Saturday night at the Pendleton firm. Every available person that had heard there was a situation, just showed up at the office to see what they could do to help. Kiki sat quietly in Ty's office watching him in action and it was an amazing thing to see. He didn't skip a beat with the set-up. What was more amazing was, everyone he called to do a part, said yes without hesitation. There was something powerful and commanding about the man. It was too much for her. She got up walked over to the desk he sat behind talking on the telephone. She sat in his lap, took the phone from his hand, and kissed him long, deep and thoroughly. She then placed the phone back in his hand and retook her seat. All the action in the room ceased. Pleased with herself, she picked up a magazine and began to read. All eyes went to Ty. After a moment of just staring at her, he put the telephone back to his ear and continued with the conversation as if it was never interrupted. Soon everyone else did the same. Kiki smiled within.

About fifteen minutes later, a man walked into the room gave Ty an envelope and walked out. "Okay people—we're set. No mistakes," He walked over to her and gave her the envelope. "You know what to do. Make me proud."

Kiki smiled. "I like you so damn much."

"Let's go people," he said with a smile on his face.

As they walked out of the door Kiki heard, his secretary Wendy say to another woman, "She's a keeper."

Kiki thought to herself, *"Damn right."*

The hotel lobby was busy. It was Saturday night in downtown Atlanta and everyone was on their way somewhere to party. Eric, on the other hand, was on his way to eliminate a threat to his family. Eric kept his head down as he walked through, to keep from being noticed. He was met at the desk by hotel security and escorted to a private room. Five minutes later the towers walked through the door with Ty and Kiki. "You ready to play little boy?" Ty asked as he walked through the door.

"I got your little boy," Eric smiled. The more time she spent around the Davies, the more she realized they are no different from any other family—they loved, they hurt, and the laughed just like everyone else.

"Kiki is going in as your legal representation. Latoya is going to do or say whatever she can to get her out of the room. According to hotel security, there are two people that have been in and out of that room all day—Latoya and Tina."

"Who is Tina?" Eric asked.

"A tech, which means there are probably cameras somewhere in the room. We are still trying to detect them and tap in, but we have a back up if that does not happen in time. Don't ask." He said before Eric could open his mouth. "You should know she has tickets on a midnight flight to LA tonight. This is a big score for her." Ty's cell phone chimed and he stepped away.

"How's Siri?" Kiki asked.

"She's good. Getting the rest she needs. If all goes well through the night, she'll be released."

Kiki smiled, "I'm glad to hear it."

"So," Eric asked as he leaned against the door, "Ty?" he raised an eyebrow.

"What about him?" Kiki beamed.

"Ah-hum," Eric cleared his throat. "I was at the hospital last night and saw you two making eye contact."

"We're um, hanging a little bit. This weekend was supposed to set things off for us, but it's been a little busy."

"His life is like that, you know. I don't know if he can slow down."

"I don't think I want him to. I like him the way he is."

Eric graced her with a huge smile.

"Damn, that thing is dangerous."

"What?"

"That smile of yours. That's how you get all those women when you're on stage. They fall for that shy, sensitive persona then you flash those pearly whites on them."

"It's a go," Ty said as he walked over to where they stood. He looked at Eric, "Keep your cool." He turned to Kiki, "If you see any signs of danger, get the hell out of there—both of you."

"Okay, give me some sugar before I go." she pulled Ty by the collar and kissed him silly.

"Baby, you have got to stop doing that in front of these people. I've got to work with them."

"I'll step in for your boss," one of the towers offered. Ty gave him a look over his shoulder that left no questions as to its meaning. "Just trying to help out boss." He smiled.

Ty turned back to Kiki. "See what I mean."

Eric and Kiki laughed.

Entering the elevator Kiki realized she was working in the blind. She did not know the details of what this Latoya woman was holding over Eric's head. She only knew Siri was connected in some way. However, Ty was concerned with Eric meeting Latoya alone and the possibility of another opportunity for blackmail. So she volunteered to go in with him. At first, Ty fought against the idea, but the more she talked the more he felt she was right. Sending someone else would make Siri vulnerable to yet another person. She, on the other hand had a vested interest in this turning out in their favor, even though she was still in the dark as to what was actually at stake.

"Are you okay?" Eric asked watching the different emotions playing across her face.

"You're the one taking a chance on losing a small fortune and you want to know if I'm alright?"

"I'll give up that and more for Siri."

Kiki smiled. "I adore love stories and this one is a whopper. How are you going to talk her into marrying a superstar? I mean marrying you will put her in front of the media and I know for a fact she is not going for that."

"I bet you five dollars."

Kiki stared at him. "Five dollars?"

"Yep,"

The elevator doors opened. "You're on." They stepped out onto the twelfth floor. "All we have to do now is get in and out of this room alive."

"You'll be cool. All Latoya wants is money," Eric said as he knocked on the door.

Latoya opened the door dressed in a long black, silk robe with a black lace teddy underneath. Eric turned to Kiki who was standing to the side of the door and could not be seen by Latoya and said with an amused look on his face, "I could be wrong." As hard as he tried, he could not hold his laughter in.

Latoya looked around the door. "What in the hell is she doing here?"

Eric was still laughing. "You're freaking kidding me?"

"I'll show how much I'm kidding. She goes or the deal is off," Latoya demanded.

Eric shrugged his shoulder," Okay. I'm tired of the game." He turned to walk away.

"I'm not," Kiki said as she pushed Latoya aside and walked into the room. "I'm just getting started. And I don't have a long time to play. I got a man waiting."

"Who in the hell is she supposed to be Eric?" Latoya yelled with her hands on her hips.

Eric looked over at Kiki who looked about ready to pounce. "She's my attorney."

"Where's Ty?"

"Unfortunately, you've graduated. You now have to deal with me." Kiki took a step closer to her. "And when I'm finished with you, you're going to wish Ty was here."

Latoya looked at Eric. "Okay, you want to play this game. One push of a button and the email goes."

"So does the five mill," Eric stated. "Your call."

Latoya did not say anything for a minute; she stood there and angrily stared at Eric. "Why are you doing this? Why couldn't you just be like every other man and take what I was offering?" She pulled her robe off and turned around. "Look at me!" she said as she flipped her hair over her shoulder. "I am beyond beautiful," she walked over and stood within inches of him, "you know, and I know, you know it. I made sure I was your type. I followed you for two years. Two years Eric, learning what you like in a woman, how the women you grant the honor of sharing your bed look and act. I knew the places you took them, the things you bought. I knew you. When I walked in that room four years ago, there was no reason for you to walk away from me. You forced me to have to settle for your brother. You could have had this," she said spreading her arms out. "You know you wanted it then just like you want it now." She smirked, "I can see it in your eyes Eric." She stepped closer, so close he could feel her breath on his cheek.

Standing off to the side, Kiki wondered if she was not there, would Eric go to this woman? She was beautiful to a fault and most men would not resist what she was offering.

Eric put his finger under her chin to look into her eyes. He saw a glimmer of triumph in her eyes as he smiled. "I do like beautiful woman, in fact they are my weakness. When you walked through that door, gracing us all with your beauty, I saw something else. I saw a conniving, scheming, gold digger walking in and just like now I wanted to get as far away from you as humanly possible." She pulled away. "What's wrong, you can't take the truth? What do you call it when someone studies your life for the soul purpose of monetary gain? When you couldn't get me to drop, you targeted the next best thing, my brother. You've gotten all you could get from him, so now your target is me again." He disgustedly looked her up and down. "What makes you think I would want to touch you, of all the women in the world? After the hell you have taken my family through. You have lost touch with reality."

"You don't get it Eric; it wasn't about the money when I came for you. It was you, I wanted. You, Eric "Silk" Davies, the man. I walked in that room to offer you my body and my love. But you threw it back in my face and now you have to pay."

"Good," Kiki declared. "Now we can get down to business."

"I'm not doing business with you," Latoya said to Kiki. "And here's a word of advice. If you have your sights on Tyrone Pendleton I hope you are ready to be an old maid, because the man is and will always be non-committal." Satisfied with the look of uncertainty she saw in Kiki's eyes Latoya turned to Eric, "Either she leaves and you make love to me or the deal is off."

Kiki looked at Eric who was looking at Latoya as if she had lost her mind. "Here are the new terms. I won't humiliate your precious Siri by selling your nude pictures to the highest bidder. All you have to do is pay me the five million I requested and make love to me. I will walk out of Jason and Sierra's life, and yours for good—if you still want me to." She sat on the bed and crossed her legs.

"Do I have to stay and watch this?" Kiki asked Eric.

Eric reached behind him and unlocked the connecting door to the next room. In walked Ty, Chief Goldman, and a female officer. "Ms. Wright you are under arrest for the attempted blackmail of Eric Davies and I'm almost certain extortion charges involving Jason Davies will follow."

"What the hell are you doing?" She jumped up off the bed as the officer approached her. "I didn't blackmail anybody. This man was propositioning me for sex."

Everyone in the room went shell shocked. "Girl, what world are you in?" Kiki asked confused.

Latoya shimmied by the officer and stood in front of the police chief. "This man and his brother have been passing

Heaven's Gate

me between them for the last few years, chief. I'm the victim here." The officer walked over and handcuffed the uncooperative Latoya.

Ty, walked over and whispered, "If I were you, I would evoke my right to remain silent at this time." He smirked and walked away.

Latoya stopped as they walked by Eric. She looked up at him with the most satisfied look. "It's not over Eric—it's not over." The officer covered her with the robe and carried her out of the room.

"She can't do anything else to you man. This is done." Ty said to Eric.

Eric shook his head. "I have a feeling it's not."

The sun was rising to a new day as Eric walked into the hospital room where Siri was resting. The nurse informed him that her mother had left around midnight and Siri had rested peacefully throughout the night. Peace. Why wasn't he feeling at peace? Latoya was locked away, Jason and TeKaya were enjoying their honeymoon, Sierra was at her new home sound asleep with Gabby and her grandmother Miriam. Ty and Kiki were, well, he was sure they were somewhere together making love. And he was with Siri, the woman that he loved beyond reason, and the very same woman that would be giving him his first child. His mind should be at peace, but it wasn't. The chilling look in Latoya's eyes flashed in his mind as he looked at Siri. And for the first time in his life, he was afraid. Not so much of Latoya, or what she might do, but of being a good father, a good husband, and a good provider.

He was so deep in thought that he did not see when Siri opened her eyes. "Having second thoughts?"

He blinked and then focused in on her. She was his weakness, his strength, his heart and his soul. "No." He kissed the tip of her nose as he took the chair beside her. "You are stuck with me for the rest of your life."

She smiled, and then became serious. "I don't know if I can deal with all the publicity or media that comes with the territory of being your wife. But now the thought of having you in my life has taken root and I will fight whatever demons there are to keep you around."

"I wore you down," he laughed. "I'm not sure which I'm happier about, you or the baby. Out of all of this madness, can you believe how blessed we are?"

"If I'm released early, I want to go to church this morning." She thought for a moment. It is Sunday, right?"

"Yes, it is, but I'm certain the doctor is going to order you to rest in bed for a few days. That mean, no church and no school."

Siri rolled her eyes. "Oh Lord, I have to call Roscoe."

"I'll call him," Eric said a little too enthusiastically.

"Okay, but I would like to have a job when you finish."

"I'll be nice," he yawned.

Siri pulled the blanket back. Eric took off his shoes and slipped into bed beside her. Gathering her in his arms, lying comfortably on his shoulder, she looked up at him. "If we have a little girl, she is going to have locs just like yours. And if we have a boy, he's going to have them, too."

He put his head on top of hers and closed his eyes. "I have to cut them soon."

"Why?" she asked shocked at the revelation.

With his eyes still closed, he smiled remembering the conversation. "My father asked me on his dying bed when was I going to cut my hair. I told him I would cut my hair when I got married."

"But I love your locs. They're a part of you."

He opened one eye. "Would you love me less without them?"

"No." She reached up and touched them. "I think I'll miss them. You know the way they cover your face when you make love to me is a turn on."

"Really," he smiled.

She nodded.

"I'll tell you what, I'll cut them for my dad and grow them back for you. How's that?"

"I think I can handle that."

"Good, now stop looking at me like that before I forget we're in a hospital and make love to you."

He closed his eyes and pulled her close; dismissing the teasing smile she flashed him.

Chapter 9

Monday morning brought an array of events, the first being the arrival of Carl at Kerri's house. He had stopped by the school to visit Siri only to be told by Cashmere that she had called in sick. To his knowledge, Siri had never called in sick and he was concerned. When he called Kerri, he was advised Siri had spent a day at the hospital and was now at Eric Davies' place recuperating. He was surprised to learn Eric had a home in Richmond and wondered if it would be okay for him to stop by to see how Siri was doing. Kerri gave him the address and called ahead to let Eric know he was coming.

To Eric's surprise, Carl did not come alone. Siri's friend Cashmere was with him.

"We don't mean to impose, but we were concerned about Siri. May we see her?" Carl asked Eric as they stood in the doorway. This could have been a very awkward moment, but it wasn't.

Eric stepped aside. "Please come in."

As they walked into the foyer, the vastness of the room took their breath away. "This is magnificent," Cashmere said as she walked over to the windows and looked out at the scenery.

"Thank you." Eric replied as he motioned for them to have a seat. "Siri should be out in a moment. The doctor put her on bed rest for a few days."

Eric sat on the sofa with his back to the window, while Carl and Cashmere sat on the sofa facing the windows. "What happened to her?" Carl asked.

"She had a bad fall. Hit her head on the footboard of the bed and it caused a slight concussion."

"What made her fall?" Carl continued to drill.

"I'll let her explain," Eric stated as Siri entered the room.

"Hello Carl," she hugged him, then turned to her friend. "Cashmere." She hugged her. "Thank you so much for coming by to see me. How was school today?"

Siri sat next to Eric as Carl and Cashmere retook their seats. As if it was the most normal thing in the world, Eric put his arms around her shoulders and pulled her close. She did nothing to resist his embrace; in fact she seemed to welcome it.

"School was fine. The children asked about you and sent these." Cashmere reached into her bag and pulled out a number of homemade cards that were all intended to wish Siri well.

Taking the cards, Siri placed them on the table. "Please tell them I said thank you."

"I will."

The room became quiet for a moment as it seemed a little tension was building between the men. "What happened, Siri?" Carl asked, not one bit concerned about irritating Eric by asking the question again.

"I received some disturbing news and became a little hysterical. I began to hyperventilate, blacked out, hit my head and that was all she wrote." She waved her hand as if to dismiss the incident.

Carl sat forward. "In all the years I've known you Siri, you've never become hysterical. Is there more to it?"

Eric stood. Carl was concerned about Siri's well being. There was no way he could be angry about that. However, the insinuation that he may have caused her injuries was a bit much. Looking down at Siri, who was holding on to his hand, he could see the pleading in her eyes to let it go. "Cashmere, I believe Carl and Siri need a moment to talk. May I show you around our home?"

"Yes," she exhaled a sigh of relief. "I think that's a wonderful idea."

The two left the room. Siri remained sitting with her legs crossed staring at Carl, whose face was impassive. "For a moment you sounded like your mother," she smiled.

His expression changed to appalled, then understanding, then he smiled. "I did." He sighed. "I'll apologize before we leave. I needed to be sure that he didn't harm you in any way."

"Eric would never raise a hand to me or any woman. I fell, hit my head. That's all there was to it." She stood, took the seat next to him, then took his hand. "Eric asked me to marry him and I said yes." She smiled. "You're the first person I've told."

Carl smiled as he squeezed her hand. "You seem so happy and you look good."

"I took your advice, and stopped running from him. It was the right thing to do. I'll have to find a way to deal with his career. It won't be easy, but we will survive."

"You know I will always be here for you. If you ever need me for anything."

"I know and I love you for it. Speaking of love, I see a little spark between you and Cashmere."

He smiled. "We are taking our time to get to know each other. I'm trying to be the gentleman and wait, but she is wearing me down. I seem to want to spend every waking moment with her."

"Ah, I think I've been replaced," Siri smiled.

Heaven's Gate

"You'll always have a special place in my heart, but Cashmere is my future, just as Eric is yours." He kissed her cheek. "You know, you really are glowing."

She stood pulling him up with her. "Thank you. Let's see if we can find Eric and Cashmere." Looking down the hallway, she shook her head. "This place is so big; I don't think I will ever find my way around." She opened the door, walked across the hallway into the other condo and could immediately hear the music. Walking through the rooms, they stopped at what would eventually be the studio and saw Eric playing the piano while Cashmere leaned against it. She looked up and watched them walk in. Carl went to stand next to Cashmere, as Siri sat on the stool next to Eric.

Eric glanced at her and continued to sing. At the end of the song he kissed Siri and then looked over at Carl. "Your concern for Siri is appreciated. As her friend you are welcome to our home anytime."

Carl extended his hand. "Please accept my apology for offending you before. I can see you care very deeply for Siri. I just wanted to make sure she was happy and safe."

Eric took his hand. "Apology accepted. We were about to have dinner. I cooked, so it's at your own risk."

They all laughed. "I think, we'll pass, but thank you for the offer." He took Cashmere's hand. "We should be going."

When the two left, Eric turned to Siri. "Okay, he's not so bad."

Siri walked into his arms. "No, he's not." She kissed his cheek. "I think he and Cashmere are going to make a great couple. He's serious and she's spicy."

They walked arm in arm back across the hallway. "She thinks he is still in love with you. But I assured her the man's eyes said something different."

"It's all in the eyes, as Nana would say."

"That's right." Eric smiled. "Know what I see in your eyes?"

"What?"

"A lifetime of love and happiness."

Maybelline Austin sat at her desk and began sorting through her mail. The day was a busy one and this was the first moment she'd had to review the items her secretary had put on her desk. Not seeing anything pertinent in the stack, she decided to check her emails. She hated the computer, but that was the way most people today chose to communicate. She preferred the good old telephone or snail mail system herself, but as an elected official, she had to be open and available for her constituents to contact her at any time. Emails or texting was the quickest form of communication. There were quite a few messages and she was about to exit when the subject line on one caught her attention. It said, *Personal and Confidential - Siri Austin.* She immediately clicked on the file. The message was simple. "Disgraceful pictures of one of your teachers." There was a slide show attachment to the message. She opened the slide show and sat back. After a number of pictures of Siri and a man flashed across the monitor, she began to laugh. "Finally, I have what I need to get Siri out of Carl's life. Finally!"

She picked up the telephone and called the school board members to set up an emergency meeting for that evening. After she made the calls, she sat back smiling as if the world had just blessed her with the gift of life. Indecent exposure would not only get her fired as a teacher, but there was no way Carl would want her back after this hit the news. She looked at the message, but could not determine who sent it. Soon she gave up searching; it wasn't important where the information came from. All that was important was that she knew exactly what to do now. She saved the pictures to a flash drive and left for the meeting. An hour later, she had convinced the board to hold a hearing to dismiss Siri Austin from her teaching position.

Kerri stepped off the elevator leading to Eric and Siri's new home. The envelope in her pursed weighed heavy on her mind. The certified letter had been delivered to the house early that morning. The return address indicated it was from the school board. The experience was reminiscent of the last time Siri was suspended from teaching. The fear that the mess with the Latoya woman had reared its ugly head again was so strong that Kerri could hardly breathe. Looking down the hallway, she saw Siri standing in the doorway waiting for her. The smiles on her daughter's face over the last few days were priceless. She would give anything not to destroy that smile, but she knew the letter was going to do just that.

"Hello Mother." Siri hugged her tight with excitement. "You have to see what Eric did. It is ridiculous, but I love him for it." She took her mother's hand and led her to the back of the condo. She opened a door next to what would eventually be the master bedroom and walked through. "Look."

Kerri stepped in and began to laugh at the sight. One half of the room was painted in blue with a crib, changing table, a rocking chair, and other baby furniture. The other side was a duplicate, only painted pink. Toys of every kind were piled up from the floor to the ceiling. "My word," was all Kerri could say as she walked through the room looking from item to item.

"Mom, I'm not going to even try to take you into the closet. It is totally ridiculous," Siri laughed.

"Where is he?" Kerri asked.

"He's in the studio working."

Kerri watched her daughter, with the big smile that reached her eyes. This is where she was supposed to be in her life, happy and carefree. "Have you been to the doctor yet?"

"I go tomorrow. If everything is okay I can return to work on Monday," Siri replied as a bit of the light left her eyes.

Kerri sighed thinking maybe this wouldn't be as bad as she thought. "May I see the studio?"

"Of course, come on." They walked out of the room and across the hall, with Siri talking a mile a minute. "He's been writing for the last three days, almost non-stop. It is so amazing to see him like this. He's in this zone," she laughed.

Kerri touched her daughter's arm before she opened the door to the studio. Siri turned to her and Kerri had to smile. "You look absolutely radiant. I'm so happy to see my daughter loving her life again."

Siri reached over and hugged her mother. "Thank you, Mother. A few months ago I would not have believed I could be this happy." She sighed and released her mother. "But now, I can't imagine my life any other way. As soon as Jason and TK get home this weekend, we're setting a date for the wedding. I'm going to marry that man and have his child. I couldn't ask for anything more."

"I'm happy to hear that. Is Eric in here?" Kerri asked as she opened the door and walked through.

For a minute Eric did not look up, he continued to write something down. He then stood and hugged Kerri. "Did I thank you today for your daughter?"

She returned the hug. "No, it's my turn to thank you for bringing her back to life." She sighed. "I need you both to have a seat."

The two looked at her strangely, but did as she asked. "Is everything alright, Mother?" Siri asked.

"I'm not sure," Kerri replied as she pulled out the envelope and gave it to Siri. "This came special delivery today."

Siri took the envelope. Seeing the address, she frowned. "I guess Maybelline is trying to get me fired for what I said."

"What did you say?" Kerri asked.

"That she was a lonely pathetic old woman that was secretly in love with her son," Eric answered for Siri.

Siri laughed. "That is not what I said. Well, not exactly in those words."

"It was close enough," he laughed.

Kerri was relieved to see that the blow to Siri was not as severe as she thought it would be. "You realize that this letter means she's convinced the board to at least have a hearing about it."

"Yes, I know." Siri replied as she read the notice. "I have to appear before the board on charges of ......" she hesitated then frowned. She looked up at Eric then back to her mother.

"What is it Siri?" Eric asked with a concerned look on his face. When she did not respond, he took the letter and finished reading it. "Indecent Exposure?" he continued to read the letter as Siri sat with her eyes closed shaking her head.

Eric picked up his blackberry from the music console and dialed Ty's number. "We are going to need you in Richmond right away. Are you free?" he asked calmly.

Siri stood and walked out of the room. She walked over to the window that overlooked the James River. Kerri walked behind her. She rubbed her daughter's arms and stood beside her. "We need TeKaya to come home and beat that woman to a pulp."

Siri looked at her mother and began to laugh. When she finished she simply shook her head and sighed. "I have never met this woman and yet she has caused more problems for me than she did for TK and TK's the one that took her man."

"Well, not really," Eric said from the doorway. "Technically, you took her man."

"What?" Siri turned and asked a little confused.

He walked over and stood near the window with the women. "The night Latoya was arrested she stated that I was her original target. Her plan was to meet and seduce me into a relationship with her. She blames me for all that has "gone wrong" in her life for the last four years. She turned to Jason as a back up, so to speak."

"What do you mean you were her target?" Siri asked.

"When you're in the business, some women put themselves in a position to get close to you in anyway they can. There is not a place I go to perform where I don't have my choice of women. My father taught us to be careful when choosing women. I learned the lesson a little too well for Latoya. I recognized her game the minute she walked in the door. Now, because of that you are paying the price. I'm so sorry, Siri."

"You keep saying that and it is so unnecessary. You can't control what that woman does, no more than I can control what Maybelline does. They are going to have to answer to a higher being. In the mean time, I can't allow them to steal my joy." She kissed Eric. "We'll go to the school board meeting on Friday. Hear what they have to say and if I lose my job—so be it. Just like before, it will give me time to concentrate on my book and my new family."

Kerri looked up at the two and knew they were going to be okay. But, there was no way she was going to allow Maybelline Austin to smear her daughter again without payback. "How would you two like a home cooked meal?"

"What did you have in mind?" Eric asked.

"Well, I couldn't help but notice that state of the art kitchen. Mind if I have a run in it?"

"Not at all. Need some help?" Siri asked as she pulled away from Eric.

He watched as the two women walked out of the room. Turning back to the window, he looked out over the river and wondered how he could turn all this turmoil into something positive.

Friday morning, as they arrived at the School Board office for the hearing, Eric wanted to leave an impression. Eric "Silk" Davies was not just any man in Siri's life. He was going to be her husband and a force to be reckoned with from this day forward. After her mother left the evening she'd brought the letter over, Eric had another visitor, a jeweler. He picked out the ring he wanted to present to Siri when he officially got down on his knees and begged her to be his wife. Yes, he'd told her and she'd said yes, but now he wanted to ask her.

The next day, he had a romantic dinner prepared for the two of them on the riverside balcony. Just as the sun set, very close to the first time he'd laid eyes on her, he serenaded her with a song he had written just for that moment, got down on one knee, and asked her to be his wife. The moment was so perfect; it brought tears to her eyes as she accepted his ring and his proposal. Now, they stood together outside the boardroom doors, hand in hand ready to face whatever was coming their way.

Ty had another agenda. His agenda was to satisfy the two women who would have his head if he failed at his mission: Kerri Kendrick and Miriam Davies. Apparently, Kerri called Miriam and invited her to the dinner she was preparing for Siri and Eric. When he boarded the plane heading to Virginia, he was surprised to see Miriam there waiting for him. On the flight to Richmond, she was very specific as to what she and Kerri wanted to take place at the school board meeting, as well as the upcoming court case against Latoya. All he could think as he watched Eric and Siri talking was that he was very happy the two mothers liked him, for he would not want to be an enemy of either of them.

Eric stood rubbing Siri's back. "Are you nervous?"

"A little. I just don't know what to expect from Maybelline. I'm sure she is going to try her best to humiliate me. Not knowing what she has is a little scary."

"Whatever she has, we will work through it together. Just remember that and this will be over soon."

"Ms. Austin, the board will see you now," a woman announced.

Together, Eric, Siri and Ty walked into the boardroom. As they looked around Siri recognized all of the members of the board, Roscoe Ford was there as the principal, and of course the ever persistent Maybelline as the complainant. The meeting began with a reading of the complaint and the request for Siri Austin to be removed permanently from her teaching position.

The floor was turned over to Maybelline to state her case. Just before she began, the doors opened and Carl walked through. He took a seat near Siri and gave his mother a look she could not decipher. She turned and began to address the board. "A few years ago a complaint was brought against Ms. Austin for indecent behavior with a minor, specifically a young man that was her student. The young man came forward and recanted his original claim against Ms. Austin. We find ourselves here again, in a situation involving Ms. Austin, regarding her behavior of a sexual nature; bringing into question yet again, her fitness to teach our children. When she was reinstated, it was clearly indicated by this board that we expected, in fact, demanded her behavior be of high moral standing if she wished to remain in her teaching position. Unfortunately, indisputable evidence has come to light that leaves this board no alternative than to request that Ms. Austin resign from her position or be released without the possibility of reinstatement." She paused and took a quick glance at Carl. "Since this information will no doubt be all over the internet soon, I don't feel it is inappropriate to show in this forum. I direct your attention to the front monitor."

All eyes turned to the monitor where the first picture of Eric and Siri appeared. "Turn that off!" Eric shouted. The pictures continued. The second and a third appeared and just as Eric made it to Maybelline, Carl stood and shouted for her to turn them off. The look he gave his mother would have burned most men where they stood. "It is beyond my understanding why you felt it necessary to show these pictures to this board!"

"The board has a right to see what type of person is standing before our children. It is our moral obligation to ensure that the teachers behave in a manner that is representative of what this board stands for—integrity, and moral decency."

"Yet this board is content to stand here and watch picture after picture of a couple during a very private moment. How decent of you. This is your way of embarrassing Siri. Did you ever think what this would do to me?"

"May I address the board?" Ty stood.
"Who are you?" A board member asked.
"Tyrone Pendleton, I am Ms. Austin's attorney."
"Yes, you have the floor."
"It's amazing to hear you speak of decency yet you put on a display of photographs that continue to invade a person's privacy. I would be very interested in knowing how you came to be in possession of such personal photographs. However, I have what I believe to be a more pressing issue. Ms. Siri Austin has been harassed by your board member, Mrs. Maybelline Austin for the last two years. I can only believe it's personal. What I can't fathom is her using this board to carry out that harassment. There have been

numerous occasions when Mrs. Austin and Mr. Ford have threatened Siri Austin and I am prepared to bring witnesses to that effect. However, I am one that believes in an eye for an eye." Ty walked over and requested the remote from Maybelline as Eric returned to an obviously distressed Siri.

Hesitantly, Maybelline handed the remote to Ty. "Let's begin with the facts. Ms. Austin's privacy was violated by a woman who is now incarcerated for the crime. And she has been violated again here. A private detective upon the request of one Latoya Wright took the pictures you just witnessed. Ms. Wright has been arrested for attempting to blackmail Eric Davies, Ms. Austin's fiancé, by threatening to expose these very pictures. At some point Ms. Wright forwarded these illegally obtained photographs to Mrs. Maybelline Austin and she saw fit to invade Ms. Austin's privacy again here. Allow me to show my solution to all of this." He hit the play button on the remote. "Here you have Maybelline Austin entering a Hotel on West Broad Street. A few minutes later we have, Mr. Roscoe Ford entering the same hotel on the same date. Here we have Mrs. Austin entering room number 223 at 3:00 pm and Roscoe Ford entering the same room at 3:15; with neither leaving before eight that evening. "

"Stop this madness!" Maybelline stood and yelled. "Turn that thing off."

"There's a perfectly good explanation for that. It was a meeting." Roscoe stammered as he stood.

"A meeting, you say?" Ty asked. "Well, let's examine that theory. Here's another day, different hotel, different time. Was this also a meeting? I think not. But none of us know what went on in those hotel rooms, because it was done in the privacy of the room. The same expectancy of privacy Siri Austin was entitled to in her own home. How does it feel to have your business displayed for all to see Mrs. Austin?"

"Nothing there is indecent. None of those pictures you have are indecent. We are both fully dressed and handling business."

"It's the kind of business that's in question Mrs. Austin. There are cameras all over hotels, shall I continue. I have quite a few.

"No!" Siri shouted. "Enough. I will resign my position effective immediately." Siri shook her head. "This is too much. No one deserves to go through this!" she cried. Eric reached up and took her hand. "No, I want this to stop now."

"I want to see what you have." Carl said to Ty. "Do you think for one moment she would stop if this were the reverse? Hell she already proved she wouldn't."

"Carl!" Maybelline shouted.

"In fact, at this time I'm calling for your resignation for indecent behavior, Mother. "

"Carl?" Maybelline and Siri shouted.

"Stop, please, stop," Siri cried out. She looked up at the people sitting in judgment of her. "Nothing you have said or shown here today negates the fact that I am a good educator. It's not as if this school board has an abundance of people waiting in line to teach at our schools. Yet, you've allowed this woman, and her personal vendetta, to rule over me for the last two years." She wiped the tears from her cheeks. "Yes, I made love to Eric in my home. Someone trespassed on my property, took pictures of us and attempted to blackmail us with the pictures. You used those very same pictures to attempt to get me to do what you want. Well, why should I at this point? You have shown nude pictures of me to every member of this board. Look around Mable, have you noticed that, other than you and I, they are all men. How in the hell do you think I feel at this moment? Or do you even give a damn? Even if Ty had nude pictures of you, I would not do to you what you just did to me." She looked at the board members. "Each of you will have to answer to a higher power for your actions here today. As for me, you've lost a damn good teacher." She turned to Eric. "I'm ready to go home."

Ty took the flash drive from the computer, reached into his pocket and gave the board members an injunction. "If those pictures appear anywhere this board will be held responsible."

Siri, Eric and Ty walked out of the board room. Carl followed behind them. "Siri!" he called out. He seemed so defeated. "I'm so sorry."

"It's not your fault Carl," she said as his mother walked out of the room.

"Carl!" Maybelline called out. "As a member of city council you just called for my resignation. The board needs you to tell them you were not serious."

"I was serious mother," he said as he turned to walk towards her. "But that is the least of your problems. As of now, you no longer have a son."

He walked out leaving a stunned Mable staring after him.

Eric turned to Ty. "Anyway we could get her into a cell with Latoya?"

"Now that would be poetic justice," Ty smiled.

Eric turned to Siri and could tell this had taken an emotional toll on her. "I know it feels as if you have no control over what's happening. But baby, take it from someone that has been there, the only way to take control back is to eliminate what your enemy has over you." She looked up at him with tears still lodged in her eyes. He cupped her face between his hands and gave her the sweetest kiss. Eric took her hand. "It's time to piss a few people off."

The next morning Jason and TeKaya returned home to Gabby telling them all the turmoil that had taken place while they were away. "Can your chief friend get me inside that jail to kick Latoya's butt. You don't mess with my sister and get away with it." TeKaya turned to Jason. "Can you get me inside that jail?"

A laughing Jason pulled out his cell phone. "No baby, I can't, but I can get Eric on the phone to see what's happening."

"Jason, I'm going to Richmond. Are you coming?" TK asked as she walked toward the steps to change her clothes.

Jason smiled as he watched the sway of her hips when she walked away. "When you ask like that, how can I refuse?" He picked up Sierra. "Hey pumpkin. You want to go see Uncle Eric?"

"Yeah," Sierra clapped her hands as Jason dialed his phone.

"Hear you've been busy while I was away," he said when Eric answered.

"Man, it was unreal," he replied in almost a whisper.

"How is Siri?"

"She's asleep, but weary. I hate what this has done to her."

"Why didn't you call me? You know I would have come home."

"That's exactly why we did not call. You and TeKaya deserved your honeymoon, uninterrupted. How's TeKaya?"

"Pissed. She is ready to break into the jail to kick Latoya's butt for messing with her sister."

"Then by all means do not tell her what the ex-mother-in-law did." He cut off the next question. "Don't ask. If I answer you, your wife will be on her way to Richmond. What we have to do now is stop this snowball from picking up any more speed. You're the PR expert, what should we do?"

"Make the story a non-story."

At eight o'clock, that evening, Jason, Ty and Kiki had assembled a group of reporters from several media outlets to announce the engagement of Eric "Silk" Davies to Siri Octavia Austin. It wasn't just a normal press conference, it was an impromptu celebration. The highlight of the evening was the private video viewing an unreleased song by Silk Davies—Heaven's Gate.

Eric spent the day in the studio getting the music just right, while TeKaya spent the day in her dark room putting the photographs into a sequence of poses of Eric and Siri. Once the music and pictures were merged together, neither Eric nor TeKaya could have imagined the final product would be so powerful, so touching, so sensual.

"Wow!" TeKaya said when the video ended. She looked at Eric, who couldn't seem to take his eyes off the monitor.

Eric turned to Siri, who sat motionless beside him as tears streamed down her face. She looked over at him, then at TeKaya. "Can I throw my wet panties at him now?"

Eric and Jason looked at the two sisters as they were nearly on the floor laughing.

Epilogue

A year later, almost to the exact day they met, Siri stood in the lobby of The Crown Plaza Hotel where her book release party was being held. The book, *Night of Seduction*, had received rave reviews prior to its release. Crimson Publishing executives were ecstatic with the pre-sales on this unknown author. Of course it didn't hurt that her husband, musical genius, Silk Davies released his CD, Heaven's Gate in conjunction with the book. In fact, everyone that attended the release party was given the CD and front row tickets to Friday's At Sunset to see Silk Davies perform.

Maxine Long watched as the camera shy Siri posed for picture after picture with executives and fans. "She has certainly come a long way from, 'the press and I don't get along', stage."

"Mmm-hmm," Kiki replied without taking her eyes off the man standing with Eric.

"Why don't you just go over there and tell the man you were wrong. You can and will move to Atlanta and take all of us out of our misery."

The words Latoya said would not leave her. As liberal as she was, there was one thing that she was just old fashioned about—she believed in love, marriage, children and the white picket fence. Tyrone did not want the wife and kids. He did not believe in love. Kiki turned to Max. "I have no idea what you are talking about."

"I'm talking about the fact that that gorgeous, successful man, Tyrone Pendleton asked you to move to Atlanta and you turned him down. Why I don't know and you don't either."

"He could move to Richmond just as easily as I could move to Atlanta." Kiki pouted. "Why is it always the woman that has to sacrifice her job and family to be with a man?"

"Did you ask him to move here? There is no sacrifice worth the love of a good man," Maxine stated.

"I agree," Siri said as she walked up. "Besides, I feel responsible for Ty being so miserable. I introduced you two. Why can't you move to Atlanta? I'll be there most of the time and TeKaya is there permanently."

"It's all happening to quick," Kiki declared.

Siri laughed. "TeKaya married Jason after one month. I married Eric after two."

"That's different, both of you fell in love at first site. Ty and I are different. He's never—said anything about—love."

Siri looked over at Tyrone. "Emotions are hard for Tyrone. But he loves you, I'm sure of that."

"I'll tell you the same thing I told him. I'm not going to uproot my life, to move in with a man that can't express himself."

"How is he in bed?" Maxine asked while raising an eyebrow.

"How is who in bed?" TeKaya walked over holding Sierra's hand.

"Tyrone," Siri replied.

TeKaya, Siri, and Maxine all turned to look at Ty. "Mmm-hmm." They all said in unison, and then laughed.

Ty looked over at Kiki who was acting as if he did not exist. He didn't understand why she'd left in such a huff. Didn't she understand the sacrifice he was making by asking her to move in with him? He never wanted to share his life with a woman—until now. Hell, he didn't even allow people to get close to him. The only ones that had were standing there next to him. He turned to find Eric and Jason both grinning at him like Cheshire cats. "What?" he asked in an irritated voice.

They laughed. "Looks like you're the topic of conversation over there," Jason answered.

"It appears you are a little on edge. What's wrong—need a woman?" Eric asked with a smile.

"I don't need anyone, especially a woman—that woman," Ty declared.

Both began to shake their heads at him. "I don't understand what happened. The night Latoya was locked up you two couldn't keep your hands off each other. What did you do?" Eric asked.

"I don't want to talk about this."

"Look man, we're here to help," Jason grinned.

"I don't need your help. Just leave it alone."

"Alright man, but I'm going home with TeKaya," Jason said as he smiled at his very pregnant wife.

"Yeah, and I'm going home with Siri. And look, both of us are smiling." He hit Ty on the shoulder. "I'm available for serenades whenever you need me."

―――~~~―――

Miriam and Kerri sat in front row seats as they waited for the concert to begin. "Can you believe we have a grandbaby and another on the way?" Kerri smiled. "Life is good."

"I'm a little sad," Miriam said as she looked around the crowd.

"Why?" Kerri looked at her friend, concerned by the statement.

"When we leave for Paris, I would like to have seen all three boys settled. It seems Tyrone is my lone holdout."

"Give him time. He's a little more intense than Jason and Eric. He'll come around."

The lights went down on the stage and the announcer came to the microphone. "Ladies and gentlemen" the announcer began. "The moment has arrived. If you came with a special someone, now is the time to pull him or her close. If you came alone, grab your neighbor. If you are still alone, I have the number to an escort service. When you leave here tonight, no one is going to want to be alone. The man referred to as, "the baby maker," "the guaranteed panty dropper" and "Mr. Get Her Wet." The man with the voice so smooth, they had to change his name. Ladies and gentlemen, put your hands together for the incomparable, Silk... Davies."

Silk appeared on stage in his white linen shirt and pants, sat at the baby grand piano and serenaded the crowd with music so sensual and soothing that it brought a hush over the crowd. During the concert, not a sound was made as he mesmerized the fans with song after song about love found and conquered. When he reached the last song, the video that had won just about every honor there was in the music industry throughout the year, played as he sang. The crowd watched and listened as he sang about the love of his life. The video consisted of pictures of him and Siri tastefully making love, then pictures of their very private wedding, followed by pictures of them together and their pregnancy. The last frame appeared and the crowd all said the same thing, "Aww." It took them a moment to realize the music had stopped and he stood at the microphone. "Allow me to introduce you to the inspiration for my music--ladies, and gentlemen, my wife Siri." The crowd applauded as Siri took center stage with her husband. The crowd erupted when he took the bundle from her arms and held the child up, for all to see. "Meet my daughter, Heaven."